BEFORE him he saw figures, a bonfire limning silhouettes. Among them, as consciousness came full upon him and he began to wish he'd never waked, was Janni, spreadeagled, staked out on the ground, his mouth open, screaming at the sky.

"Ah," he heard, "Nikodemos. So kind of you to join us."

Then a woman's face swam before him, beautiful, though that just made it worse. It was the Nisibisi witch and she was smiling, itself an awful sign. A score of minions ringed her, creatures roused from graves, and two with ophidian eyes and lipless mouths whose skins had a greenish cast.

She began to tell him softly the things she wished to know. He only stared back at her in silence: Tempus's plans and state of mind were things he knew little of; he couldn't have stopped this if he'd wanted to; he didn't know enough. But when at length, knowing it, he closed his eyes again, she came up close and pried them open, impaling his lids with wooden splinters so that he would see what made Janni cry. . . .

JANET MORRIS
TEMPUS

BAEN BOOKS

TEMPUS

A Baen Books Original

Baen Publishing Enterprises
260 Fifth Avenue
New York, N.Y. 10001

First printing, April 1987

Acknowledgments: Parts of this work have been published previously in somewhat different form as follows: "An End to Dreaming," *Whispers* #5, © 1982, by permission Stuart Schiff; "Vashanka's Minion," *Tales from the Vulgar Unicorn*, Ace 1980; "A Man and His God," *Shadows of Sanctuary*, Ace 1981; "Wizard Weather," *Storm Season*, Ace 1982, permission Berkley; "High Moon," *Face of Chaos*, Ace 1983, permission Berkley; "Hell to Pay," *The Dead of Winter*, Ace 1985. The following are original to this volume: *Desperately Seeking Niko; A Trick of Memory; A Better Class of Enemy; For Love of a Ghost; Beginner's Luck; Blood and Honor; Dream Lord; Tempus.*

(Thieves' World® and Sanctuary® are trademarks belonging to Robert Lynn Asprin and Lynn Abbey.)

ISBN: 0-671-65631-7

Cover art by Gary Ruddell

Printed in the United States of America

Distributed by
SIMON & SCHUSTER
1230 Avenue of the Americas
New York, N.Y. 10020

Contents

DESPERATELY SEEKING NIKO

Niko was haunted, the adepts of Bandara decided, and shook their bald heads in shame and consternation. All over the main island of Bandara, and throughout the subsidiary islands of the sea-locked chain, wiser men pondered the fate of the prodigal son who had returned.

Bandara was not an easy place to return to—its wards were strong and its defenses many. It could hide from the common worlds whose periphery it inhabited. It could refuse to be reached from the northern shore close by, or the troubled lands to its east. It could do this because it was a mystical place, a nexus of dimensional flux, like its faraway sister chain, Aškelon's archipelago of Meridian. But it never did—it never had, in all its years, completely disappeared.

The land of Meridian had that habit of disappearing, but the archipelago was ruled by Aškelon the archmage, one of the spirits that haunted Niko, the young Bandaran fighter. In "the World" as Niko and his kind called the common worlds beyond the misty isles, no one still lived who remembered that Bandara

1

could—and might—disappear. No one human, that is.

Once in darker ages, Bandara had broken away from a horrid and self-destructive world, leaving only mislabeled maps to remind men that it had ever been. Like pages flipped in a picture book, it had sorted through the loci available for its manifestation, and chosen this common world in which it now sat, low in the water, swaddled in mist.

No one human remembered that Bandara—the place itself, its soil and its bedrock and its mountain peaks—was mystical in its essence and protective of the life that thrived there. But others did.

Others such as Aškelon, lord of dreams, knew what Bandara was. It was the opposite of his domain and yet its twin. It was the obverse and equal expression of inverted principles: where Meridian houses a dark lord, ruled dream and nightmare, and had power over the subconscious of mortal men, Bandara hosted the secular adepts of pure degree, remembered the elder gods but worshipped only God in Man, and taught the disciplines of conscious power.

The Aškelonians called it magic, dark force. The Bandarans called it mystery, mastery. And that polarization stabilized everything in between—the manifold dimensions of human struggle and human defect; the embedded heavens and hells that man creates; the very difference between conscious thought and primal action.

Some on Bandara were not blunt: Meridian represented all that was dark and evil and out of control; Bandara fostered willful good, the bright light of truth, the struggle to perfect godhead in mortal man.

The two, from time immemorial, had coexisted on many planes without ever having collided. Now a battered Bandaran fighter named Nikodemos had come home and changed all that.

Niko had sortied into the world and become embroiled in dark battles—with Aškelon, the very lord of dreams himself. And then Nikodemos had returned, bringing a shard of darkness with him that hung over Bandara like a pall.

Two adepts on a high peak whispered together, staring out into the mist swathing a sea that had once had farther shores, but might not have them anymore. If Niko, who was called Stealth in the World, was truly haunted—if Aškelon or his minions followed the young man here—Bandara might disappear.

It was a gargantuan worry. It was a problem these adepts had not faced in countless ages. It was the worst possible result of the best conceivable impulse: Niko, the finest of the fighting adepts ever to venture into the World, had come home with all his demons chasing after him.

The two adepts who stood watch were cold and wet and shivering, but they hardly blinked; they built no fire; they sought no blanket on their wind-whipped peak. Their eyes scanned the occluded distance for a ship, a dark spot, a patch of evil tacking shoreward.

For their prescience told them that Aškelon himself was on his way here, seeking Niko.

Ennina (Lord's Eye) was the smallest of Bandara's six islands; she nestled in the harbor created by the larger isles like a child. Here Niko always came, when the World became too horrid, its venality too unconscionable, its burdens more than he could lift.

This time, as once before, he'd brought new students—children to learn what could be learned nowhere else. When he'd set out on the journey hither, he'd thought that was his reason. Now he knew it was only an excuse.

Once he'd given his charges over to the masters on the main island, Ennina had drawn him like a lodestone and he'd known why he'd come home.

He'd secured his old cabin, with its lawns of gravel and its view of the cliffs and sea. He'd tended his gravel "ponds" with his rake and sat under his whispering pines and watched the willows by his stream weep quietly. And he had wept as well.

Once he'd thought he'd never come back here. He'd been ousted for bringing an evil image upon the place. When return to Bandara had been forbidden, it had cut like no knife he'd ever known. When he'd been forgiven, it had been like salvation.

And yet, home on his cliffside, in retreat, he found no rest. The outside world deviled him; promises he'd made disturbed him.

He'd given his word to meet a man somewhere, and the time was drawing near. He'd told Tempus, his Worldly commander, that he'd rejoin the band on a certain date, at a certain place. And now, if he did not want to go, if he felt weak and insufficient to his tasks in the World, what difference did that make? He had given his word.

He'd given his word to a man who had his allegiance, in proper Sacred Band fashion. He could not fail to go. No matter the danger, no matter his weariness, no matter the cry in his soul for peace, he must leave here.

Most times, Bandara made him restless, after it had done its revivifying work. This time, Niko was not impatient to return to the World. He was still tired, aching in his heart and his bones, and a venture into the thoughtless evil of the uncivilized mainland was one to be met with resolve and fierce pleasure.

You took your strength, your mystery, your spirit

and your skill out into the World and you challenged the evil of that World until it wore you down. Then you came home, restored your internal equilibrium, and did the same again.

This was Niko's mystery, his special skill. He was a devotee of *maat*, of balance and equilibrium, of truth and the scales of justice. He was, on occasion, justice incarnate, when justice must be dispensed with a sword.

Maat should have been forcing him out into the World by now. He should have been ready. He should have been disdainful of Ennina and the harbor view below him. But he was not. This time, Niko didn't want to leave. In his mind's eye he could see Tempus, his commander—the man to whom, above all others, he was sworn. He could see Tempus's fine Trôs horse and another man, an emperor called Theron, who'd decreed an expedition that Tempus was to lead.

Niko had agreed to join that expeditionary force, yet now he could not summon the strength to do so. His legs were leaden, his heart was torn, his eyelids heavy.

Too often, when he should have been working with his rake to order the gravel in his ponds and thus order his thoughts and his heart, he would fall asleep. And this troubled him, because in sleep he was vulnerable to Aškelon, the hideous dream lord who plagued him.

Tempus, Niko's commander, didn't sleep and now Niko thought he understood why. When last he'd dozed off, leaning on his rake in the middle of his gravel pond, he'd dreamed that Tempus had come here to see him, and both of them had wept upon the stones at his feet.

Tempus didn't weep. Tempus was immortal, implacable, impenetrable. Tempus was also, in a way that no Bandaran adept could be, Niko's teacher. Tempus's long slitted eyes taught Niko, *Don't do as I did; don't trade your soul away*. Tempus's hard mouth taught Niko what despair was in store for a man who asked too much of his fellows. *People disappoint*, Tempus had cautioned him. And yet, the accursed Tempus had taught Niko something more: the value of indefatigability; the honor in struggle against insurmountable odds, the perfection of mortal spirit out of strife.

Tempus never turned away from injustice, never left a problem for another to solve. Tempus never let the pain or difficulty of an undertaking persuade him not to pursue a resolution his heart thought was right. Tempus never gave up.

But then, Tempus was immortal. Tempus's strength never gave out. His heart, despite the cynicism of his glance, never quavered. To his men, he was Vengeance and Power. To himself, he was a constant disappointment. To Niko, he was a beacon and a specter: even Tempus had admitted that Niko was in danger of becoming like Tempus himself.

Like the man his men called variously the Riddler, the Sleepless One, and the Black, from his temper. Niko did not want to be any of these things. Niko merely wanted, as his Bandaran training had taught him, to be the best man he could be. The most honorable. The most capable. The most effective. And, possibly, if he lived long enough, the most wise.

Wisdom, Niko thought as he leaned his cheek against his long-handled rake, cannot be had without price. And that price is blood. The sound of it in your veins. The pound of it in your head. The volume of it in a human body; the sickness when you've spilled it. Nothing he knew of, enunciated life like death. And Niko knew death like a sister—she was his true partner in a phenomenal World.

So, if wisdom was out there, to be bought with experience, with danger and risk and striving, what was he doing here, quailing like a coward, dawdling, wishing he didn't have to leave?

Was it age, a creeping weakness in his very bones? He was not yet thirty. Men who fight in the World age on a different schedule than the turning of the earth, but he thought it was not that. He had given up everything for Bandara, one more time, and this time Bandara was not giving up everything for him.

No adepts had come to sit with him in warm fellowship and conversation. No scribe had come to take down anecdotes of what he'd learned in the World. It was as if no one wanted to know what he'd done out there. And that was almost like having done nothing—or having done something shameful. He didn't understand it.

But he was too proud to ask a question whose answer he might not like. Perhaps they disapproved of Niko's time in Tempus's service. Of his pairbond with Sacred Band fighters. Of his warring up Wizardwall and his private battle with a Nisibisi witch. Witches were obscene, unspeakable, dishonorable, but so was war. Any war. And he'd been trained for war by these very adepts. His was a fighting order.

There is no possibility of bringing freedom, or truth, or justice into the World without strife. There must be a corps that will battle for righteousness, for there are endless battalions who serve unrighteousness. On Bandara, some learned to fight in the World so that others would never have to. He had taken on the duty willingly. If he no longer could discharge it, he could tell himself that he'd served his time, that someone younger, someone with unsullied ideals, would take his place. But that was letting his enemy win, for what Niko had learned about life in the World was priceless; he could not be replaced.

Soldiers for disorder would triumph in the end if men like Niko were exhausted by their very numbers, by their youthful fanaticism, brute force and their unthinking commitment to chaos.

His hands gripped his rake so tightly that he ached. He lifted it ankle high and drove it hard into the ground. He knew what he should do—pack up and leave. He simply didn't have the energy to do it.

And he couldn't blame the hierarchy on Bandara. If he was unrefreshed, it was a lack in himself, not in others. He was not responsible for their performance, only for his own. He must be impeccable in his own eyes, as perfect as meditation and self-examination could make him. Then he could leave.

If no one from the main island ever came here and said, "Niko, you've done well. Tell your exploits for our records and leave, unburdened and refreshed," he still must find a way to become strong enough to go.

He must overcome his doubts, for he was beginning to doubt that uncomprehending and ungrateful men were worth his sacrifice. He must overcome his fear of sleep—of what lurked in his dreams. And he must overcome the creeping cynicism that made him care that Tempus might be right: if Aškelon was trying to make a minion out of Niko, as the primal Storm God had made a minion out of Tempus, it shouldn't matter.

Men live, and then they die. It is the quality of the process of living which matters, that and that alone.

With an effort of will as great as he would have needed to lift his cabin from its foundations, Niko began raking the gravel at the center of his pond into

a smooth and ordered pattern. When he had done
that, he would pack up and depart. The gravel ponds
were the symbol of man in the World, as well as man
on Bandara.

If he could bring order to his pond, he could bring
order to his heart. When he no longer craved anything carnal—not revenge by action or inaction, not
a confrontation or an end of confrontation with Aškelon
or with any woman or witch—then he could stride
into the charnal house of human contest without
flinching.

Slowly, from the middle of the pond, Niko began
working his rake. And above, a cloud scudded across
the sun and darkened the day. He did not look up.
There was Aškelon, and the World, and the Nisibisi
witch who loved him, and Tempus and the Sacred
Band—out there, somewhere, waiting.

There was Niko, high on his cliff at Ennina, and
Niko's maat, and his soul and will and bright purpose,
here on Bandara, preparing. As he slowly and carefully moved outward, bare feet refusing to disturb
the balance of the pattern he was making, he began
to see the balance in what awaited, and what must
be left behind.

An equal and opposite sacrifice was what he needed.
An inner peace through strife was how he'd get it.
He was certain, by the time he had come to the edge
of his gravel pond and looked back to see the neatly
raked spiral, that he could find the strength to try.

Over the whole of his gravel, no footstep marred
the pattern. No pebble was out of place. No rake-
furrow wobbled. And the sun emerged from behind
the clouds.

Behind him, a voice said, "Nikodemos, called
Stealth, it is time for us to talk."

Niko turned and there, wraithlike in irridescent

robes, was a master from the main island, the man who had taken Niko's dead teacher's place.

"I thought no one would come," Niko said harshly. "I waited and now I am nearly ready to leave."

"You are not ready to leave," said the old man severely. His face was wizened like a roast turkey's skin and yet his eyes were as live as white-hot coals. "You are ready to begin preparing to leave."

Niko stepped away from the gravel pond, a hot flush creeping up his neck. If he'd known the adept's name, he would have used it. But he did not, and he must wait until it was given—if it was. He said, "I can use all the help I can get." It was an insolent thing to say, without honorifics and bluntly, but Niko didn't like being snuck up on, and there was something in the old master's bearing . . .

"You are not ready because you will receive a visitor, unless we can prevent it." Hot eyes burned him.

Niko didn't look away, but he didn't ask who. Any visitor to Bandara uninvited was a travesty; Niko had invited no one. And he didn't want to hear which of the many Worldly powers that contested over him it might be: Tempus, an unbound witch or wizard, or Aškelon himself. Because Niko's maat told him it was the dream lord, and that, somehow, with Aškelon came all the others.

So his maat spoke to him, a whispering certainty inside his head that caused him to stare unspeakingly at the adept.

And the old man said, "Niko, are you willing to penetrate a deeper mystery—learn things about yourself and your destiny, about the past and the future—to prepare you to battle in the World this time? Dangerous things, for a dangerous undertaking? Without them, you are not . . . will not . . . be ready."

Niko's palms were suddenly slippery on the handle of his rake. "I . . . knew that. Sensed it. I've been feeling unready to leave, yet I must. Soon."

"We know. You haven't answered me."

Of course they knew. And Niko realized that it was not him the adepts had been shunning, but his ghosts—those creatures from the World who chased him. And he said, "Whatever the risk, I will take it gladly for knowledge."

It was an old, ritual statement. But without it, no enlightenment could be undertaken.

Now, Niko's rehabilitation could begin.

By the time the sun had set, the teacher was weary, wary and frustrated.

Niko lay before him on the pallet in his little cabin, every muscle relaxed, eyes open wide. But the student could not reach the deep level of meditation that the teacher required.

"It's something," Niko said softly, staring up at the beams of his ceiling, "that I learned while fighting the Nisibisi witch—not to let someone put me into a trance. I'm sorry, I'm trying to cooperate."

The Bandaran adept was sitting crosslegged, but his knees did not touch the floor. Niko could have sworn that his buttocks didn't rest on the boards, either—that he floated, inches above the ground.

There was, from this teacher, an emanation of power, but also one of desperation. And that was making things worse. Niko said, "Let me try it myself. Give me a few minutes to go to my rest-place, and then meet me there." He'd done this before, though never in controlled circumstances.

Niko's "rest-place" was a gift of the mystery of maat, a spiritual meadow he'd created in his mind, and surrounded with words, a place where he could totally relax—or once it had been so. It had been invaded, during his battles with the supernatural, by other creatures, other minds. To invite someone to your rest-place was nearly sacrilege.

But Niko could see no other way to reach the mental state the teacher insisted he must reach.

He waited for a reply, got none, and took it as assent.

So Nikodemos began the process. He had trained his mind to find his spot as a dog finds its place by the hearth or a fox its den. He closed his eyes and further relaxed his body, starting with his toes. When he could feel his pulse in his toes, he commanded those toes to relax completely, and to tingle with energy. When he had done that, he moved his attention to his feet, then to his knees, and slowly up his body.

Muscles twitched and ticked as he worked, but he understood that this was necessary, a release of tension. It was as if he pulled a warm, wonderful blanket up over himself, a blanket under which nothing could hurt him.

When he had pulled that blanket up over his head, he told himself that he would maintain this perfectly relaxed state until he willed it otherwise, and directed his mind to go, on the count of three, to his rest-place.

He had built it long ago, from the fabric of a dimension no man understood, but many men could use. It was bordered by mountains and a stream ran through it. It was star-shaped and ever green. Once he had truly relaxed he could return there anytime by directing himself, on the count of three, to do so and then visualizing each number until, on the recitation of the last one, he could open his eyes and see the special, blue-green grass of that meadow.

The grass tickled his knees today, and the smell of the breeze was soft and sweet. There had been carnage here once, a battle that had raged even here. For an instant he saw charred earth and blood in his stream. But he cleared those from his fundament with a determined effort.

This is my place, into which no evil can enter, into which no harm will come. Here I am in control of everything and in danger from nothing. Here all that happens will be beneficial to my body and my soul. Here I will find the solutions to my problems and remember them when I return to the world. It was a familiar litany, one from the beginnings of his training. Reciting it was like meeting an old and sorely-missed friend.

Having done that, he proceeded through his ritual as if he were still a novice. He focused on the grass tickling his knees and bowed his head, opening his eyes very slowly to see what was around his feet. Since what he saw then was merely grass and insects, harmless ants and dandelions and grasshoppers, he raised his head more.

In the back of his mind fear rustled—fear that the monsters that once had invaded this place would be shown to him, but he asserted control: this was his place; he was master here. And there were no monsters.

Better still, there was no Aškelon, lord of dreams, and no dead partners from hard-fought wars. There was not even a lost pet, only his meadow, and his mountains, and a warm sun beating down.

He said to the breeze, "I'm ready and I invite you, teacher," and knew that the sound was heard in the cabin where his physical body lay.

The teacher did not materialize from thin air in Niko's rest-place. He came striding out of a copse at the northernmost point of the meadow.

And waved.

And came to sit with him, their knees a handbreath apart.

The teacher said, "Aškelon seeks you, and it endangers us all."

Here, these things could be said without dithering. Here, problems were not for solving. Here, Niko could control even his own fear. He replied, "I have dealt with the dream lord before and lived."

"We want to help you, if you would be freed of this curse."

"I'm not sure that it is a curse . . . yet. But I, too, know that my burdens are too heavy."

"It is your association with Tempus that brings all this about. You could be his successor. Powers know that. You are being molded, tested. We can stop it."

"Stop witches and warlocks and seventh-level adepts, perhaps. But stop twelfth-plane lords—I doubt it."

"Doubt is optional here, is it not?" said the teacher sharply. "Is it that you want to become like Tempus, whom you love?"

Niko tried to deny it, but the words wouldn't come. He said, "Tempus is lonely, pressed beyond measure, suffering beyond limit. He needs help."

"You are a mortal youth. It is not your responsibility."

"He and I are pair-bound . . . brothers."

"You cannot be a brother to what he is," said the teacher. "Look, I will show you."

Then the ancient adept raised his hand, palm toward Niko.

Transiently, Niko felt overwhelming fear and tried to break away, to lower his eyes, to bolt from his rest-place. But then a calm descended, and in the palm of the Bandaran adept, Niko began to see a different place, a distant time, and people whom he thought he recognized.

And then it was as if he were sucked down into other minds and bodies, another time and place.

All his rest-place and the adept who sat there with him dissolved, but for the palm before him, which became a door into another world.

And then the palm too was gone, and Niko was transported more intimately and completely than he had ever thought to be. . . .

AN END TO DREAMING

He was the most powerful sorceror in the whole world, and he was her quarry.

He was called Aškelon of Meridian, and he ruled an archipelago labeled on mouldering maps simply: "Aškelon's," and marked with a skull. None who sailed into the amber mist shrouding the honeyed sea which lapped his domain had ever returned to dispute either the naming, or the posting of dire warnings along the sketchily charted chain of submerged mountains which were his.

She was Cime the Free Agent, and she was going to destroy him. It was nothing personal. She had never met him. She lingered long before his colossus, hewn from basalt, overlooking the western sea, studying his likeness which peered ever toward the ruddy, rising sun. She prepared. She spent a season staring into the heavy-lidded stone eyes, meditating. She committed the harsh, wind-chiseled profile to memory, and from memory it trekked into her dreams, proffering nightmares and fantasies while in whose power she cried out for the cleanliness of simple terror. She learned his secret language from crum-

16

bling palimpsests of sandstone, a language so tortuous and occluded that silver streaked her ebony hair while she was about it. She researched his legends, performed the rites of gods he had served in a time so misty in mind that its days were numbered in reverse of the days of Man.

She trekked the seven continents, spent her summers in hoary vaults.

When she found in the only remaining archive left unsearched the last lines of a tablet whose beginning she had read at the outset of her quest, she was nearly divested of resources.

But she mastered the instructions she had sought. And if she sold more than just her favors to obtain the two diamond needles, each long as her forearm from wrist to elbow and sleeved in leather, which pinned up her nightsmile hair, then she knew the bargain shrewd. He was worth any price. He was Aškelon.

When the solar eclipse begins, in the hundredth-year summer as Aškelon, Lord of Meridian counts time, the topaz mists around the archipelago draw in their skirts and the sky ripples with unnamed colors and the Lord Aškelon works a summoning, petitioning the Stormbringer to send him a Froth Daughter who for a while will chase the years from his eyes.

But this hundredth-year, Cime the Free Agent was waiting.

She lay on a reed raft, rocked gently by the amber waves, to view the islands' coming. They are not always there, some say; they are only not always seen, contend others.

Cime lay on her stomach clothed only in the diamond, leather-wrapped rods which she had thrust through her piled-up mane, and watched the mist boil up in a spout of molten gold from the ocean. She

larded her yet-supple body for the swim while overhead the moon shouldered its way before the cinna-
bar sun. The amber sea darkened; rolled ocher;
sienna; vermillion-black. Above the islands girt with
mist, hellfires beckoned, shivering like flaming cur-
tains across the false dusk.

She had come naked because the ensorceled fog
would strip her if she were not. She had come on the
reed raft because even at this distance from her desti-
nation wood would sop like paper, iron nails rust to
dust, copper turn brittle enough to shatter at a sigh.
She had come with every filling in her head changed
to porcelain, for in Aškelon's domain gold was the
mud from which bricks were baked.

When the sun began to slide from under the moon,
she dove headfirst into the water.

It had been possible that he might come to her,
that his magic would detect her aforetime and he
would himself give chase. As her form knifed the
waves, she heaved a soft sigh of relief: it was no
longer possible.

The ancient eyes of the colossus whose profile split
the winds on a distant shore danced before her as
she swam. She had traded her youth for the secret of
his undoing, but all she really knew of Aškelon was
that he would be unlike any man, mortal or mage,
whom she had ever met.

White seals came and cavorted in the suddenly
glasslike sea. Sworded mentor-fish leaped purple on
her left and right. Azure porpoises caressed her in
amorous play.

Above her head, day regained its hold upon the
sky. But as she entered the mist, the restless aurora
grew even brighter, while the islands glided close
from out of the swaddling pink-gold haze that reached
upward toward the vault of heaven.

A score of strokes within the fog, she could no

longer see the sky at all, just the pale play of the
aurora on a dome of lavender-fleeced cloud that arched
over the becalmed harbor.

A score more strokes, and the mentor-fish were
gone.

As she approached a barque moored at one of the
crystal quays, the porpoises sped seaward.

When she detoured leftward toward a staircase
leading up from the sea, the seals sighed softly and
went their own way.

The barque was fashioned in the semblance of a
winged lion, his ruby paws outstretched to rake the
waves. The crimson sail was furled, the silks of its
pavillion drawn up. Oars glinted in their ports. Men's
laughter touched her ears, and she dove deep and
swam submerged until her breath gave out.

When she broke the surface, a figure surmounted
the wide stairs' summit, wreathed in dark smoke.

The steps of silver-shot crystal were mossed below
the water-line. She trod carefully, sluicing seaweeds
from her as she climbed, conscious of the slap of his
sandals, descending.

The stairs seemed molded, rather than hewn. She
sang a song she had learned for the occasion, a song
that had not been sung for an age.

The slapping sandals ceased their whisper on the
stone.

Cime's skin, gazed upon, quivered. Limbs and
muscles, scrutinized from above, lost grace. She became aware of her breathing, and that water had
lodged in her right ear.

Still singing, she raised her head in time to see his
smile's final flash.

Then she paused, speaking desperate encourage-
ment to her knees.

He was not at all what she had expected.

Now the likeness of Aškelon carved into the western cliffs is grey near to black. Its brow is furrowed and its nose is a beak of hauteur and its mouth curls within a flowing beard like an angry seaserpent. Its eyes are white and pale. They stare out at the sea with a proprietary gaze whose claim seems staked in hell. Its cheeks are undercut with deep carven hollows in which demons raise their broods. The shoulders slope into the mountain and bear a giant, double-headed adze upon them. Some swear that the fists uncurl on stormy nights to crush unsuspecting vessels in their grasp.

The fists were the same, dark with the kiss of salt winds, seared by the unending seasons. But the face, and the form . . .

Cime sang her soft fierce song with greater fervor, while in his limbo the sorcerer, unprepared, knew nothing.

. . . Aškelon's face was angled, hung with shadow, dark with trial. But the somber skin and the black hair, traced with stars of grey whipping back from a gently rising brow had not the death in them that she had seen in the stone. The round profile was not so sharp; the curl of lip not so cruel; the line of chin, bared of beard, had no hint of intimidation in it. The eyes of Aškelon of Meridian, however, were pale: they were light as fine silver, with dark rings around them as if chased. And in those colorless eyes rode sharp shards of sorrow, inky eons of loneliness, and a compassion deep enough to baptize the world anew.

But Cime, climbing mechanically the dozen steps that separated them, did not cease her song.

She reached up into her hair and pulled free the two rods of diamond sheathed in hide. She stripped them and cast aside the leather tubes, and brought the two points together before her body so that their tips touched.

Then she stopped her song, one step below him.

Aškelon, Lord of Meridian, shivered and continued the motion he had started before the first strains of the song imprisoned him: he swept off his cloak, the color of dried blood, and took a final step downward.

He faced her there, the cloak extended, his eyes yet full of joy and welcome.

"Aškelon," Cime said, "if it is for me that you hold jubilee, I salute you." She knew he could not see the needle-sharp wands, that he saw only her outstretched hands. She knew also that the melodies of flute and string, the bubbling laughter that came ever closer, were the welcome the people of the golden city held out to their new mistress. She dared not look away from him. Yet what she saw in that face tore her heart.

The pale eyes held her. The hand grasping the cloak outstretched. Around his wrist was a band of obsidian rimmed with silver. In its center was a snowflake of purest white.

"Froth Daughter, our bethrothal barque awaits," said he with the tiniest frown. "Praise be to the Storm-bringer for answering my plea."

"Sorcerer," she retorted, catching his outstretched wrist between the glowing points of the diamond wands, "I am here to sing you the song of Last Storm. I am no Froth Daughter, but a daughter of Man. Too long have you held the world in thrall. These people, your servants, shall be free. The archipelago shall be free. And you, too, shall be free: free to go to your death."

He knew her before that last. He could not move his wrist from what seemed to him the grasp of thin air. Her hands appeared to hover on either side of his arm. The cloak dropped from his nerveless fingers and turned dark sopping moisture from the crystal stair.

"Free Agent," he said wonderingly, with no hint of accusation in his voice. He did not lunge at her, pull back, or even try to jerk his hand away. He merely stood looking at her from out of those silver pits of weariness. "Free Agent, I had thought there were no more of you. It seems I was mistaken. What is your name?"

And when she did not answer, nor thrust the needles' diamond tips through his wrist and the jeweled band called the Heart of Aškelon, he prodded.

"Come now, have I not even the right to know the name of my executioner?" So calm was Aškelon, so magnificent was that countenance in contemplation of death, that still Cime could not sing, nor even make the tiny twisting motion with her fingers which would consign his spirit to endless toil in the service of his age-old masters.

"I am Cime," said the Free Agent. "And you are the last."

"So, then, are you."

"That is true," she said, suddenly longing to lift the shadows from the corners of his mouth.

"There will be nothing left for you," spoke the sorcerer softly. "There will be no dreams, any longer."

"So I have heard it said. But there will be no sorcerers, either."

"And no Free Agents."

"I do not mind that," she replied, and began to fear herself. She rolled the needles once in her fingers, and the Lord Aškelon shuddered. The needles' tips drove a hair's breadth into the obsidian band where the snowflake design had its center, and at the point on his wrist's underside equidistant.

"There will be darkness, and madness, and death. There will be such penance in the land of Man as you cannot conceive. There will be no healing for the tired mind, no wonder for the ailing spirit. Nothing.

Just empty sleep. You rob the spirits of us all, little sister. Make no end to dreaming." His brows were drawn over diamond eyes that etched their message on her soul.

The song burst from her lips and her shoulders convulsed. The needles shattered obsidian like eggshell, biting deep into flesh to meet in the bone of the sorcerer's wrist.

The ground heaved. A moan of anguish came from the golden houses that bestarred the quayside. The cobbles of precious stones crumbled, and their dust changed to mud upon the ground. The crystal quays turned to sand and slid into the sea. The sounds of jubilee shrilled until they were no longer music. All that could be heard was the screech of angry gulls and seals barking from the clay cliffs on whose bottommost ledge they stood.

Cime sang the song's refrain.

In the harbor, where the lion-prowed barque had been, floated a basking shark.

The golden clouds blew away on a fierce grey wind, and a cinder from a far-off city pricked Cime's eye.

She dared not take hand from wand to rub it, for Aškelon's wrist was yet impaled between her fingers. Hoarsely, Cime sang on.

The stinking wind ruffled his black hair, blew it around his face. About his feet lay the cloak, at his waist he still bore the kirtle of brownish-purple. He was not yet a pile of mud nor a mound of sand or a sea robin flopping between her legs. Cime sang the final lines, and jerked the diamond wands from his wrist.

Blood welled there. The shards of the Heart of Aškelon fell from his wrist to the clay, and the blood from his wound dripped onto them. He looked at her, and shook his head wearily. Grasping the injured limb with his good hand, he turned full round, inspecting his city's ruins. Then he knelt down and retrieved the sopping cloak and with a strip torn from it bound his wound.

Kneeling on one knee, he gathered up the splinters of obsidian from the clay.

He did not rise.

"Take your leave, Cime, once Free Agent. Go on. You need not stay to see me spill my life upon the beach."

She looked down on the Lord of Meridian, whose great form was racked with tremors, at his deep, wounded eyes in which were engraved all the dreams of a race.

She did as he asked. She walked away down the wrack-strewn shore, among its rotting, thousand-legged amber jellyfish, carefully skirting the oily, scummed tide.

Once she stopped, to pick up the leather sheaths for the diamond pins. With them she bound up her hair. Holding her breath in the foul air, she waded into the choppy, brownish water, then struck out for her reed raft.

A TRICK OF MEMORY

"What has *she* to do with anything?" said Niko before the vision had truly faded. "A trick of memory, an adept's game, that's all this is. Nothing more." And he raised his head and opened his eyes . . .

. . . to see his rest-place about him, as solid as the pallet on which his body must be sleeping still, somewhere minds away. For an instant he trembled there, in his star-shaped meadow, fearful for his fleshly robes.

"Your body is safe, right where you left it," said the adept across from him, the wizened brown and ancient man whose hand was still raised to Niko's face. But now the fingers curled down, almost a fist, closing the door that opened through the master's palm.

This whole sense of being physically in his rest-place unnerved Nikodemos. Before, when this had happened, it had been because evil had entered here. He'd bled here and fought here and returned to his physical form with scars he'd earned here.

Fear usually made his rest-place grow grainy, insubstantial. Sometimes it could jerk him back to wakefulness. But not today. Today, as had sometimes happened in the past when Niko was deep in trouble, he was as physically present in his place of mental relaxation as he'd ever been on any battlefield.

He stared at the master and the adept stared back. In those eyes he saw only sharp-honed purpose, no malefic glint, but no mercy either. This was a lesson the adept before him was determined to teach.

Niko squared his shoulders and shifted aching knees. He knew his legs were straight, somewhere else where his body lay, but here his knees were bent for too long, and the strain was as real as it could be.

He could die here, he'd learned that. He could bleed here, he knew from past experience. Danger was as real here as in the World. And he'd brought any consequences upon himself by inviting the Bandaran master into his private place.

"You haven't answered me," Niko accused the adept. "What has Tempus's sister got to do with me? What can be learned from a creature of such nature?"

"These are the questions," said the adept without a smile. "You have the answers."

"I don't. She's . . . committed to destruction. For ideology. For intolerance. Become an octave of the evil she purports to fight."

"Exactly," nodded the adept. "There are no right or wrong ideologies, only ideologues; no good and evil sides, only good and evil people. Eradication of a race is rightly termed genocide, and bigots in all disguises become worse than what they hate. Has she not, since then, taken up with wizards? Fallen in with archmages? Become no better—perhaps worse— than what she fought to destroy in your dream?"

"Is that what it was—a dream? A dream within a dream. It felt like . . . memory."

"For you, it was a dream. For them, it was life,

and is now memory. This Aškelon you encountered there, is he the terrible dream lord before whom you shudder and quail, afraid of his very affection?"

"Whose side are you on?" Niko demanded.

"Exactly," smiled the adept. "Exactly."

Then Niko remembered everything the adept had just said, and blushed. Confusion rose up in him like an ague, making his head swim. He closed his eyes before it, remembering the Heart of Aškelon, the pain on its owner's face, and the closed-hearted woman who threatened the very realm of dream for something once perceived as principle, but finally no more than habit.

Niko shook his head there in his rest-place. Not only was that woman one he'd shunned in life, but she was one the Riddler called "sister." She'd run afoul of every piece of moral tripe she hid behind, by the time Niko had met her. He'd never understood the hard and unbending Cime, or the reason Tempus, who feared nothing else, feared her.

Now he did. She was a lesson in humility, a walking proof that no ethos, pursued without thought or mercy, is ethical. And he realized why he'd seen the dream, or memory, or whatever it was: she'd become indistinguishable from what she battled hardest; she'd taken up the arms of her enemies and lost everything that differentiated her from them, in the name of oath and righteousness.

She'd done as much evil fighting evil as evil had ever done. And that hit home: Niko could not risk losing sight of his own humanity, losing the ability to see clearly, to deliver mercy, to rise above his own prejudice.

Aškelon, in that moment a trick of memory had provided, was not a villain, in Niko's way of thinking.

And when he thought that thought, the adept

nodded as if he'd spoken aloud, and said: "That's right, Nikodemos. Now look here, and learn another thing about passion, prejudice, and the art of war."

Again, before Niko's eyes, the palm of the adept opened, its fingers uncurling to reveal a door through which Niko had to step. . . .

VASHANKA'S MINION

— *1* —

The storm swept down on Sanctuary in unnatural fury, as if to punish the thieves for their misdeeds. Its hailstones were large as fists. They pummeled Wideway and broke windows on the Street of Red Lanterns and collapsed the temple of Ils, most powerful of the conquered Ilsigs' gods.

The lightning it brought snapped up from the hills and down from the devilish skies and wherever it spat the world shuddered and rolled. It licked round the dome of Prince Kadakithis's palace and when it was gone, the Storm God Vashanka's name was seared into the stone in huge hieratic letters visible from the harbor. It slithered in the window of Jubal's walled estate and circled round the bulky slavetrader's chair while he sat in it, turning his black face blue with terror.

It danced on a high hill between the slaver's estate and the cowering town, where a mercenary named Tempus schooled his new Syrese horse in the art of death. He had bought the tarnished silver beast sight unseen, sending to a man whose father's life he had once saved.

"Easy," he advised the horse, who slipped in a sharp turn, throwing mud up into his rider's face. Tempus cursed the mud and the rain and the hours he would need to spend on his tack when the lesson was done. As for the screaming, stumbling hawk-masked man who fled iron-shod hooves in ever-shortening circles, he had no gods to pray to—he just howled.

The horse wheeled and hopped; its rider clung tightly, reins flapping loose, using only his knees to guide his mount. If the slaver who kept a private army must flaunt the fact, then the mercenary-cum-Guardsman would reduce its ranks. He would teach Jubal the overweening flesh merchant that he who is too arrogant, is lost. He saw it as part of his duty to the Ranke Prince-Governor he was sworn to protect. Tempus had taken down a dozen hawk-masks. This one, stumbling gibbering, would make thirteen.

"Kill," suggested the mercenary, tiring of his sport in the face of the storm.

The flattened ears of the misty horse flickered, came forward. It lunged, neck out. Teeth and hooves thunked into flesh. Screaming. Then screaming stopped.

Tempus let the horse pummel the corpse awhile, stroking the beast's neck and cooing soft praise. When bones showed in a lightning flash, he backed the horse off and set it at a walk toward the walled city.

It was then that the lightning came circling round man and mount.

"Stand, stand." The horse, though he shook like a newborn foal, stood. The searing red light violated Tempus's tight-shut lids and made his eyes tear. An awful voice rang inside his head, deep and thunderous: *"You are mine."*

"I have never doubted it," grated the mercenary.

"You have doubted it repeatedly," growled the

voice querulously, if thunder can be said to carp.
"*You have been unruly, faithless though you pledged
me your troth. You have been, since you renounced
your inheritance, a mage, a philospher, an auditing
Adept of the Order of the Blue Star, a—*"

"Look here, God. I have also been a cuckold, a
foot-soldier in the ranks, a general at the end of that.
I have bedded more iron in flesh than any ten other
men who have lived as long as I. Now you ring me
round with thunder and compass me with lightning
though I am here to expand Your worship among
these infidels. I am building Your accursed temple as
fast as I can. I am no priest, to be terrified by loud
words and bright manifestations. Get Thee hence,
and leave this slum unenlightened. They do not deserve me, and they do not deserve You!"

A gust sighed fiercely, flapping Tempus's woolens
against his mail beneath.

"*I have sent you hither to build me a temple among
the heathens, O sleepless one! A temple you will build!*"

"A temple I will build. Yes, sir, Vashanka, lord of
the Edge and the Point. If You leave me alone to do
it." Damn pushy tutelary god. "You blind my horse,
O God, and I will put him under Your threshold
instead of the enemies slain in battle Your ritual
demands. Then we will see who comes to worship
there."

"*Do not trifle with me, Man.*"

"Then let me be. I am doing the best I can. There
is no room for foreign gods in the hearts of these
Sanctuarites. The Ilsig gods they were born under
have seen to that. Do something amazing: strike the
fear of You into them."

"*I cannot even make you cower, O impudent
human!*"

"Even Your visitations get old, after three hundred fifty years. Go scare the locals. This horse will founder, standing hot in the rain."

The thunder changed its tune, becoming canny. *"Go you to the harbor, My son, and look upon what My Majesty hath wrought! And into the Maze, where I am making My power known!"*

With that, the corral of lightning vanished, the thunder ceased, and the clouds blew away on a west wind, so that the full moon shone upon the land.

"Too much krrf," the mercenary who had sold himself for a Hell Hound sighed. "Hell Hound" was what the citizenry called the Prince's Guard; as far as Tempus was concerned. Sanctuary was Hell. The only thing that made it bearable was krrf, his drug of choice. Rubbing a clammy palm across his mouth, he dug in his human-hide belt until searching fingers found a little silver box he always carried. Flipping it open, he took a pinch of black Caronne krrf and, clenching his fist, piled the dust into the hollow between his first thumb joint and the fleshy muscle leading to his knuckle. He sniffed deeply, sighed, and repeated the process, inundating his other nostril.

"Too much damn krrf," he chuckled, for the krrf had never been stepped on—he did not buy adulterated drugs—and all six and a half feet of him tingled from its kiss. One of these days he would have to stop using it—the same day he lay down his sword.

He felt for its hilt, patted it. He had taken to calling it his "Wriggly-be-good," since he had come to this Godforsaken warren of magicians and changelings and thieves. Then, the initial euphoria of the drug past, he kneed his horse homeward.

It was the krrf, not the instructions of the lightning or any fear of Vashanka, that made him go by way of the harbor. He was walking out his horse before taking it to the stable the Hell Hounds shared with the barracks personnel. What had ever possessed him to come down-country among the Ilsigs? It was not for his fee, which was exorbitant, that he had come, or for the sake of those interests in the Rankan Capital who underwrote him—those who hated the Emperor so much that they were willing to back such a loser as Kadakithis, if they could do it without becoming the brunt of too many jokes. It was not for the temple, though he was pleased to build it. It was some old, residual empathy in Tempus for a prince so inept as to be known far and wide as "Kitty" which had made him come. Tempus had walked away from *his* primogeniture in Azehur, a long time ago, leaving the throne to his brother, who was not compromised by palace politics. He had deposited a treatise on the nature of being in the temple of a favored goddess, and he had left. Had he ever, really, been that young? Young as Prince Kadakithis, whom even the Wrigglies disparaged?

Tempus had been around in the days when the Ilsigs had been the Enemy: the Wrigglies. He had been on every battlefield in the Rankan-Ilsig conflict. He had spitted more Ilsigs than most men, watched them writhe soundlessly until they died. Some said he had coined their derogatory nickname, but he had not, though he had doubtless helped spread it . . .

He rode down Wideway, and he rode past the docks. A ship was being made fast, and a crowd had gathered round it. He squeezed the horse's barrel, urging it into the press. With only four of his fellow Hell Hounds in Sanctuary, and a local garrison whose personnel never ventured out in groups of less than six, it was natural for him to take a look.

He did not like what he saw of the man who was being helped from the storm-wracked ship that had come miraculously to port with no sail intact, who murmured through pale cruel lips to the surrounding

Ilsigs, then climbed into a Rankan litter bound for the palace.

He spurred the horse. "Who?" he demanded of the eunuch-master whose path he suddenly barred.

"Aspect, the archmage," lisped the palace lackey, "if it's any business of yours."

Behind the lackey and the quartet of ebony slaves the shoulder-borne litter trembled. The view-curtain with Kitty's device on it was drawn back, fell loose again.

"Out of my way, Hound," squeaked the enraged little pastry of a eunuch-master.

"Don't get flapped, Eunice," said Tempus, wishing he were in Caronne, wishing he had never met a god, wishing he were anywhere else. *Oh, Kitty, you have done it this time*. Alain Aspect, yet! Alchemist extraordinaire, assassin among magicians, dispeller of enchantments, in a town that ran on contract sorcery?

"Back, back, back," he counseled the horse, who twitched its ears and turned its head around reproachfully, but obeyed him.

He heard titters among the eunuchs, another behind in the crowd. He swung round in his saddle. "Hakiem, if I hear any stories about me I do not like, I will know whose tongue to hang on my belt."

The bent, news-nosed storyteller, standing amid the children who always clustered round him, stopped laughing. His rheumy eyes met Tempus's. "I have a story I would like to tell you, Hell Hound. One you would like to hear, I humbly imagine."

"What is it, then, old man?"

"Come closer, Hell Hound, and say what you will pay."

"How can I tell you how much it's worth until I hear?" The horse snorted, raised his head, sniffed a rank, evil breeze come suddenly from the stinking Downwind beach.

"We must haggle."

"Somebody else, then, old man. I have a long night ahead." He patted the horse, watching the crowd of Ilsigs surging round, their heads level with his hips.

"That is the first time I have seen *him* backed off": a stage-whisper reached Tempus through the buzz of the crowd. He looked for the source of it, could not find one culprit more likely than the rest. There would be a lot more of that sort of talk, when word spread. But he did not interfere with sorcerers. Never again. He had done it once, thinking his tutelary god could protect him. His hand went to his hip, squeezed. Beneath his dun woolens and beneath his ringmail he wore a woman's scarf. He never took it off. It was faded and it was ragged and it reminded him never to argue with a warlock. It was all he had left of her, who had been the subject of his dispute with a mage.

Long ago in Azehur . . .

He sighed, a rattling sound, in a voice hoarse and gravelly from endless battlefield commands. "Have it your way tonight, then, Wriggly. And hope you live 'til morning." He named a price. The storyteller named another. The difference was split.

The old man came close and put his hand on the horse's neck. "The lightning came and the thunder rolled and when it was gone the temple of Ils was no more. The Prince has bought the aid of a mighty enchanter, whom even the bravest of the Hell Hounds fears. A woman was washed up naked and half drowned on the Downwinders' beach and in her hair were pins of diamond."

"Pins?"

"Rods, then."

"Wonderful. What else?"

"The red-head from Amoli's Lily Garden died at moonrise."

He knew very well what whore the old man meant. He did not like the story, so far. He growled. "You had better astound me, quick, for the price you're asking."

"Between the Vulgar Unicorn and the tenement on the corner an entire building appeared on that vacant lot, you know the one."

"I know it."

"Astounding?"

"Interesting. What else?"

"It is rather fancy, with a gilded dome. It has two doors, and above them two signs that read, 'Men,' and 'Women.' "

Vashanka had kept his word, then.

"Inside it, so the patrons of the Unicorn say, they sell weapons. Very special weapons. And the price is dear."

"What has this to do with me?"

"Some folk who have gone in there have not come out. And some have come out and turned one upon the other, dueling to the death. Some have merely slain whomsoever crossed their paths. Yet, word is spreading, and Ilsig and Rankan queue up like brothers before its doors. Since some of those who were standing in line were hawk-masks, I thought it good that you should know."

"I am touched, old man. I had no idea you cared." He threw the copper coins to the storyteller's feet and reined the horse sideways so abruptly it reared. When its feet touched the ground, he set it at a collected canter through the crowd, letting the rabble scatter before its iron-shod hooves as best they might.

— 2 —

In Sanctuary, enchantment ruled. No sorcerer believed in gods. But they believed in the Law of Correspondences, and they believed in evil. Thus, since every negative must have its positive, they *implied* gods. Give a god an inch and he will take your soul. That was what the commoners and the second-rate prestidigitators lined up outside the Weaponshop of Vashanka did not realize, and that was why no respectable magician or Hazard Class Enchanter stood among them.

In they filed, men to Tempus's left, toward the Vulgar Unicorn, and women to his right, toward the tenement on the corner.

Personally, Tempus did not feel it wise or dignified for a god to engage in a commercial venture. From across the street, he took notes on who came and went.

Tempus was not sure whether he was going in there, or not.

A shadow joined the queue, disengaged, walked toward the Vulgar Unicorn in the tricky light of fading stars. It saw him, hesitated, took one step back.

Tempus leaned forward, his elbow on his pommel, and crooked a finger. "Hanse, I would like a word with you."

The youth cat-walked toward him, errant torchlight from the Unicorn's open door twinkling on his weapons. From ankle to shoulder, Shadowspawn bristled with armaments.

"What is it with you, Tempus? Always on my tail. There are bigger frogs than this one in Sanctuary's pond."

"Are you not going to buy anything tonight?"

"I'll make do with what I have, thanks. I do *not* swithe with sorcerers."

"Steal something for me?" Tempus whispered, leaning down. The boy had black hair, black eyes, and blacker prospects in this desperados' demesne.

"I'm listening."

"Two diamond rods from the lady who washed up on the beach tonight."

"Why?"

"I won't ask you how, and you won't ask me why, or we'll forget it." He sat up straight in his saddle.

"Forget it, then," toughed Shadowspawn, deciding he wanted nothing to do with this Hell Hound.

"Call it a prank, a jest at the expense of an old girlfriend."

The thief edged around where Tempus could not see him, into a dapple of deepest dark. He named a price.

The Hell Hound did not argue. Rather, he paid half in advance.

"I've heard you don't really work for Kitty. I've heard your dues to the mercenaries' guild are right up to date, and that Kitty knows better than to give you any orders. If you are not arguing about my price, it must be too low."

Silence.

"Is it true that you roughed up that whore who died tonight? That Amoli is so afraid of you that you do whatever you want in her place and never pay?"

Tempus chuckled, a sound like the cracking of dry ice. "I will take you there, when you deliver, and you can see for yourself what I do."

There was no answer from the shadow, just a skittering of stones.

Yes, I will take you there, young one. And yes, you are right. About everything. You should have asked for more.

— 3 —

Tempus lingered there still, eating a boxed lunch from the Unicorn's kitchen, when a voice from above his head said, "The deal is off. That girl is a sorceress, if a pretty one. I'll not chance ensorcelment to lift baubles I don't covet, and for a pittance!"

Girl? The woman was nearly his own age, unless another set of diamond rods existed, and he doubted that. He yawned, not reaching up to take the purse that dangled over the lee of the roof, "I am disappointed. I thought Shadowspawn could steal."

The innuendo was not lost on the invisible thief. The purse was withdrawn. An impalpable something told him he was once again alone, but for the clients of Vashanka's Weaponshop. Things would be interesting in Sanctuary, for a good little while to come. He had counted twenty-three purchasers able to walk away with their mystical armaments. Four had died while he watched, intrigued.

It was possible that a career Hell Hound such as Zalbar might have intervened. But Tempus wore Vashanka's amulet about his neck, and, if he did not agree with Him, he would at least bear with his god.

The woman he was waiting for showed there at dusk. He liked dusk; he liked it for killing and he liked it for loving. Sometimes, if he was very lucky, the dusk made him tired and he could nap. A man who has been cursed by an archmage and pressed into service by a god does not sleep much. Sleep was something he chased like other men chased women. Women, in general, bored him, unless they were taken in battle, or unless they were whores.

This woman, her black hair brushing her doeskin-clad shoulders, was an exception.

He called her name, very softly. Then again: "Cime." She turned, and at last he was sure. He had thought Hakiem could mean no other: he had not been wrong.

Her eyes were gray as his horse. Silver shot her hair, but she was yet comely. Her hands rose, hesitated, covered a mouth pretending to hardness and tight with fear. He recognized the aborted motion of her hands: toward her head, forgetful that the rods she sought were no longer there.

He did not move in his saddle, or speak again. He let her decide, glance quickly about the street, then come to him.

When her hand touched the horse's bridle, he said: "It bites."

"Because you taught it to. It will not bite me." She held it by the muzzle, squeezing the pressure points that rode the skin there. The horse raised his head slightly, moaned, and stood shivering.

"What seek you in there?" He inclined his head toward Vashanka's; a lock of copper hair fell over one eye.

"The tools of my trade were stolen.'

"Have you money?"

"Some. Not enough."

"Come with me."

"Never again."

"You have kept your vow, then?"

"I slay sorcerers. I cannot suffer any man to touch me except a client. I dare no love; I am chaste of heart."

"All these aching years?"

She smiled. It pulled her mouth in hard at its corners and he saw aging no potion or cosmetic spell could hide. "Every one. And you? You did not take the Blue Star, or I would see it on your brow. What discipline serves your will?"

"None. Revenge is fruitless. The past is only alive in us. I am not meant for sorcery. I love logic too well."

"So, you are yet damned?"

"If that is what you call it, I suppose—yes. I work for the Storm God, sometimes. I do a lot of wars."

"What brought you here, Cle—"

"Tempus, now. It keeps me in perspective. I am building a temple for Him." He pointed to Vashanka's Weaponshop, across the street. His finger shook. He hoped she had not seen. "You must not ply your trades here. I have employment as a Hell Hound. Appearances must be preserved. Do not pit us against one another. It would be too sour a memory."

"For whomever survived? Can it be you love me still?" Her eyes were full of wonder.

"No," he said, but cleared his throat. "Stay out of there. I know His service well. I would not recommend it. I will get you back what you have lost. Meet me at the Lily Garden tonight at midnight, and you will have them. I promise. Just take down no sorcerers between now and then. If you do, I will not return them, and you cannot get others."

"Bitter, are you not? If I do what you are too weak to do, what harm is there in that?" Her right eyebrow raised. It hurt him to watch her.

"We are the harm. And we are the harmed, as well. I am afraid that you may have to break your fast, so be prepared. I will reason with myself, but I promise nothing."

She sighed. "I was wrong. You have not changed one bit."

"Let go of my horse."

She did.

He wanted to tell her to let go of his heart, but he was struck mute. He wheeled his mount and clattered down the street. He had no intention of leaving. He just waited in a nearby alley until she was gone.

Then he hailed a passing soldier, and sent a message to the palace.

When the sun danced above the Vulgar Unicorn's improbably engaged weather vane, support troops arrived, and Kadakithis's new warlock, Aspect, was with them.

"Since last night, and this is the first report you have seen fit to make?" The sorcerer's pale lips flushed. His eyes burned within his shadowed cowl.

"I hope you and Kadakithis had a talk."

"We did, we did. You are not still angry at the world after all these years?"

"I am yet living. I have your kind to blame or thank, whichever."

"Do you not think it strange that we have been thrown together as—equals?"

"I think that is not the right word for it, Aspect. What are you about, here?"

"Now, now, Hell Hound—"

"Tempus."

"Yes, Tempus. You have not lost your fabled sense of irony. I hope it is a comfort."

"Quite, actually. Do not interfere with the gods, guildbrother of my nemesis."

"Our prince is justifiably worried. Those weapons—"

"—equal out the balance between the oppressors and the oppressed. Most of Sanctuary cannot afford your services, or the prices of even the lowliest members of the Enchanters' Guild. Let it be. We will get the weapons back, as their wielders meet their fates."

"I have to report to Kitt—to Kadakithis."

"Then report that I am handling it." Behind the magician, he could see the ranks whispering. Thirty men, the archmage had brought. Too many.

"You and I have more in common than in dispute, Tempus. Let us join forces."

"I would sooner bed an Ilsig matron."

"Well, I am going in there." The archmage shook his head and the cowl fell back. He was pretty, ageless, a blond. "With or without you."

"Be my guest," Tempus offered.

The archmage looked at him strangely. "We do the same services in the world, you and I. Killing, whether with natural or supernatural weapons, is still killing. You are no better than I."

"Assuredly not, except that I will outlive you. And I will make sure you do not get your requisite burial ritual."

"You would not!"

"Like you said, I yet bear my grudge—against every one of you."

With a curse that made the ranks clap their hands to their helmeted ears, the archmage swished into the street, across it, and through the door marked "Men" without another word. It was his motioned command which made the troops follow.

A waitress Tempus knew came out when the gibbous moon was high, to ask him if he was hungry. She brought him fish and he ate it, watching the doors.

When he had just about finished, a terrible rumble crawled up the street, tremors following in its wake. He slid from his horse and held its muzzle, and the reins up under its bit. The doors of Vashanka's Weaponshop grew shimmery, began taking color. Above, the moon went behind a cloud. The little dome on the shop rocked, grew cracks, crazed, steamed. The doors were ruby red, and melting. Awful wails and screams and the smell of sulphur and ozone filled the night.

Patrons began streaming out of the Vulgar Unicorn, drinks in hand. They stayed well back from the rocking building, which howled as it stressed larger, growing turgid, effluescing spectrums which sheeted and snapped and snarled. The doors went molten white, then they were gone. A figure was limned in the left-hand doorway, and it was trying to climb empty air. It flamed and screeched, dancing, crumbling, facing the street but unable to pass the invisible barrier against which it pounded. It stank: the smell of roasting flesh was overwhelming. Behind it, helmets crumpled, dripped onto the contorted faces of soldiers whose mustaches had begun to flare.

The mage who tried to break down the invisible door had no fists; he had pounded them away. The ranks were char and ash in falling effigy of damnation. The doors which had been invisible began to cool to white, then to gold, then to red.

The street was utterly silent. Only the snorts of his horse and the squeals of the domed structure could be heard. The squeals fell off to growls and shudders. The doors cooled, turned dark.

People muttered, drifted back into the Unicorn with mumbled wardings, tracing signs and taking many backward looks.

Tempus, who could have saved thirty innocent soldiers and one guilty magician, got out his silver box and sniffed some krrf.

He had to be at the Lily Garden soon.

When he got there, the mixed elation of drug and death had faded.

What if Shadowspawn did not appear with the rods? What if the girl Cime did not come to get them back? What if he still could hurt, as he had not hurt for more than three hundred years?

He had had a message from the palace, from Prince Kadakithis himself. He was not going up there, just yet. He did not want to answer any questions about the archmage's demise. He did not want to appear involved. His only chance to help the Prince-Governor effectively lay in working his own way. Those were his terms, and under those terms Kitty's supporters in the Rankan capital had employed him to come down here and play Hell Hound and see what he could do. There were no wars, anywhere. He had been bored, his days stretching out never-ending, bleak. So he had concerned himself with Kitty, for something to do. The building of Vashanka's temple he oversaw for himself more than Kadakithis, who understood the necessity of elevating the state cult above the Ilsig gods, but believed only in wizardry, and his noble Ranke blood.

He was not happy about the spectacle at Vashanka's Weaponshop. Sloppy business, this sideshow melting and unmelting. The archmage must have been talented, to make his struggles visible to those outside.

Wisdom is to know the thought which steers all things through all things, a friend of his who was a philosopher had once said to him. The thought that was steering all things through Sanctuary was muddled, unclear.

That was the hitch, the catch, the problem with employing the supernatural in a natural milieu. Things got confused. With so many spells at work, the fabric of causality was overly strained. Add the gods, and Evil and Good faced each other across a board game whose extent was the phenomenal world. He wished the gods would stay in their heavens and the sorcerers in their hells.

Oh, he had heard endless persiflage about simultaneity; iteration—the constant redefining of the now by checking it against the future—; alchemical laws of consonance. When he had been a student of philosophy and Cime had been a maiden, he had learned the axiom that Mind is unlimited and self-controlled, but all the other things are connected; that nothing is completely separated off from any other thing, nor are things divided one from the other, except Mind.

The sorcerers put it another way: they called the consciousness of all things into service, according to the laws of magic.

Not philosphy, nor theology, nor thaumaturgy held the answer for Tempus; he had turned away from them, each and all. But he could not forget what he had learned.

And none of the adepts like to admit that no servitor can be hired without wages. The wages of unnatural life are unnatural death.

He wished he could wake up in Azehur, with his family, and know that he had dreamed this impious dream.

But instead he came to Amoli's whorehouse, the Lily Garden. Almost, but not quite, he rode the horse up its stairs. Resisting the temptation, he reflected that in every age he had ever studied, doomcryers abounded. No millenium is attractive to the man immured in it; enough prophecies have been made in antiquity that one who desires, in any age, to take the position that Apocalypse is at hand can easily defend it. He would not join that dour Order; he would not worry about anything but Tempus, and the matter awaiting his attention.

Inside Amoli's, Hanse the thief sat in full swagger, a pubecent girl on each knee.

"Ah," she waved. "I have something for you." Shadowspawn tumbled both girls off of him, and stood, stretching widely, so that every arm-dagger and belted sticker and thigh-sheath creaked softly. The girls at his feet stayed there, staring up at Tempus wide-eyed. One whimpered to Shadowspawn and clutched his thigh.

"'Room key,'" Tempus snapped to no one in particular, and held out his hand. The concierge, not Amoli, brought it to him.

"Hanse?"

"Coming." He extended a hand to one girl.

"Alone."

"You are not my type," said the thief, suspicious.

"I need just a moment of your evening. You can do what you wish with the rest."

Tempus looked at the key, headed off toward a staircase leading to the room which bore a corresponding number.

He heard the soft tread of Shadowspawn close behind.

When the exchange had been made, the thief departed, satisfied with both his payment and his gratuity, but not quite sure that Tempus appreciated the trouble to which he had put himself, or that he had gotten the best of the bargain they had made.

He saw the woman he had robbed before she saw him, and ended up in a different girl's room than the one he had chosen, in order to avoid a scene. When he had heard her steps pass by, stop before the door behind which the big Hell Hound waited, he made preclusive threats to the woman whose mouth he had stopped with the flat of his hand, and slipped downstairs to spend his money somewhere else, discreetly.

If he had stayed, he might have found out what the diamond rods were really worth; he might have found out what the sour-eyed mercenary with his high brow, suddenly so deeply creased, and his lightly carried mass, which seemed tonight too heavy, was worried about. Or perhaps he could have fathomed Tempus's enigmatic parting words:

"I would help you if I could, backstreeter," Tempus had rumbled. "If I had met you long ago or if you liked horses, there would be a chance. You have done me a great service. More than that pouch holds. I am seldom in any man's debt, but you, I own, can call me anytime."

"You paid me, Hell Hound. I am content," Hanse had demurred, confused by weakness where he had never imagined it might dwell. Then he saw the Hell Hound fish out a snuffbox of krrf, and thought he understood.

But later, he went back to Amoli's and hung around the steps, cautiously petting the big man's horse, the krrf he had sniffed making him willing to dodge the beast's square, yellow teeth.

— *4* —

She had come to him, had Cime. She was what she was, what she had always been.

It was Tempus who was changed: Vashanka had entered into him, the Storm God who was Lord of Weapons who was Lord of Rape who was Lord of War who was Lord of Death's Gate.

He could not take her, gently. So spoke not his physical impotence, as he might have expected, but the cold wash of wisdom. He would not despoil her; Vashanka would accept no less.

She knocked and entered and said, "Let me see them," so sure he would have the stolen diamonds that her fingers were already busy on the lacings of her Ilsig leathers.

He held up a hide-wrapped bundle, slimmer than her wrist, shorter than her forearm. "Here. How were they thieved?"

"Your voice is hoarser than I have ever heard it," she replied, and: "I needed money; there was this man . . . actually, there were a few; but there was a tough, a streetbrawler. I should have known—he is half my apparent age. What would such as he want with a middle-aged whore? And he agreed to pay the price I asked, without quibbling. *Then* he robbed me." She looked around, her eyes, as he remembered them, clear windows to her thoughts: She was appalled.

"The low estate into which I have sunk?"

She knew what he meant. Her nostrils shivered, taking in the musty reek of the soiled bedding on which he sprawled fully clothed, smelling easily as foul. "The devolution of us both. That I would be here, under these circumstances, is surely as pathetic as you."

"Thanks. I needed that. Don't."

"I thought you wanted me." She ceased unlacing, looked at him, her tunic open to her waist.

"I did. I don't. Have some krrf." On his hips rode her scarf; if she saw it, then she would comprehend his degradation too fully. So he had not removed it, hoping its presence would remind him, if he weakened and his thoughts drowned in lust, that *this* woman he must not violate.

She sat on the quilt, one doe-gloved leg tucked under her.

"You jest," she breathed, then, eyes narrowed, took the krrf.

"It will be ill with you, afterward, should I touch you."

Her fingers ran along the flap of hide wrapped over her wands. "I am receiving payment." She tapped the package. "And I may not owe debts."

"The boy who pilfered these, did it at my behest."

"Must you pander for me?"

He winced. "Why do you not go home?" She smelled of salt and honey and he thought desperately that she was here only because he forced the issue: to pay her debt.

She leaned forward, touched his lips with a finger. "For the same reason that you do not. Home is changed, gone to time."

"Do you know that?" He jerked his head away, cracking it against the bed's wooden headboard.

"I believe it."

"I cannot believe anything, any more. I surely cannot believe that your hand is saying what it seems to be saying."

"I cannot," she said, between kisses at his throat he could not, somehow, fend off, "leave . . . with . . . debts . . . owing."

"Sorry," he said firmly, and got out from under her hands. "I am just not in the mood."

She shrugged, unwrapped the wands, and wound her hair up with them. "Surely, you will regret this, later."

"Maybe you are right," he sighed heavily. "But that is my problem. I release you from any debt. We are even. I remember past gifts, given when you still knew how to give freely." There was no way in the world he was going to hurt her. He would not strip before her. With those two constraints, he had no option. He chased her out of there. He was as cruel about it as he could manage to be, for both their sakes.

Then he yelled downstairs for service.

When he descended the steps in the cool night air, a movement startled him, on the gray's off side.

"It is me, Shadowspawn."

"It is I, Shadowspawn," he corrected, huskily. His face averted, he mounted from the wrong side. The horse whickered disapprovingly. "What is it, snipe?"

As clouds covered the moon, Tempus seemed to pull all night's shadows round him. Hanse might have the name, but this Tempus had the skill. Hanse shivered. There were no Shadow Lords any longer . . . "I was admiring your horse. Bunch of hawk-masks rode by, saw the horse, looked interested. I looked proprietary. The horse looked mean. The hawk-masks rode away. I just thought I'd see if you showed soon, and let you know."

A movement at the edge of his field of vision warned him, even as the horse's ears twitched at the click of iron on stone. "You should have kept going, it seems," said Tempus quietly, as the first of the hawk-masks edged his horse out past the intersection, and others followed. Two. Three. Four. Two more.

"Mothers," whispered Cudget Swearoath's prodigy, embarrassed at not having realized that he was not the only one waiting for Tempus.

"This is not your fight, junior."

"I'm aware of that. Let's see if they are."

Blue night: Blue hawk-masks: The sparking thunder of six sets of hooves rushing toward the two of them. Whickering. The gleam of frothing teeth and bared weapons: iron clanging in a jumble of shuddering, straining horses. The kill-trained gray's challenge to another stallion: Hooves thudding on flesh and great mouths gaped, snapping: A blaring death-clarion from a horse whose jugular had been severed. Always watching the boy: Keeping the gray between the hawk-masks and a thief who just happened to get involved; who just happened to kill two of them with thrown knives: one through an eye and the other blade he recalled clearly: sticking out a slug-white throat. Tempus would remember even the whores' ambivalent screams of thrill and horror, delight and disgust. He had plenty of time to sort it out.

Time to draw his own sword, to target the rider of

his choice, feel his hilt go warm and pulsing in his hand. He really did not like to take unfair advantage. The iron sword glowed pink like a baby's skin or a just-born day. Then it began to react in his grip. The gray's reins, wrapped around the pommel, flapped loosely; he told it where he wanted it with gritted words, with a pressing knee, with his shifting weight. One hawk-mask had a greenish tinge to him: protected. Tempus's sword would not listen to such talk: it slit charms like butter, armor like silk. A blue wing whistled above his head, thrown by a compatriot of the man who fell so slowly with his guts pouring out over his saddle like cold molasses. While that hawk-mask's horse was in midair between two strides Tempus's sword licked up and changed the color of the foe-seeking boomerang. Pink, now, not blue. He was content to let it return its death to the hand that threw it. That left just two.

One had the thief engaged, and the youth had drawn his wicked, twenty-inch Ibarsi knife, too short to be more than a temporizer against the hawk-mask's sword, too broad to be thrown. Backed against the Lily Garden's wall, there was just time for Tempus to flicker the horse over there and split the hawk-mask's head down to his collarbones. Gray brains splattered him. The thrust of the hawk-mask, undiminished by death, shattered on the flat of the long, curved knife Shadowspawn held up in a two-fisted desperate block.

"Behind you!"

Tempus had known the one last hawk-mask was there. But this was not the boy's battle. Tempus had made a choice. He ducked and threw his weight sideways, reining the horse down with all his might. The sword, a singing one, sonata'd over his head, shearing hairs. His horse, overbalanced, fell heavily, screaming, pitching, rolling onto his left leg. Pinned for an instant, he saw white anguish, then the last hawk-mask was leaping down to finish him, and the gray scrambled to its feet. "Kill," he shouted, his blade yet at ready, but lying in the dirt. His leg flared once again, then quieted. He tried, gained his knees, dust in his eyes. The horse reared and lunged. The hawk-mask struck blindly, arms above his head, sword reaching for gray, soft underbelly. He tried to save it. He tried. He tackled the hawk-mask with the singing sword. Too late, too late: horse fluids showered him. Bellows of agony pealed in his ears. The horse and the hawk-mask and Tempus went down together, thrashing.

When Tempus sorted it out, he allowed that the horse had killed the hawk-mask at the same time the hawk-mask had disemboweled the horse.

But he had to finish it. It lay there thrashing pathetically, deep groans coming from it. He stood over it uncertainly, then knelt and stroked its muzzle. It snapped at him, eyes rolling, demanding to die. He acceded, and the dust in his eyes hurt so much they watered profusely.

Its legs were still kicking weakly when he heard a movement, turned on his good leg, and stared.

Shadowspawn was methodically stripping the hawk-masks of their arms and valuables.

Hanse did not notice Tempus, as he limped away. Or he pretended he did not. Whichever, there was nothing left to say.

— 5 —

When he reached the weapons shop, his leg hardly pained him. It was numb; it no longer throbbed. It would heal flawlessly, as any wound he took always healed. Tempus hated it.

Up to the Weaponshop's door he strode, as the dawn spilled gore onto Sanctuary's alleys.

He kicked it; it opened wide. How he despised supernal battle, and himself when his preternatural abilities came into play.

"Hear me, Vashanka! I have had enough! Get this sidewalk stand out of here!"

There was no answer. Within, everything was dim as dusk, dim as the pit of unknowingness which spawned day and night and endless striving.

There were no weapons here for him to see, no counter, no proprietor, no rack of armaments pulsing and humming expectantly. But then, he already had his. One to a customer was the rule: one body; one mind; one swing through life.

He trod mists tarnished like the gray horse's coat. He trod a long corridor with light at its ending, pink like new beginnings, pink like his iron sword when Vashanka lifted it by Tempus's hand. He shied away from his duality; a man does not look closely at a curse of his own choosing. He was what he was, vessel of his god. But he had his own body, and that particular body was aching; and he had his own mind, and that particular mind was dank and dark like the dusk and the dusty death he dealt.

"Where are You, Vashanka, O Slaughter Lord?"

Right here, resounded the voice within his head. But Tempus was not going to listen to any internal voice. Tempus wanted confrontation.

"Materialize, you bastard!"

I already have; one body; one mind; one life—in every sphere.

"I am not you!" Tempus screamed through clenched teeth, willing firm footing beneath his sinking feet.

No, you are not. But I am you, sometimes, said the nimbus-wreathed figure striding toward him over gilt-edged clouds. Vashanka: two meters tall with hair

the color of yarrow honey and a high brow free from
lines.

"Oh, no . . ."

You wanted to see Me. Look upon Me, servant!

"Not so close, Pillager. Not so much resemblance.
Do not torture me, my god! Let me blame it all on
you—not *be* you!"

So many years, and you yet seek self-delusion?

"Definitely. As do You, if You think to gather
worshipers in this fashion! O Berserker God, You
cannot roast their mages before them: they are all
dependent on sorcery. You cannot terrify them thusly,
and expect them to come to You. Weapons will not
woo them; they are not men of the armies. They are
thieves, and pirates, and prostitutes! You have gone
too far, and not far enough!"

*Speaking of prostitutes, did you see your sister?
Look at me!*

Tempus had to obey. He faced the manifestation
of Vashanka, and recalled that he could not take a
woman in gentleness, that he could but war. He saw
his battles, ranks parading in endless eyes of storm
and blood bath. He saw the Storm God's consort,
His own sister whom He raped eternally, moaning
on Her coach in anguish that Her blood brother
would ravish Her so.

Vashanka laughed.

Tempus snarled wordlessly through frozen lips.

You should have let us have her.

"Never!" Tempus howled. Then: "O God, leave
off! You are not increasing your reputation among
these mortals, nor mine! This was an ill-considered
venture from the outset. Go back to Your heaven
and wait. I will build Your temple better without
Your maniacal aid. You have lost all sense of proportion. The Sanctuarites will not worship one who
makes of their town a battlefield!"

Tempus, do not be wroth with Me. I have My own troubles, you know. I have to get away every now and again. And you have not been warring, whined the god, *for so very long. I am bored and I am lonely.*

"And you have caused the death of my horse!" Tempus spat, and broke free of Vashanka, wrenching his mind loose from the mirror mind of his god with an effort of will greater than any he had ever mounted before. He turned in his steps and began to retrace them. The god called to him over his shoulder, but he did not look back. He put his feet in the smudges they had left in the clouds as he had walked among them, and the farther he trudged, the more substantial those clouds became.

He trekked into lighter darkness, into a soft, new sunrise, into a pink and lavender morning which was almost Sanctuary's. He continued to walk until the smell of dead fish and Downwind pollution assailed his nostrils. He strode on, until a weed tripped him and he fell to his knees in the middle of a damp and vacant lot.

He heard a cruel laugh, and as he looked up he was thinking that he had not made it back at all—that Vashanka was not through punishing him.

But to his right was the Vulgar Unicorn, to his left the palimpsest tenement wall. And before him stood one of the palace eunuchs, come seeking him with a summons from Kittycat to discuss what might be done about the weapons shop said to be manifesting next to the Vulgar Unicorn.

"Tell Kadakithis," said Tempus, arduously gaining his feet, "that I will be there presently. As you can see . . ." He waved around him, where no structure stood or even could be proved ever to have stood. ". . . there is no longer any weapons shop. Therefore, there is no longer any problem, nor any urgency to attend to it. There is, however, one very irritable Hell Hound in this vacant lot who wants to be left alone."

The blue-black eunuch exposed perfect, argent teeth. "Yes, yes, master," he soothed the honey-haired man. "I can see that this is so."

Tempus ignored the eunuch's rosy, outstretched palm, and his sneer at the Hell Hound pretending to negotiate the humpy turf without pain. Accursed Wriggly!

As the round-rumped eunuch sauntered off, Tempus decided the Vulgar Unicorn would do as well as anyplace to sit and sniff krrf and wait for his leg to finish healing. It ought to take about an hour—unless Vashanka was more angry at him than he estimated, in which case it might take a couple of days.

Shying from that dismal prospect, he pursued diverse thoughts. But he fared little better. Where he was going to get another horse like the one he had lost, he could not conjecture, any more than he could recall the exact moment when the last dissolving wisps of Vashanka's Weaponshop blurred away into the mists of dawn.

A BETTER CLASS OF ENEMY

This time, when the memory faded, Niko could not meet his teacher's eyes. He was uncomfortable, as if he'd eavesdropped at some keyhole for no reason but prurient interest.

And when he did look up, he began to protest: "This has nothing to do with me! They're each other's curse—so what? Tempus had said that many times! And as for the dead sorcerer—" He shrugged his shoulders and his chin jutted. "What of that? You wouldn't have welcomed Aspect here, not to save his life. And all the Sacred Banders know of Tempus's special relationship with the Stormgod."

"Why protest to me?" said the adept mildly. And smiled a tiny, knowing smile.

Niko was sweating, even in his rest-place where a cool breeze blew. He didn't want to know so intimately of the Riddler's struggles. He didn't want to be privy to what went on between the sorcerer-slayer and her brother. He said defensively, "He did it for her—did it to save her. That's the way of it with them."

"He did what he did for himself, out of thought-

58

lessness and grudge—out of vengeance. And because
Aspect was a better class of enemy, one worth his
time and trouble."

"That wasn't him, not Aspect. That was the god.
And politics."

The adept laughed a derisive laugh that rustled
the needles on every tree in Niko's rest-place and
made his teeth water. "So, like lesser men who have
never learned your graces, you blame venality on
gods and politics? Gods are nothing without their
worshippers; they act on the affairs and the passions
of men. They are an excuse for evil-doing, a recepta-
cle of responsibility. And politics—how are politics
to blame? Are they alive? Willful? Self-aware or capable of anything on their own? Are they even ideas?
I say they are none of these, just a way to organize
prejudice and men behind it. Gods and politics are
the tools with which the godless and unprincipled
manipulate the gullible."

"I fought on Wizardwall. You can't tell me that
gods aren't real." Niko crossed his arms and glared.

"They are as real as men will make them, as powerful as their believers' love. Why do you think
Aškelon covets you? Why do you think the Stormgods
give Tempus such power? To leech from you the
belief that is the very cornerstone of their being, the
love that keeps them bold, the fear that keeps them
strong, and the conflict among men that keeps their
names alive. Die never for a god, Nikodemos who
should know better—not your soldiers' god, nor any
other."

"We venerate the older gods here—Enlil among
the rest."

"Venerate, not blindly serve. Venerate because
they are ancient and in some ways, wise. But the day
that none believeth in them, gods perish. So we keep
names alive to keep gods alive. But the only sacrifice

a god wants is the sacrifice his worshippers want. And in gods' names, more evil has been done than in evil's own."

"No man thinks he's evil?" Niko was increasingly uncomfortable. The adept had his own purpose, one which might not be as pure as it seemed.

"No man knows what another man thinks, except here, in this way. In this place, there is only the evil you perceive, Nikodemos."

"You haven't been here long enough to be that sure." Niko remembered the gate that had opened here once, allowing horrors to enter, ravening beasts. "And if you are trying to show me Tempus in an unacceptable light, leave off. He is my sworn commander, and his dealings with his sister and with the wizard-class are none of my affair."

"Are they not? Are you not free? Could you not shake off the Aškelonian influence in a second if you truly believed you could? Or should? If you were not harboring ghosts in your rest-place and unclean urges in your heart, could you not have benefited from your time on Ennina? Become rested? Become ready to return to the World?"

"But it's different out there," said Niko with exasperation. "It's easy to sit here and say these things, to talk of choices that *should* be made. There's no 'should' out there, only must and can't, live and die, win and lose. No matter what I think, the World has its own ideas about what will happen in it. And Tempus is in no way to blame for anything I've done—or not done. He loves me like no other."

"Is that so? Then look here, and say that after you've seen what you should see."

Should, again. But Niko looked squarely into the palm of the adept, his chin held high, all his defenses roused. Whatever this adept wanted, it had more to do with Bandaran stricture than the World beyond.

But he'd always known that; whenever he was ready to leave, Bandaran dogma and the World's chaos collided in him, making him unfit for either.

There was nothing this adept could show him that would make any difference in how Niko felt about Tempus, or about himself, or about the Sacred Band oath he'd taken.

Or so he thought until he was sucked into the becoming maw that opened in the old adept's palm . . .

A MAN AND HIS GOD

Solstice storms and heat lightning beat upon Sanctuary, washing the dust from the gutters and from the faces of the mercenaries drifting through town on their way north where (seers proclaimed and rumor corroborated) the Rankan Empire would soon be hiring multitudes, readying for war.

The storms doused cookfires west of town, where the camp followers and artificers that Sanctuary's ramshackle facilities could not hold had overflowed. There squatted, under stinking ill-tanned hide pavilions, custom weaponers catering to mercenaries whose eyes were keener than the most carefully wax-forged iron and whose panoplies must bespeak their whereabouts in battle to their comrades; their deadly efficacy to strangers and combatants; the dear cost of their hire to prospective employers. Fine corselets, cuirasses ancient and modern, custom's best axes and swords, and helmetry with crests dyed to order could be had in Sanctuary that summer; but the downwind breeze had never smelled fouler than after wending through their press.

Here and there among the steaming firepots siege-crafters and commanders of fortifications drilled their engineers, lest from idleness picked men be suborned by rival leaders seeking to upgrade their corps. To keep order here, the Emperor's half-brother Kadakithis had only a handful of Rankan Hell Hounds in his personal guard, and a local garrison staffed by indigenous Ilsigs, conquered but not assimilated. The Rankans called the Ilsigs "Wrigglies," and the Wrigglies called the Rankans naked barbarians and their women worse, and not even the rain could cool the fires of that age-old rivalry.

On the landspit north of the lighthouse, rain had stopped work on Prince Kadakithis's new palace. Only a man and horse, both bronze, both of heroic proportions, rode the beach. Doom criers of Sanctuary, who once had proclaimed their town "just left of heaven," had changed their tune: they had dubbed Sanctuary Death's Gate and the lone man, called Tempus, Death Himself.

He was not. He was a mercenary, envoy of a Rankan faction desirous of making a change in Emperors; he was a Hell Hound, by Kadakithis's good offices; and marshal of palace security, because the prince, not meant to triumph in his Governorship/exile, was understaffed. Of late Tempus had become a royal architect, for which he was as qualified as any man about, having fortified more towns than Kadakithis had years. The prince had proposed the site; the soldier examined it and found it good. Not satisfied, he had made it better, dredging deep with oxen along the shore while his imported fortifications crews raised double walls of baked brick filled with rubble and faced with stone. When complete, these would be deeply crenelated for archers, studded with gatehouses, double-gated and sheer. Even incomplete, the walls which barred the folk from spit and lighthouse grinned with a death's head smirk toward the town, enclosing granaries and stables and newly whited barracks and a spring for fresh water: if War came hither, Tempus proposed to make Him welcome for a long and arduous seige.

The fey, god's breath weather might have stopped work on the construction, but Tempus worked without respite, always: it eased the soul of the man who could not sleep and who had turned his back upon his god. This day, he awaited the arrival of Kadakithis and that of his own anonymous Rankan contact, to introduce emissary to possible figurehead, to put the two together and see what might be seen.

When he had arranged the meeting, he had yet walked in the shelter of the god Vashanka's arm. Now, things had changed for him and he no longer cared to serve Vashanka, the Storm God, who regulated kingship. If he could, he was gong to contrive to be relieved of his various commissions and of his honor bond to Kadakithis, freed to go among the mercenaries to whom his soul belonged (since he had it back) and put together a cohort to take north and lease to the highest bidder. He wanted to wade thigh-deep in gore and guts and see if, just by chance, he might manage to find his way back through the shimmering dimensional gate beyond which the god had long ago thrust him, back into the world and into the age to which he was born.

Since he knew the chances of that were less than Kadakithis becoming Emperor of Upper and Lower Ranke, and since the god's gloss of rationality was gone from him, leaving him in the embrace of the curse, yet lingering, which he had originally become the god's suppliant to thwart, he would settle for a small mercenary corps of his own choosing, from which to begin building an army that would not be a puerile jest, as Kadakithis's forces were at present.

For this he had been contacted, to this he had agreed. It remained only to see to it that Kadakithis agreed.

The mercenary who was a Hell Hound scolded the horse, who did not like its new weighted shoes or the water surging around its knees, white as its stockings. Like the horse, Kadakithis was only potential in quest of actualization; like the horse, Kadakithis feared the wrong things, and placed his trust in himself only, an untenable arrogance in horse or man, when the horse must go to battle and the man also. Tempus collected the horse up under him, shifting his weight, pulling the red-bronze beast's head in against its chest, until the combination of his guidance and the toe-weights on its hooves and the waves' kiss showed the horse what he wanted. Tempus could feel it in the stallion's gait; he did not need to see the result: like a dancer, the sorrel lifted each leg high. Then it gave a quizzical snort as it sensed the power to be gained from such a stride: school was in session. Perhaps, despite the four white socks, the horse would suit. He lifted it with a touch and a squeeze of his knees into a canter no faster than another horse might walk. "Good, good," he told it, and from the beach came the *pat-pat* of applause.

Clouds split; sunrays danced over the wrack-strewn shore and over the bronze stallion and its rider, stripped down to plated loinguard, making a rainbow about them. Tempus looked up, landward to where a lone eunuch clapped pink palms together from one of Prince Kadakithis's chariots. The rainbow disappeared, the clouds suppressed the sun, and in a wrap of shadow of the enigmatic Hell Hound (who the eunuch knew from his own experience to be capable of regenerating a severed limb and thus veritably eternal; and who was indubitably deadlier than all the mercenaries descended on Sanctuary like flies upon a day-old carcass) trotted the horse up the beach to where the eunuch in the chariot was waiting on solid ground.

"What are you doing here, Sissy? Where is your lord, Kadakithis?" Tempus stopped his horse well back from the irascible pair of blacks in their traces. This eunuch was near their color: a Wriggly. Cut young and deftly, his answer came in a sweet alto:

"Lord Marshal, most daunting of Hell Hounds, I bring you His Majesty's apologies, and true word, if you will heed it."

The eunuch, no more than seventeen, gazed at him longingly. Kadakithis had accepted this fancy toy from Jubal, the slaver, despite the slavemaster's own brand on its high rump, and the deeper dangers implied by the identity of its fashioner. Tempus had marked it, when first he heard its lilting voice in the palace, for he had heard that voice before. Foolish, haughty, or merely pressed beyond a bedwarmer's ability to cope: no matter; this creature of Jubal's, he had long wanted. Jubal and Tempus had been making private war, the more fierce for being undeclared, since Tempus had first come to Sanctuary and seen the swaggering, masked killers Jubal kept on staff terrorizing whom they chose on the town's west side. Tempus had made those masked murderers his private game stock, the west end of Sanctuary his personal preserve, and the campaign was on. Time and again, he had despatched them. But tactics change, and Jubal's had become too treacherous for Tempus to endure, especially now with the northern insurrection half out of its egg of rumor. He said to the parted lips awaiting his permission to speak and to the deer-soft eyes doting on his every move that the eunuch might dismantle the car, prostrate itself before him, and from there deliver its message.

It did all of those, quivering with delight like a dog enraptured by the smallest attention, and said with its forehead to the sand: "My lord, the Prince bids me say he has been detained by Certain Persons, and will be late, but means to attend you. If you were to ask me why that was, then I would have no choice but to admit to you that the three most mighty magicians, those whose names cannot be spoken, came down upon the summer palace in billows of blackest smoke and foul odors, and that the fountains ran red and the sculptures wept and cried, and frogs jumped upon my lord in his bath, all because the Hazards are afraid that you might move to free the slayer-of-sorcerers called Cime before she comes to trial. Although my master assured them that you would not, that you had said nothing to him about this woman, when I left they still were not satisfied, but were shaking walls and raising shades and doing all manner of wizardly things to demonstrate their concern."

The eunuch fell quiet, awaiting leave to rise. For an instant there was total silence, then the sound of Tempus's slithering dismount. Then he said: "Let us see your brand, pretty one," and with a wiggling of its upthrust rump the eunuch hastened to obey.

It took Tempus longer than he had estimated to wrest a confession from the Wriggly, from the Ilsia who was the last of his line and at the end of his line. It did not make cries of pleasure or betrayal or agony, but accepted its destiny as good Wrigglies always did, writhing soundlessly.

When he let it go, though the blood was running down its legs and it saw the intestine like wet parchment caught in his fingernails, it wept with relief, promising to deliver exhortation posthaste to Kadakithis. It kissed his hand, pressing his palm against its beardless cheek, never realizing that it was, itself, his message, or that it would be dead before sunset.

— 2 —

Kneeling to wash his arm in the surf, he found himself singing a best-forgotten funerary dirge in the ancient argot all mercenaries learn. But his voice was gavelly and his memories were treacherous thickets full of barbs, and he stopped as soon as he realized he sang. The eunuch would die because he remembered its voice from the workshop of despicable Kurd, the frail and filthy vivisectionist, while he had been an experimental animal therein. He remembered other things too: he remembererd the sear of the branding iron and the smell of flesh burning and the voices of two fellow guardsmen, the Hell-Hounds Zalbar and Razkuli, piercing the drug-mist through holes they poked in his stupor. And he recalled a protracted and hurtful healing, shut away from any who might be overawed to see a man regrow a limb. Mending, he had brooded, seeking a certainty, some redress fit to his grievance. But he had not been sure enough to act. Now, after hearing the eunuch's tale, he was certain. When Tempus was certain, Destiny got out its ledger.

But what to write therein? His instinct told him it was Black Jubal he wanted, not the two Hell-Hounds; that Razkuli was a nonentity and Zalbar, like a saw horse, was merely in need of schooling. Those two had single-handedly arranged for Tempus's snuff to be drugged, for him to be branded, his tongue to be cut out, then sold off to wicked little Kurd, there to languish interminably under the knife? He could not credit it. Yet the eunuch had said—and in such straits no one lies—that though Jubal had gone to Zalbar for help in dealing with Tempus, the slave trader had known nothing of what fate the Hell-Hounds had in mind for their colleague. Never mind it; crimes were voluminous.

But if not Jubal, then who had written Tempus's itinerary for Hell? It sounded, suspiciously, like the god's work. Since he had turned his back upon the god, things had gone from bad to worse. And if Vashanka had not turned His face away from Tempus even while he lay helpless, the god had not stirred to rescue him (though any limb lopped off him still grew back, any wound he took healed relatively quickly, as men judge such things). No, Vashanka, his tutelary, had not hastened to aid him. The speed of Tempus's healing was always in direct proportion to the pleasure the god was taking in His servant. Vashanka's terrible rebuke had made the man wax terrible, also. Curses and unholy insults rang down from the mind of the god and up from the mind of the man who then had no tongue left with which to scream. It had taken Hanse the thief, young Shadowspawn, chance-met and hardly known, to extricate him from interminable torture. That and an earlier service meant that now he owed more debt than he liked to Shadowspawn, and Shadowspawn knew more about Tempus than even that backstreeter could want to know, so that the thief's eyes slid away, sick and mistrustful, when Tempus would chance upon him in the Maze.

But even then, Tempus's break with divinity was not complete. Not until he had found, upon his belated return to duty—whole and unscarred—that his sister Cime had been apprehended slaying sorcerers wantonly in their beds had he thrown the amulet of Vashanka, which he had worn since former times, out to sea from this very shore. Zalbar, had he known what was punishment and what was not, would not have bothered engaging the vivisectionist's services, but merely announced in person that he had Cime in custody, and her diamond rods locked away in the Hall of Judgment awaiting her disposition.

He growled to himself, thinking about her, her black

hair winged with gray, in Sanctuary's unsegregated dungeons where any syphilitic rapist could have her at will, while he must not touch her at all, or raise hand to help her lest he start forces in motion he could not control. His break with the god stemmed from her presence in Sanctuary, as his endless wandering as Vashanka's minion had stemmed from an altercation he had had over her with a mage. If he went down into the pits and took her, the god would be placated; he had no desire to reopen relations with Vashanka, who had turned His face away from His servant. If Tempus brought her out under his own aegis, he would have the entire Mageguild at his throat; he wanted no quarrel with the Adepts. He had told her not to slay them here, where he must maintain order and the letter of the law.

By the time Kadakithis arrived in that very same chariot, its braces sticky with Wriggly blood, Tempus was in a humor darker than the drying clots, fully as dark as the odd, round cloud coming fast from the northeast.

Kadakithis's noble Rankan visage was suffused with rage, so that his skin was darker than his pale hair: "But *why?* In the name of all the gods, what did the poor little creature ever do to you? You owe me a eunuch, and an explanation." He tapped his lacquered nails on the chariot's bronze rim.

"I have a perfect replacement in mind," smiled Tempus smoothly, "my lord. As for why . . . all eunuchs are duplicitous. This one was an information conduit to Jubal. Unless you would like to invite the slaver to policy sessions and let him stand behind those ivory screens where your favorites eavesdrop as they choose, I have acted well within my prerogatives as marshal. If my name is attached to your palace security, then your palace *will be* secure."

"Bastard! How dare you even imply that *I* should

apologize to *you*? When will you treat me with the proper amount of respect? You tell me all eunuchs are teacherous, the very breath after offering me another one!"

"I am giving you respect. Reverence I reserve for better men than I. When you have attained that dignity we shall both know it: you will not have to ask. Until then, either trust or discharge me." He waited, to see if the prince would speak. Then he continued: "As to the eunuch I offer as replacement, I want you to arrange for his training. You like Jubal's work; send to him saying yours has met with an accident and you wish to tender another into his care to be similarly instructed. Tell him you paid a lot of money for it, and you have high hopes."

"You have such a eunuch?"

"I will have it."

"And you expect me to conscion your sending of an agent in there—aye, to aid you—without knowing your plan, or even the specifics of the Wriggly's confession?"

"Should you know, my lord, you would have to approve, or disapprove. As it lies, you are free of onus."

The two men regarded each other, checked hostility jumping between them like Vashanka's own lightning in the long, dangerous pause.

Kadakithis flicked his purple mantle over his shoulder. He squinted past Tempus, into the waning day. "What kind of cloud is that?"

Tempus swung around in his saddle, then back. "That should be our friend from Ranke."

The prince nodded. "Before he arrives, then, let us discuss the matter of the female prisoner Cime."

Tempus's horse snorted and threw its head, dancing in place. "There is nothing to discuss."

"But . . . ? Why did you not come to me about it? I could have done something, previously. Now, I cannot . . ."

"I did not ask you. I am not asking you." His voice was a blade on whetstone, so that Kadakithis pulled himself up straight. "It is not for me to take a hand."

"Your own sister? You will not intervene?"

"Believe what you will, *prince*. I will not sift through gossip with any man, be he prince or king."

The prince lost hold, then, having been "princed" too often back in Ranke, and berated the Hell Hound.

The man sat quite still upon the horse the prince had given him, garbed only in his loinguard though the day was fading, letting his gaze full of festering shadows rest in the prince's until Kadakithis trailed off, saying, ". . . the trouble with you is that anything they say about you could be true, so a man knows not what to believe."

"Believe in accordance with your heart," the voice like grinding stone suggested, while the dark cloud came to hover over the beach.

It settled, seemingly, into the sand, and the horses shied back, necks outstretched, nostrils huge. Tempus had his sorrel up alongside the chariot team and was leaning down to take the lead-horse's bridle when an earsplitting clarion came from the cloud's translucent center.

The Hell Hound raised his head then, and Kadakithis saw him shiver, saw his brow arch, saw a flicker of deepset eyes within their caves of bone and lid. Then again Tempus spoke to the chariot horses, who swiveled their ears toward him and took his counsel, and he let loose the lead-horse's bridle and spurred his own between Kadakithis's chariot and what came out of the cinereous cloud which had been so long descending upon them in opposition to the prevailing wind.

The man on the horse who could be seen within the cloud waved: a flash of scarlet glove, a swirl of burgundy cloak. Behind his tasseled steed he led another, and it was this second gray horse who again

challenged the other stallions on the beach, its eyes
full of fire. Farther back within the cloud, stonework
could be seen, masonry like none in Sanctuary, a sky
more blue and hills move virile than any Kadakithis
knew.

The first horse, reins flapping, was emerging, nose
and neck casting shadows upon solid Sanctuary sand;
then its hooves scattered grains, and the whole of the
beast, and its rider, and the second horse he led on a
long tether, stood corporeal and motionless before
the Hell Hound, while behind, the cloud whirled in
upon itself and was gone with an audible "pop."

"Greetings, Riddler," said the rider in burgundy
and scarlet, as he doffed his helmet with its blood-
dark crest to Tempus.

"I did not expect *you*, Abarsis. What could be so
urgent?"

"I heard about the Trôs horse's death, so I thought
to bring you another, better auspiced, I hope. Since
I was coming anyway, our friends suggested I bring
what you require. I have long wanted to meet you."
Spurring his mount forward, he held out his hand.

Red stallion and iron gray snaked arched necks,
thrusting forth clacking teeth, wide-gaped jaws emit-
ting squeals to go with flattened ears and rolling
eyes. Above horse hostilities could be heard snatches
of low wordplay, parry and riposte: ". . . disappointed
that you could not build the temple." ". . . welcome
to take my place here and try. The foundations of the
temple grounds are defiled, the priest in charge more
corrupt than even politics warrants. I wash my
hands . . ." ". . . with the warring imminent, how
can you . . . ?" "Theomachy is no longer my burden."
"That cannot be so." ". . . hear about the insurrection,
or take my leave!" ". . . His name is unpronounceable,
and that of his empire, but I think we all shall learn
it so well we will mumble it in our sleep . . ." "I don't

sleep. It is a matter of the right field officers, and men young enough not to have fought upcountry the last time." "I am meeting some Sacred Band members here, my old team. Can you provision us?" "Here? Well enough to get to the capital and do it better. Let me be the first to . . ."

Kadakithis, forgotten, cleared his throat.

Both men stared at the prince severely, as if a child had interrupted adults. Tempus bowed low in his saddle, arm outswept. The rider in reds with the burnished cuirass tucked his helmet under his arm and approached the chariot, handing the second horse's tether to Tempus as he passed by.

"Abarsis, presently of Ranke," said the dark, cultured voice of the armored man, whose hair swung black and glossy on a young bull's neck. His line was old, one of court graces and bas-relief faces and upswept, regal eyes that were disconcertingly wise and as gray-blue as the huge horse Tempus held with some difficulty. Ignoring the squeals of just-met stallions, the man continued: "Lord Prince, may all be well with you, with your endeavors and your holdings, eternally. I bear reaffirmation of our bond to you." He held out a purse, fat with coin.

Tempus winced, imperceptibly, and took wraps of the gray horse's tether, drawing its head close with great care, until he could bring his fist down hard between its ears to quiet it.

"What is this? There is enough money here to raise an army!" scowled Kadakithis, tossing the pouch lightly in his palm.

A polite and perfect smile lit the northern face, so warmly handsome, of the Rankan emissary. "Have you not told him, then, O Riddler?"

"No, I thought so, but got no opportunity. Also, I am not sure whether we *will* raise it, or whether that is my severance pay." He threw a leg over the sorrel's neck and slid down it, butt to horse, dropped its reins and walked away down the beach with his new Trôs horse in hand.

The Rankan hooked his helmet carefully on one of the saddle's silver rosettes. "You two are not getting on, I take it. Prince Kadakithis, you must be easy with him. Treat him as he does his horses; he needs a gentle hand."

"He needs his comeuppance. He has become insufferable! What is this money? Has he told you I am for sale? I am not!"

"He has turned his back on his god and the god is letting him run. When he is exhausted, the god will take him back. You found him pleasant enough, previously, I would wager. He has been set upon by your own staff, men to whom he was sworn and who gave oaths to him. What do you expect? He will not rest easy until he has made that matter right."

"What is this? My men? You mean that long unexplained absence of his? I admit he is changed. But how do you know what he would not tell me?"

A smile like sunrise lit the elegant face of the armored man. "The god tells me what I need to know. How would it be, for him to come running to you with tales of feuding among your ranks like a child to his father? His honor precludes it. As for the . . . funds . . . you hold, when we sent him here, it was with the understanding that should he feel you would make a king, he would so inform us. This, I was told you knew."

"In principle. But I cannot take a gift so large."

"Take a loan, as others before you have had to do. There is no time now for courtship. To be capable of *becoming* a king insures no seat of kingship, these days. A king must be more than a man, he must be a hero. It takes many men to make a hero, and special times. Opportunities approach, with the upcountry insurrection and a new Empire rising beyond the northern range. Were you to distinguish yourself in combat, or field an army that did, we who seek a change could rally around you publicly. You cannot do it with what you have, the Emperor has seen to that."

"At what rate am I expected to pay back this loan?"

"Equal value, nothing more. If the prince, my lord, will have patience, I will explain all to Your Majesty's satisfaction. That, truly, is why I am come."

"Explain away, then."

"First, one small digression, which touches a deeper truth. You must have some idea who and what the man you call Tempus is; I am sure you have heard it from your wizards and from his enemies among the officials of the Mageguild. Let me add to that this: Where he goes, the god scatters His blessings. By the cosmological rules of state cult and kingship, He has invested this endeavor with divine sanction by his presence. Though he and the god have their differences, without him, no chance remains that you might triumph. My father found that out. Even sick with his curse, he is too valuable to waste, unappreciated. If you would rather remain a princeling forever, and let the Empire slide into ruin apace, just tell me and I will take word home. We will forget this matter of the kingship and this corollary matter of a small standing army, and I will release Tempus. He would as soon it, I assure you."

"Your *father*? Who in the God's Eye *are* you?"

"Ah, my arrogance is unforgivable; I thought you would know me. We are all so full of ourselves, these days, it is no wonder events have come to such a pass. I am Man of the God in Upper Ranke, Sole Friend to the Mercenaries, the hero, Son of the Defender, and so forth."

"High Priest of Vashanka."

"In the Upper Land."

"My family and yours thinned each other's line," stated Kadakithis baldly, no apology, no regret in his words. Yet he looked differently upon the other, thinking they were of an age, both wielding wooden swords in shady courts while the slaughter raged, far off at the fronts.

"Unto eradication," remarked the dark young man. "But we did not contest, and now there is a different enemy, a common threat. It is enough."

"'And you and Tempus have never met?'"

"He knew my father. And when I was ten, and my father died and our armies were disbanded, he found a home for me. Later, when I came to the god and the mercenaries' guild, I tried to see him. He would not meet with me." He shrugged, looking over his shoulder at the man walking the blue-gray horse into blue-gray shadows falling over the blue-black sea. "Everyone has his hero, you know. A god is not enough for a whole man; he craves a fleshly model. When he sent to me for a horse, and the god approved it, I was elated. Now, perhaps, I can do more. The horse may not have died in vain, after all."

"I do not understand you, Priest."

"My Lord, do not make me too holy. I am Vashanka's priest: I know many requiems and oaths, and thirty-three ways to fire a warrior's bier. They call me Stepson, in the mercenaries' guild. I would be pleased if you would call me that, and let me talk to you at greater length about a future in which your destiny and the wishes of the Storm God, our Lord, could come to be the same."

"I am not sure I can find room in my heart for such a god; it is difficult enough to pretend to piety," grated Kadakithis, squinting after Tempus in the dusk.

"You will, you will," promised the priest, and

dismounted his horse to approach Tempus's ground-
tied sorrel. Abarsis reached down, running his
hand along the beast's white-stocking'd leg. "Look,
Prince," he said, craning his neck up to see Kadakithis's
face as his fingers tugged at the gold chain wedged in
the weight-cleat on the horse's shoe. At the end of
the chain, sandy but shining gold, was an amulet.
"The god wants him back."

— *3* —

The mercenaries drifted into Sanctuary dusty from
their westward trek or blue-lipped from their rough
sea passage and wherever they went they made hellish what before had been merely dissolute. The Maze
was no longer safe for pickpocket or pander; usurer
and sorcerer scuttled in haste from street to doorway, where before they had swaggered virtually un-
challenged, crime lords in fear of nothing.

Now the whores walked bowlegged, dreamy-eyed,
parading their new finery in the early hours of the
morning while most mercenaries slept; the taverns
changed shifts but feared to close their doors, lest a
mercenary find that an excuse to take offense. Even
so early in the day, the inns were full of brawls and
the gutters full of casualties. The garrison soldiers
and the Hell Hounds could not be omnipresent:
wherever they were not, mercenaries took sport, and
they were not in the Maze this morning.

Though Sanctuary had never been so prosperous,
every guild and union and citizen's group had sent
representatives to the palace at sunrise to complain.

Lastel, a/k/a One-Thumb, could not understand
why the Sanctuarites were so unhappy. Lastel was
very happy: he was alive and back at the Vulgar
Unicorn tending bar, and the Unicorn was making

money, and money made Lastel happy, always. Being
alive was something Lastel had not fully appreciated
until recently, when he had spent aeons dying a
subjective death in thrall to a spell he had paid to
have laid upon his own person, a spell turned against
him by the sons of its deceased creator, Mizraith of
the Hazard class, and dispelled by he-knew-not-whom.
Though every night he expected his mysterious benefactor to sidle up to the bar and demand payment, no
one ever came and said: "Lastel, I saved you. I am
the one. Now, show your gratitude." But he knew
very well that someday soon, someone would. He
did not let this irritation besmirch his happiness. He
had gotten a new shipment of Caronne krrf (black,
pure drug, foil stamped, a full weight of it, enough to
set every mercenary in Sanctury at the kill) and it was
so good that he considered refraining from offering it
on the market. Having considered, he decided to
keep it all for himself, and so was very happy indeed,
no matter how many fistfights broke out in the bar,
or how high the sun was, these days, before he got to
bed . . .

Tempus, too, was happy that morning, with the
magnificent Trôs horse under him and signs of war
all around him. Despite the hour, he saw enough
rough hoplites and dour artillery fighters with their
crank-bows (whose springs were plaited from wom-
en's hair) and their quarrels (barbed and poisoned) to
let him know he was not dreaming: these did not
bestir themselves from daydreams! The war was real
to them. And any one of them could be his. He felt
his troop-levy money cuddled tight against his groin,
and he whistled tunelessly as the Trôs horse threaded
his way toward the Vulgar Unicorn.

One-Thumb was not going to be happy much
longer.

Tempus left the Trôs horse on its own recognizance, dropping the reins and telling it, "Stay." Anyone who thought it merely ripe for stealing would learn a lesson about the strain which is bred only in Syr from the original line of Trôs's.

There were a few locals in the Unicorn, most snoring over tables along with other, bagged trash ready to be dragged out into the street.

One-Thumb was behind his bar, big shoulders slumped, washing mugs while watching everything through the bronze mirror he had had installed over his stock.

Tempus let his heels crack against the board and his armor clatter: he had dressed for this, from a box he had thought he might never again open. The wrestler's body which Lastel had built came alert, pirouetted smoothly to face him, staring unabashedly at the nearly god-sized apparition in leopard-skin mantle and helmet set with boar's tusks, wearing an antique enameled breastplate and bearing a bow of ibex-horn morticed with a golden grip.

"*What* in Azyuna's twat are *you?*" bellowed One-Thumb, as every waking customer he had hastened to depart.

"I," said Tempus, reaching the bar and removing his helmet so that his yarrow-honey hair spilled forth, "am Tempus. We have not chanced to meet." He held out a hand whose wrist bore a golden bracer.

"Marshal," acknowledged One-Thumb, carefully, his pate creasing with his frown. "It is good to know you are on our side. But you cannot come in here . . . My—"

"I am here, *Lastel*. While you were so inexplicably absent, I was often here, and received the courtesy of service without charge. But now I am not here to eat or drink with those who recognize me for one who is fully as corrupt as are they themselves. There are those who know where you were, *Lastel*, and why—and *one* who broke the curse that bound you. Truly, if you had cared, you could have found out." Twice, Tempus called One-Thumb by his true name, which no palace personage or Mazedweller should have known enough to do.

"Marshal, let us go to my office." Lastel fairly ramped behind his bar.

"No time, krrf-dealer. Mizraith's sons, Stefab and Marype; Markmor: those three and more were slain by the woman Cime who is in the pits awaiting sentence. I thought that you should know."

"What are you saying?" You want me to break her out? Do it yourself."

"No one," said the Hell Hound, "can break anyone out of the place. *I* am in charge of security there. If she were to escape, I would be very busy explaining to Kadakithis what went wrong. And tonight I am having a reunion here with fifty of my old friends from the mercenaries' guild. I would not want anything to spoil it. And, too, I ask no man to take me on faith, or go where I have not been." He grinned like the Destroyer, gesturing around. "You had better order in extra. And half a piece of krrf, your courtesy to me, of course. Once you have seen my men well in hand, you will be better able to conjecture what might happen should they get *out* of hand, and weigh your alternatives. Most men I solicit find it to their benefit to work in accord with me. Should you deem it so for you, we will fix a time, and discuss it."

Not the cipher's meaning, nor the plan it shrouded, nor the threat that gave it teeth were lost on the man who did not like to be called "Lastel" in the Maze. He bellowed: "You are addled. You cannot do this. I cannot do that! As for krrf, I know nothing about . . . any . . . krrf."

But the man was gone, and Lastel was trembling

with rage, thinking he had been in purgatory too
long; it had eroded his nerves!

— *4* —

When the dusk cooled the Maze, Shadowspawn
ducked into the Unicorn. One-Thumb was not in
evidence; Two-Thumbs was behind the bar.

He sat with the wall supporting him, where the
story-teller liked to sit, and watched the door, waiting for the crowd to thicken, tongues to loosen, some
caravan driver to boast of his wares. The mercenaries
were no boon to a thief, but dangerous playmates,
like Kadakithis's palace women. He did not want to
be intrigued; he was being distracted moment by
moment. As a consequence, he was very careful to
keep his mind on business, so that he would not
come up hungry next Ilsday, when his funds, if not
increased, would run out.

Shadowspawn was dark as iron and sharp like a
hawk; a cranked crossbow, loaded with cold bronze
and quarrels to spare. He wore knives where a pro-
fessional wears them, and sapphire and gold and
crimson to draw the eye from his treasured blades.

Sanctuary had spawned him: he was hers, and he
had thought nothing she did could surprise him. But
when the mercenaries arrived as do clients to a strum-
pet's house, he had been hurt like a whore's bastard
when first he learns how his mother feeds him.

It was better, now; he understood the new rules.

One rule was: get up and give them your seat.
Hanse *gave* no one his seat. He might recall pressing
business elsewhere, or see someone he just had to
hasten over to greet. Tonight, he remembered nothing earlier forgotten; he saw no one he cared to
bestir himself to meet. He prepared to defend his

place as seven mercenaries filled the doorway with plumes and pelts and hilts and mail, and looked his way. But they went in a group to the bar, though one, in a black mantle, with iron at chest and head and wrists, pointed directly to him like a man sighting his arrow along an outstretched arm.

The man talked to Two-Thumbs awhile, took off his helmet with its horsehair crests that seemed blood-red, and approached Hanse's table alone. A shiver coursed the thief's flesh, from the top of his black thatch to his toetips.

The mercenary reached him in a dozen swinging strides, drawing a stabbing sword as he came on. If not for the fact that the other hand held a mug, Shadowspawn would have aired iron by the time the man (or youth from his smooth, heart-shaped face) spoke: "Shadowspawn, called Hanse? I am Stepson, called Abarsis. I have been hoping to find you." With a grin full of dazzling teeth, the mercenary put the ivory-hilted sword flat in the wet-rings on the table, and sat, both hands well in evidence, clasped under his chin.

Hanse gripped his beltknife tightly. Then the panic-flash receded, and time passed, instead of piling all its instants terrifyingly on top of one another. Hanse knew that he was no coward, that he was plagued by flashbacks from the two times he had been tapped with the fearstick of Vashanka, but his chest was heaving, and the mercenary might see. He slumped back, for camouflage. The mercenary with the expensive taste in accouterments could be no older than he. And yet, only a king's son could afford such a blade as that before him. He reached out hesitantly to touch its silvered guard, its garnet pommel, his gaze locked in the sellsword's soulless pale one, his hand slipping closer and closer to the elegant sword of its own accord.

"Ah, you do like it then," said Stepson. "I was not sure. You will take it, I hope. It is customary in my country, when meeting a man who has performed heroically to the benefit of one's house, to give a small token." He withdrew a silver scabbard from his belt, laid it with the sword, which Hanse put down as if burned.

"What did I ever do for you?"

"Did you not rescue the Riddler from great peril?"

"Who?"

The tanned face grinned ingeniously. "A truly brave man does not boast. I understand. Or is it a deeper thing? That—" He leaned forward; he smelled sweet like new-mown hay."—is truly what I need to know. Do you comprehend me?"

Hanse gave him an eagle's look, and shook his head slowly, his fingers flat on the table, near the magnificent sword that the mercenary Stepson had offered to give him. *The Riddler?* He knew no one of that name.

"Are you protecting him? There is no need, not from me. Tell me, Shadowspawn, are you and Tempus lovers?"

"Mother—!" His favorite knife leapt into his palm, unbidden. He looked at it in his own grasp in consternation, and dropped his other hand over it and began paring his nails. *Tempus! The Riddler!* Hanse's eyes caressed the covetable blade. "I helped him out, once or twice, that's all."

"That is good," the youth across from him approved. "Then we will not have to fight over him. And, too, we could work a certain bargain, service for service, that would make me happy and you, I modestly estimate, a gentleman of ease for at least six months."

"I'm listening," said Shadowspawn, taking a chance, commending his knife to its sheath. The short sword too, he handled, fitting it in the scabbard and drawing it out, fascinated by the alert scrutiny of Abarsis the Stepson's six companions.

When he began hearing the words "diamond rods" and "Hall of Judgment" he waxed uneasy. But by then, he could not see any way that he could allow himself to appear less than heroic in the pale, blue-gray eyes of the Stepson. Not when the amount of money Stepson had offered hung in the balance, not when the nobly fashioned sword he had been given as if it were merely serviceable proclaimed the flashy mercenary's ability to *pay* that amount. But, too, if he would pay that, he would pay more. Hanse was not so enthralled by the mecenaries' mystique to hasten into one's pay without some good Sanctuary barter. Watching Stepson's six formidable companions, waiting like purebred hunting dogs curried for show, he spied a certain litheness about them, an uncanny cleanliness of limb and nearness of girded hips. Close friends, these. Very close.

Abarsis's sonorous voice had ceased, waiting for Hanse's response. The disconcertingly pale eyes followed Hanse's stare, frank now, to his companions.

"Will you say yea, then, friend of the Riddler? And become my friend, also? These other friends of mine await only your willingness to embrace you as a brother."

"I own," Hanse muttered.

Abarsis raised one winged brow. "So?" They are members of a Sacred Band, my old one; most prized officers; heroes, every pair." He judged Hanse's face. "Can it be you do not have the custom, in the south? From your mien I must believe it." His voice was liquid, like deep running water. "These men, to me and to their chosen partners, have sworn to foresake life before honor, to stand and never retreat, to fall where they fight if need be, shoulder to shoulder. There is no more hallowed tryst than theirs. Had I a thousand such, I would rule the earth."

"Which one is yours?" Hanse tried not to sneer, to be conversational, unshaken, but his eyes could find no comfortable place to rest, so that at last he took up the gift-sword and examined the hieratic writing on its blade.

"None. I left them, long ago, when my partner went up to heaven. Now I have hired them back, to serve a need. It is strictly a love of spirit, Hanse, that is required. And only in Sacred Bands is a mercenary asked so much."

"Still, it's not my style."

"You sound disappointed."

"I am. In your offer. Pay me twice that, and I will get the items you desire. As for your friends, I don't care if you bugger them each twice daily. Just as long as it's not part of my job and no one thinks I am joining any organizations."

A swift, appreciative smile touched Abarsis. "Twice, then. I am at your mercy."

"I stole those diamond rods once before, for Tem—, for the Riddler. He'll just give them back to her, after she does whatever it is she does for him. I had her once, and she did nothing for me that any other whore would not do."

"You *what?* Ah, you do not know about them, then? Their legend, their curse?"

"Legend? Curse? I *knew* she was a sorceress. Tell me about it! Am I in any danger? You can forget the whole idea, about the rods. I keep shut of sorcery."

"Hardly sorcery, no need to worry. They cannot transmit any of it. When he was young and she was a virgin, he was a prince and a fool of ideals. I heard it that the god is his true father, and thus she is *not* his sibling, but you know how legends are. As a princess, her sire looked for an advantageous marriage. An archmage of a power not seen anymore made an offer, at about the time the Riddler renounced his claim to the throne and retired to a philosopher's cave. She went to him begging aid, some way out of an unacceptable situation, and convinced him that should she be deflowered, the mage would not want her, and of all men the Riddler was the only one she trusted with the task; anyone else would despoil her. She seduced him easily, for he had loved her all his young life and that unacceptable attraction to flesh of his flesh was part of what drove him from his primogeniture. She loved nothing but herself; some things never change. He was wise enough to know he brought destruction upon himself, but men are prone to ruin for women. In passion, he could not think clearly; when it left him he went to Vashanka's altar and threw himself upon it, consigning his fate to the god. The god took him up, and when the Archamage appeared with four eyes spitting fire and four mouths breathing fearful curses, the god's aegis partly shielded him. Yet, the curse holds. He wanders eternally bringing death to whomever loves him and being spurned by whomsoever he shall love. She must offer herself for pay to any comer, take no gift of kindness on pain of showing all her awful years, incapable of giving love as she has always been. So thus, the gods, too, are barred to her, and she is truly damned."

Hanse just stared at Stepson, whose voice had grown husky in the telling, when the mercenary left off.

"Now, will you help me? Please. He would want it to be you."

Hanse made a sign.

"*Would* want it to be me?" the thief frowned. "He does not *know* about this?" There came the sound of Shadowspawn's bench scraping back.

Abarsis reached out to touch the thief's shoulder, a move quick as lightning and soft as a butterfly's landing. "One must do for a friend what the friend cannot do for himself. With such a man, opportunities of this sort come seldom. If not for him, or for your price, or for whatever you hold sacred, do this thing for me, and I will be eternally in your debt."

A sibilant sound, part impatience, part exasperation, part irritation, came sliding down Shadowspawn's hawkish nose.

"Hanse?"

"You are going to *surprise* him with this deed, done? What if he has no taste for surprises? What if you are wrong, and he refrains from aiding her because he prefers her right where she is? And besides, I am staying away from him and his affairs."

"No surprise: I will tell him once I have arranged it. I will make you one more offer: Half again the doubled fee you suggested, to ease your doubts. But that is my final bid."

Shadowspawn squinted at the heartshaped face of Stepson. Then, without a word, he scooped up the short stabbing sword in its silver sheath, and found it a home in his belt. "Done," said Hanse.

"Good. Then, will you meet my companions?" The long-fingered, graceful hand of Stepson, called Abarsis, made a gesture that brought them, all smiles and manly welcomes, from their exile by the bar.

— 5 —

Kurd, the vivisectionist who had tried his skills on Tempus, was found a fair way from his adobe workshop, his gut stretched out for thirty feet before him: he had been dragged by the entrails; the hole cut in his belly to pull the intestines out was made by an expert: a mercenary had to be at fault. But there were so many mercenaries in Sanctuary, and so few friends of the vivisectionist, that the matter was not pursued.

The matter of the Hell Hound Razkuli's head, however, was much more serious. Zalbar (who knew why both had died and at whose hands, and who feared for his own life) went to Kadakithis with his friend's staring eyes under one arm, sick and still tasting vomit, and told the prince how Tempus had come riding through the gates at dawn and called up to him where he was checking pass-bys in the gatehouse: "Zalbar, I've a message for you."

"Yo!" Zalbar had waved.

"Catch," Tempus laughed, and threw something up to him while the gray horse reared, uttered a shrill, demonic scream, and clattered off by the time Zalbar's hand had said *head: human;* and his eyes had said, *head: Razkuli's* and then begun to fill with tears.

Kadakithis listened to his story, looking beyond him out the window the entire time. When Zalbar had finished, the prince said, "Well, I don't know what you expected, trying to take him down so clumsily."

"But he said it was a message for me," Zalbar entreated, caught his own pleading tone, scowled and straightened up.

"Then take it to heart, man. I can't allow you two to continue feuding. If it is anything other than simple feuding, I do not want to know about it. Stepson, called Abarsis, told me to expect something like this! I demand a stop to it!"

"*Stepson!*" Tall, lank Zalbar snarled like a man invoking a vengeful god in close fighting. "An ex-Sacred Bander looking for glory and death with honor, in no particular order! *Stepson* told you? The Slaughter Priest? My lord prince, you are keeping deadly company these days! Are all the gods of the armies in

Sanctuary, then, along with their familiars, the mercenary hordes? I had wanted to discuss with you what could be done to curb them—"

"Zalbar," interrupted Kadakithis firmly. "In the matter of gods, I hold firm: I do not believe in them. In the matter of mercenaries, let them be. You broach subjects too sensitive for your station. In the matter of Tempus, I will talk to him. You change your attitude. Now, if that is *all* . . . ?"

It *was* all. It was nearly the end of Zalbar the Hell Hound's entire career: he almost struck his commander-in-chief. But he refrained, though he could not utter even a civil goodbye. He went to his billet and he went into the town, and he worked wrath out of himself, as best he could. The dregs he washed away with drink, and after that he went to visit Myrtis, the whoremistress of Aphrodisia House who knew how to soothe him. And she, seeing his heart breaking and his fists shaking, asked him nothing about why he had come, after staying away so long, but took him to her breast and healed what she might of his hurts, remembering that all the protection he provided her and good he did for her, he did because of a love spell she had bought and cast on him longsince, and thus she owed him at least one night to match his dreams.

— *6* —

Tempus had gone among his own kind, after he left the barracks. He had checked in at the guild hostel north of the palace, once again in leopard and bronze and iron, and he was welcome there.

Why he had kept himself from it for so long, he could not have reasoned, unless it was that without these friends of former times the camaraderie would not have been as sweet.

He went to the sideboard and got hot mulled wine from a krater, sprinkling in goat's cheese and grain, and took the posset to a corner, so the men could come to him as they would.

The problem of the eunuch was still unsolved; finding a suitable replacement was not going to be easy: there were not many eunuchs in the mercenaries' guild. The clubroom was red as dying day and dark as backlit mountains, and he felt better for having come. So, when Abarsis, high priest of Upper Ranke, left his companions and approached, but did not sit among, the mercenaries Tempus had collected, he said to the nine that he would see them at the appointed time, and to the iron-clad one:

"Life to you, Stepson. Please join me."

"Life to you, Riddler, and everlasting glory." Cup in hand, he sipped pure water, eyes hardly darker never leaving Tempus's face. "Is it Sanctuary that has driven you to drink?" He indicated the posset.

"The dry soul is wisest? Not at the Empire's anus, where the water is chancy. Anyway, those things I said long ago and far away: do not hold me to any of that."

The smooth cheek of Stepson ticced. "I must," he murmured. "You are the man I have emulated. All my life I have listened after word of you and collected intelligence of you and studied what you left us in legend and stone in the north. Listen: 'War is sire of all and king of all, and some He has made gods and some men, some bond and some free'. Or: 'War is ours in common; strife is justice; all things come into being and pass away through strife.' You see, I know your work, even those other names you have used. Do not make me speak them. I would work with you, O Sleepless One. It will be the pinnacle of my career." He flashed Tempus a bolt of naked entreaty, then his gaze flickered away and he rushed on: "You need me. Who else will suit? Who else here has a brand and gelding's scars? *And* time in the arena as a gladiator, like Jubal himself? Who could intrigue him, much less seduce him among these? And though I—"

"No."

Abarsis dug in his belt and tossed a golden amulet onto the table. "The god will not give you up; this was caught in the sorrel's new shoe. That teacher of mine whom you remember . . . ?"

"I know the man," Tempus said grimly.

"He thinks that Sanctuary is the end point of existence; that those who come here are damned beyond redemption; that Sanctuary is Hell."

"Then how is it, Stepson," said Tempus almost kindly, "that folk experience fleshly death here? So far as I know, I am the only soul in Sanctuary who suffers eternally, with the possible exception of my sister, who may not have a soul. Learn not to listen to what people say, priest. A man's own mistakes are load enough, without adding others'."

"Then *let me* be your choice! There is no time to find some other eunuch." He said it flatly, without bitterness, a man fielding logic. "I can also bring you a few fighters whom you might not know and who would not dare, on their own, to approach you. My Sacred Band yearns to serve you. You dispense your favor to provincials and foreigners who barely recognize their honor! Give it to me, who craves little else . . . ! The prince who would be king will not expose me, but pass me on to Jubal as an untrained boy. I am a little old for it, but in Sanctuary, those niceties seem not to matter. I have increased your lot here. You owe me this opportunity."

Tempus stirred his cooling posset with a finger. "That prince . . ." Changing the subject, he sighed glumly, a sound like rattling bones. "He will never be a Great King, such as your father. Can you tell me why the god is taking such an interest?"

"The god will tell you, when you make the Trôs horse a sacrifice. Or some person. Then He will be mollified. You know the ritual. If it be a man you choose, I will gladly volunteer . . . Ah, you understand me, now? I do not want to frighten you . . ."

"Take no thought of it."

"Then . . . though I risk your displeasure, yet I say it: I love you. One night with you would be a surfeit, to work under you is my long-held dream. Let me do this, which none can do better, which no *whole* man can do for you at all!"

"I cede you the privilege, since you value it so; but there is no telling what Jubal's hired hawk-masks might do to the eunuch we send in there."

"With your blessing and the god's, I am fearless. And you will be close by, busy attacking Black Jubal's fortress. While you are arresting the slavemaster for his treasonous spying, whosoever will make good the woman's escape. I understand your thought; I have arranged for the retrieval of her weapons."

Tempus chuckled. "I hardly know what to say."

"Say you look kindly upon me, that I am more than a bad memory to you."

Shaking his head, Tempus took the amulet Abarsis held out to him. "Come then, Stepson, we will see what part of your glorious expectations we can fulfill."

— 7 —

It was said, ever after, that the Storm God took part in the sack of the slaver's estate. Lightning crawled along the gatehouses of its defensive wall and rolled in balls through the inner court and turned the oaken gates to ash. The ground rumbled and buckled and bucked and great crumbling cracks appeared in its inner sanctum, where the slaver dallied with the glossy-haired eunuch Kadakithis had just sent up for training. It was profligate waste to make a fancy boy out of such a slave: the arena had muscled him up and time had grown him up, and to squeeze the two or three remaining years of that sort of pleasure out of him seemed to the slaver a pity. If truth be known, blood like his came so rarely to the slavepens that gelding him was a sin against future generations: had Jubal gotten him early on—when the cuts had been made, at nine, or ten—he would have raised him with the great pains and put him to stud. But his brand and tawny skin smacked of northern mountains and high wizards' keeps where the wars had raged so savagely that no man was proud to remember what had been done there, on either side.

Eventually, he left the eunuch chained by the neck to the foot of his bed and went to see what the yelling and the shouting and the blue flashes and the quivering floorboards could possibly mean.

What he saw from his threshold he did not understand, but he came striding back, stripping off his robe as he passed by the bed, rushing to arm himself and do battle against the infernal forces of this enemy, and, it seemed, the whole of the night.

Naptha fireballs came shooting over his walls into the courtyard; flaming arrows torqued from spring-wound bows; javelins and swordplay glittered nastily, singing as they slew in soft sussurrussings Jubal had hoped never to hear there.

It was eerily quiet: no shouting, not from his hawk-masks, or the adversaries; the fire crackled and the horses snorted and groaned like the men where they fell.

Jubal recollected the sinking feeling he had had in his stomach when Zalbar had confided to him that the bellows of anguish emanating from the vivisectionist's workshop were the Hell Hound Tempus's agonies, the forebodings he had endured when a group of his beleagured sellswords went after the man who killed those who wore the mask of Jubal's service for sport, and failed to down him.

That night, it was too late for thinking. There was time enough only for wading into the thick of battle (if he could just find it: the attack was from every side, out of darkness); hollering orders; mustering point leaders (two); and appointing replacements for the dead (three). Then he heard whoops and abysmal screams and realized that someone had let the slaves out of their pens; those who had nothing to lose bore haphazard arms, but sought only death with vengeance. Jubal, seeing wide, white rimmed eyes and murderous mouths and the new eunuch from Kadakithis's palace dancing ahead of the pack of them, started to run. The key to its collar had been in his robe; he remembered discarding it, within the eunuch's reach.

He ran in a private wash of terror, in a bubble through which other sounds hardly penetrated, but where his breathing reverberated stentorian, rasping, and his heart gonged loud in his ears. He ran looking back over his shoulder, and he saw some leopard-pelted apparition with a horn bow in hand come sliding down the gatehouse wall. He ran until he reached the stable, until he stumbled over a dead hawk-mask, and then he heard everything, cacaphonously, that had been so muted before: swords rasping; panoplies rattling; bodies thudding and greaved men running; quarrels whispering bright death as they passed through the dark press; javelins ringing as they struck helm or shield suddenly limned in lurid fiery light.

Fire? Behind Jubal flame licked out the stable windows and horses whistled their death screams.

The heat was singeing. He drew his sword and turned in a fluid motion, judging himself as he was wont to do when the crowds had been about him in applauding tiers and he must kill to live to kill another day, and do so pleasingly.

He felt the trill of it, the immediacy of it, the joy of the arena, and as the pack of freed slaves came shouting, he picked out the prince's eunuch and reached to wrest a spear from the dead hawk-mask's grip. He hefted it, left handed, to cast, just as the man in leopard pelt and cuirass and a dozen mercenaries came between him and the slaves, cutting him off from his final refuge, the stairs to the westward wall.

Behind him, the flames seemed hotter, so that he was glad he had not stopped for armor. He threw the spear, and it rammed home in the eunuch's gut.

The leopard leader came forward, alone, sword tip gesturing three times, leftward.

Was it Tempus, beneath that frightful armor? Jubal raised his own blade to his brow in acceptance, and moved to where his antagonist indicated, but the leopard leader was talking over his shoulder to his front-line mercenaries, three of whom were clustered around the downed eunuch. Then one archer came abreast of the leader, touched his leopard pelt. And that bowman kept a nocked arrow on Jubal, while the leader sheathed his sword and walked away, to join the little knot around the eunuch.

Someone had broken off the haft; Jubal heard the grunt and the snap of wood and saw the shaft discarded. Then arrows whizzed in quick succession into both his knees and beyond the shattering pain, he knew nothing more.

— *8* —

Tempus knelt over Abarsis, bleeding out his life

naked in the dirt. "Get me light," he rasped. Tossing his helmet aside, he bent down until his cheek touched Stepson's knotted, hairless belly. The whole bronze head of the spear, barbs and all, was deep in him. Under his lowest rib, the shattered haft stuck out, quivering as he breathed. The torch was brought; the better light told Tempus there was no use in cutting the spearhead loose; one flange was up under the low rib; vital fluids oozed out with the youth's blood. Out of age-old custom, Tempus lay his mouth upon the wound and sucked the blood and swallowed it, then raised his head and shook it to those who waited with a hot blade and hopeful, silent faces. "Get him some water, no wine. And give him some air."

They moved back and as the Sacred Bander who had been holding Abarsis's head put it down, the wounded one murmured; he coughed, and his frame shuddered, one hand clutching spasmodically at the spear. "Rest now, Stepson. You have got your wish. You will be my sacrifice to the god." He covered the youth's nakedness with his mantle, taking the gory hand from the broken haft, letting it fasten on his own.

Then the blue-gray eyes of Abarsis opened in a face pale with pain, and something else: "I am not frightened, with you and the god beside me."

Tempus put an arm under his head and gathered him up, pulling him across his lap. "Hush, now."

"Soon, soon," said the paling lips. "I did well for you. Tell me so . . . that you are content. O Riddler, so well do I love you, I go to my god singing your praises. When I meet my father, I will tell him . . . I . . . fought beside you."

"Go with more than that, Stepson," whispered Tempus, and leaned forward, and kissed him gently on the mouth, and Abarsis breathed out his soul while their lips yet touched.

— *9* —

Now, Hanse had gotten the rods with no difficulty, as Stepson had promised he would be able to do, citing Tempus's control of palace personnel as surety. And afterward, the young mercenary's invitation to come and watch them fight up at Jubal's rang in his head until, to banish it, he went out to take a look.

He knew it was foolish to go, for it was foolish even to *know*, but he knew that he wanted to be able to say, "Yes, I saw. It was wonderful," the next time he saw the young mercenary, so he went very carefully and cautiously. If he were stopped, he would have all of Stepson's Sacred Band as witnesses that he had been at Jubal's, and nowhere near the palace and its Hall of Judgment.

He knew those excuses were flimsy, but he wanted to go, and he did not want to delve into why: the lure of mercenary life was heady in his nostrils; if he admitted how sweet it seemed, he might be lost. If he went, perchance he would see something not so sweet, or so intoxicating, something which would wash away all this talk of friendship and honor. So he went, and hid on the roof of a gatehouse abandoned in the confusion. Thus he saw all that transpired.

When he could in safety leave his roost, he followed the pair of gray horses bearing Tempus and the corpse ridgeward, stealing the first mount he came to that looked likely.

The sun was risen when Tempus reached the ridgetop and called out behind: "Whoever you are, ride up," and set about gathering branches to make a bier.

Hanse rode to the edge of the outcropping of rock on which Tempus piled wood and said: "Well, accursed one, are you and your god replete? Stepson told me all about it."

The man straightened up, eyes like flames, and put his hand to the small of his back: "What do you want, Shadowspawn? A man who is respectful does not sling insults over the ears of the dead. If you are here for him, then welcome. If you are here for me, I assure you, your timing is ill."

"I *am* here for him, *friend*. What think you, that I would come here to console you in your grief when it was his love for you that he died of? He asked me," Hanse continued, not dismounting, "to get these. He was going to give them to you." He reached for the diamond rods, wrapped in hide, he had stolen.

"Stay your hand, and your feelings. Both are misplaced. Do not judge what you do not understand. As for the rods, Abarsis was mistaken as to what I wanted done with them. If you are finishing your first mercenary's commission, then give them to One-Thumb. Tell him they are for his benefactor. Then it is done. Someone of the Sacred Band will seek you out and pay you. Do not worry about that. Now, if you would honor Abarsis, dismount." The struggle for control obvious in Tempus's face was chilling, where nothing unintentional was ever seen. "Otherwise, please leave now, friend, *while* we are yet friends. I am in no mood for living boys today."

So Hanse slid from the horse and stalked over to the corpse stage-whispering, "Mouth me no swill, Doomface. If this is how your friends fare, I'd as soon be relieved of the honor" and slipped back the shroud. "His eyes are open." Shadowspawn reached out to close them.

"Don't. Let him see where he goes."

They glared a time at each other above the staring corpse while a red-tailed hawk circled overhead, its shadow caressing the pale, dead face.

Then Hanse knelt stiffly, took a coin from his belt, slid it between Stepson's slightly parted lips, and murmured something low. Rising, he turned and strode to his stolen horse and scrambled clumsily astride, reining it round and away without a single backward glance.

When Tempus had the bier all made, and Abarsis arranged on it to the last glossy hair, and a spark nursed to consuming flame, he stood with clenched fists and watering eyes in the billows of smoke. And through his tears, he saw the boy's father, fighting oblivious from his car, his charioteer fallen between his legs, that time Tempus had hacked off an enemy's arm to save him from the ax it swung; he saw the witchbitch of a sorceress the king had wed in the black hills to make alliance with what could not be had by force; he saw the aftermath of that, when the wild woman's spawn was out of her and every loyal general took a hand in her murder before she laid their commander out in state. He saw the boy, wizard-haired and wise, running to Tempus's chariot for a ride, grasping his neck, laughing, kissing like the northern boys had no shame to do; all this before the Great King discharged his armies and retired home to peace, and Tempus rode south to Ranke, an Empire hardly whelped and shaky on its prodigious feet. And Tempus saw the field he had taken against a monarch, once his leige: Masters change. He had not been there when they had got the Great King, dragged him down from his car and begun the Unending Deaths that proved the Rankans barbarians second to none. It was said by those who *were* there that he stood it well enough until his son was castrated before his eyes, given off to a slaver with ready collar . . . When he had heard, Tempus had gone searching among the sacked towns of the north, where Ranke wrought infamy into example, legends better

than sharp javelins at discouraging resistance. And
he saw Abarsis in the slaver's kennel, the boy's look
of horror that a man of the armies would see what
had been done to him. No glimmer of joy invaded
the gaunt child's face turned up to him. No eager
hands outflung to their redeemer; a small, spent
hero shuffled across soiled straw to meet him, slave's
eyes gaging without fear just what he might expect
from this man, who had once been among his father's
most valued, but was now only one more Rankan
enemy. Tempus remembered picking the child up in
his arms, hating how little he weighed, how sharp
his bones were; and that moment when Abarsis at
last believed he was safe. About a boy's tears, Abarsis
had sworn Tempus to secrecy. About the rest, the
less said, the better. He had found him foster parents, in the rocky west by the sea temples where
Tempus himself was born, and where the gods still
made miracles upon occasion. He had hoped somehow the gods would heal what love could not. Now,
they had done it.

He nodded, having passed recollection like poi-
son, watching the fire burn down. Then, for the sake
of the soul of Stepson, called Abarsis, and under the
aegis of his flesh, Tempus humbled himself before
Vashanka and came again into the service of his god.

— *10* —

Hanse, hidden below on a shelf, listening and
partaking of the funeral in his own fashion, upon
realizing what he was overhearing, spurred the horse
out of there as if the very god whose thunderous
voice had heard were after him.

He did not stop until he reached the Vulgar Unicorn. There he shot off the horse in a dismount

which was a fall disguised as a vault, slapped the beast smartly away, telling it hissingly to go home, and slipped inside with such relief as his favorite knife must feel when he sheathed it.

"One-Thumb," Hanse called out, making for the bar, "What is going on out there?" There had been soldierly commotion at the Common Gate.

"You haven't heard?" scoffed the night-turned-day barman. "Some prisoners escaped from the palace dungeon, certain articles were thieved from the Hall of Judgment, and none of the regular security officers were around to get their scoldings."

Looking at the mirror behind the bar, Hanse saw the ugly man grin without humor. Gaze locked to mirror-gaze, Hanse drew the hide-wrapped bundle from his tunic. "These are for you. You are supposed to give them to your benefactor." He shrugged to the mirror.

One-Thumb turned and wiped the dishrag along the shining bar and when the rag was gone, the small bundle was gone, also. "Now, what do you want to get involved in something like this for? You think you're moving up? You're not. Next time, when it's this sort of thing come round the back. Or, better, don't come at all. I thought you had more sense."

Hanse's hand smacked flat and loud upon the bar. "I have taken enough offal for one day, cup-bearer. Now I tell you what you do, Wide-Belly: You take what I brought you and your sage counsel, and you wrap it all together, and then you squat on it!" And stiff-kneed as a roused cat, Shadowspawn stalked away, toward the door, saying over his shoulder: "As for sense, I thought *you* had more."

"I have my business to think of," called out One-Thumb, too boldly for a whine.

"Ah, yes! So have I, so have I."

— *11* —

Lavender and lemon dawn light bedizened the white-washed barracks' walls and colored the palace parade grounds.

Tempus had been working all night, out at Jubal's estate where he was quartering his mercenaries away from town and Hell Hounds and Ilsig garrison personnel. He had fifty there, but twenty of them were paired members of three different Sacred Bands: Stepson's legacy to him. The twenty had convinced the thirty nonallied operatives that "Stepsons" would be a good name for their squaddron, and for the cohort it would eventually command should things go as everyone hoped.

He would keep the Sacred Band teams and spread the rest throughout the regular army, and throughout the prince's domain. They would find what clay they chose, and mold a division from it of which the spirit of Abarsis, if it were not too busy fighting theomachy's battles in heaven, could look upon with pride.

The men had done Tempus proud, already, that night at Jubal's, and thereafter; and this evening when he had turned the corner round the slave barracks the men were refitting for livestock, there it had been, a love-note written in lamb's blood two cubits high on the encircling protective wall: *"War is all and king of all, and all things come into being out of strife."*

Albeit they had not gotten it exactly right, he had smiled, for though the world and the boyhood from out of which he had said such audacious thing was gone to time, Stepson, called Abarsis, and his legacy of example and followers made Tempus think that perhaps (oh just perhaps) he, Tempus, had not been so young, or so foolish, as he had lately come to think that he had been. And if thus the man, then his epoch, too, was freed of memory's hindsightful taint.

And the god and he were reconciled: This pushed away his curse and the shadow of distress it cast ever before him. His troubles with the prince had subsided. Zalbar had come through his test of fire and returned to stand his duty, thinking deeply, walking quietly. His courage would mend. Tempus knew his sort.

Jubal's disposition he had left to Kadakithis. He had wanted to take the famous ex-gladiator's measure in single combat, but there was no fitness in it now, since the man would never be quick on his feet, should he live to regain the use of them.

Not that the world was as ridiculously beautiful as was the arrogant summer morning which did not understand that it was a Sanctuary morning and therefore should at least be gory, garish, or full of flies buzzing about his head. No, one could find a few thorns in one's path, still. There was Shadowspawn, called Hanse, exhibiting unseemly and proprietary grief over Abarsis whenever it served him, yet not taking a billet among the Stepsons that Tempus had offered. Privately, Tempus thought he might yet come to it, that he was trying to step twice into the same river. When his feet chilled enough, he would step out onto the banks of manhood. If he could sit a horse better, perhaps his pride would let him join in where now, because of that, he could only sneer.

Hanse, too, must find his own path. He was not Tempus's problem, though Tempus would gladly take on that burden should Shadowspawn ever indicate a desire to have help toting it.

His sister, Cime, however, *was* his problem, his

alone, and the enormity of that conundrum had him casting about for any possible solution, taking pat answers up and putting them down like gods move seeds from field to field. He could kill her, rape her, deport her; he could not ignore her, forget her, or suffer along without confronting her.

That she and One-Thumb had become enamored of one another was something he had not counted on. Such a thing had never occurred to him.

Tempus felt the god rustling around in him, the deep cavernous sensing in his most private skull that told him the deity was going to speak. "*Silently!*" he warned the god. They were uneasy with each other, yet, like two lovers after a trial separation.

We can take her, mildly, and then she will leave. You cannot tolerate her presence. Drive her off. I will help thee, spake Vashanka.

"Must you be so predictable, Pillager?" Tempus mumbled under his breath, so that Abarsis's Trôs horse swivelled its ears back to eavesdrop. He slapped its neck, and told it to continue on straight and smartly. They were headed toward Lastel's modest eastside estate.

Constancy is one of My attributes, jibed the god in Tempus's head meaningfully.

'You are not getting her, O Ravening One. You who are never satisfied, in this one thing, will not triumph. What would we have between us to keep it clear who is whom? I cannot allow it."

You will, said Vashanka so loud in his head that he winced in his saddle and the Trôs horse broke stride, looking reproachfully about at him to see what that shift of weight could possibly be construed to mean.

Tempus stopped the horse in the middle of the cool shadowed way on that beautiful morning and sat stiffly a long while, conducting an internal battle which had no resolution.

After a time, he swung the horse back in its tracks, kicked it into a lope toward the barracks from which he had just come. Let her stay with One-Thumb, if she would. She had come between him and his god before. He was not ready to give her to the god, and he was not ready to give himself back into the hands of his curse, rip asunder what had been so laboriously patched together and at such great cost. He thought of Abarsis, and Kadakithis, and the refractory upcountry peoples, and he promised Vashanka any other woman the god should care to choose before sundown. Cime would keep, no doubt, right where she was. He would see to it that Lastel saw to her.

Abarsis's Trôs horse snorted softly, as if in agreement, single-footing through Sanctuary's better streets toward the barracks. But the Trôs horse could not have known that by this simple decision its rider had attained to a greater victory than in all the wars of all the empires he had ever labored to increase. No, the Trôs horse whose belly quivered between Tempus's knees as it issued a blaring trumpet to the dusty air did so not because of its rider's triumph over self and god, but out of pure high spirits, as horses always will praise a fine day dawned.

FOR LOVE OF A GHOST

This time, when the adept's palm closed and Niko was returned to himself and his rest-place, tears glittered in his eyes. Not only had he seen Abarsis, his former commander, but also himself—through Tempus's eyes.

The experience was more than disconcerting. It was intrusive, unwelcome. He felt as if he'd been peeking through floorboards. His Sacred Band oath conflicted with such inner knowledge of Tempus, the man to whom, on Abarsis's death, he'd sworn it.

Niko was a Stepson; had been one of the paired fighters in the Vulgar Unicorn that day when Tempus was found by Abarsis. It made his heart sore to see it all again, without the softening mists of selective memory, without the mitigation that time can bring.

He said to the adept who peered at him owlishly, "You're wrong if you think you can turn my heart from Tempus with this 'lesson.' Whatever he thinks of himself, or of us, he is still what we need him to be. It makes no difference."

"Really?" responded the teacher. "You are wrong,

student. It makes—will make—a great difference to you. From now on and for all time. Knowledge is never wasted. You will look upon these soldiers and their doings with the eyes of a man, not a boy."

"I gave my word. My allegiance is firm. Nothing will change it. I am a Sacred Bander, in the World. Don't make me choose between them, and you." *You* in this case meant the whole Bandaran school, which seemed now to be part and parcel of this onslaught upon Niko's loyalty.

For that was what he perceived here. He did not want to know Tempus so intimately, never had claimed the rights to his leader's innermost thoughts. It didn't matter if Tempus, in his sad and blackened heart, thought every man who served under him to be an ass in fighter's clothing. They still served their purpose, served it well.

Niko added, "Tempus would not attempt to turn me from Bandara. Why is Bandara trying to turn me from Tempus?"

"Bandara wants only the best for you, Nikodemos," said the man whose face now seemed like some animated walnut shell, so deep were the furrows of its wrinkles. "Bandara wants you to know yourself. Know your friends. Know your enemies. An end to hero-worship is in order. You cannot reach your own full potential until you come out from under the shadow of the Riddler. You must be yourself, or else you will become a parody of him."

And then Niko thought he understood: the adepts believed that Niko was in danger of becoming Tempus's successor—of being coopted by Aškelon, or worse. These divisive visions were their attempt at immunizing his soul against a fate they perceived to be no better than a plague.

"I won't," Niko said through gritted teeth. "I can't. I've tried to let it happen—with Aškelon, with the witch, with the northern wizards—to get it over with." It was a lie, some of that. In Mygdonia, fighting with Tempus against the undead, he'd plain run out of strength. In Free Nisibis, with the warrior priest Bashir by his side, he'd been wooed by the adherents of Enlil, the primal Stormgod of the mountain fighters.

And when a witch had tried to claim him as a lover, he'd wished he could surrender. But through it all, his maat had been like an anchor, a stanchion binding him to higher ground. Once opened to it, he could never sink unknowing into folly. He'd wished, often enough in those days, that he could.

Watching the adept watch him, waiting for an answer, he saw faces superimposed over that nut-brown countenance: that of the beleaguered prince-governor; that of the raffish young thief—both of whom Tempus had so badly wanted to help. But no one could put wisdom into the prince or into the delinquent backstreeter, who was controlled by a selfish, evil and primitive Ilsigi god. And no one could mitigate Tempus's curse. No good deed went unpunished, when Tempus was the do-gooder.

Niko had promised himself never to shun the Riddler; never to be ungrateful; never to force Tempus to disappoint him.

And in the things that mattered, Tempus never had. Throughout the long campaign against magic that had brought Niko home, finally, to rest when it had ended, Tempus had never betrayed him. Never. Not even when Niko, under the spell of this or that power, had been less than his oath required. And the Sacred Band oath was rigorous, its adherents continually tested.

You stood with your partner, despite all hardship. You withheld judgment. You were part of a family, and understood it so.

Families were prone to internecine disputes of the most vituperous sort, disagreements of the greatest magnitude, fallings in and fallings out. But after all was said and done, a family was a family still.

The band was more a family to Niko than the Bandaran adepts, who'd ousted him once and then, when it was convenient, taken him back. The band had a bond that was unbroken even by death.

Abarsis was proof of that. Abarsis had been everything to Niko. The adept did not realize what pain he'd caused. But then, the adept didn't know that Abarsis fought the band's battles still, in heaven.

Niko said, "If you do not understand what you are showing me, you'd best leave off. This is *my* rest-place. I suffer you to be here only so long as what you do here is beneficial. Show me that you meddle where you do not belong, and I will oust you from here as quickly as you can close your tale-telling palm." His eyes were glittering with tears unshed— tears for Abarsis. And with rebellion—over being manipulated. And with pathos—knowing the death of Abarsis in life had been enough.

Knowing what Tempus had suffered was more than Niko felt he had to bear. Did the adept realize he was cementing, rather than weakening, the bond between Niko and his left-side leader? Did he even understand the term?

The adept stared at him unspeaking until Niko added, "You *don't* know what you're doing, do you? You don't comprehend the World—that's why you live here in seclusion. Yours is not the fighter's code. Aškelon, for all I know, manipulates you and yours through trance and dream."

It was an accusation of some weight.

The adept straightened up a bit and for the first time his knees seemed to brush the grass of Niko's rest-place. Then the old man nodded and murmured,

"Good, think what you will. But *think*. And watch. And listen. Before we talk again."

This time, as the palm of the Bandaran master opened and a shimmering began to draw Niko into it, he almost fought the process. But he could not. Somehow, though it was painful, though it was even dangerous to learn what he should not know, Niko needed to see what the adept would show him next. . .

WIZARD WEATHER

— 1 —

In the archmage's sumptuous purple bedroom, the woman astride him took two pins from her silver-shot hair. It was dark—his choice; and damp with cloying shadows—his romanticism. A conjured moon in a spellbound sky was being swallowed by effigy-clouds where the vaulted roof indubitably yet arced, even as he shuddered under the tutored and inexorable attentions of the girl Lastel had brought to his party. She had refused to tell him her name because he would not give his, but had told him what she would do for him so eloquently with her eyes and her body that he had spent the entire evening figuring out a way the two of them might slip up here unnoticed. Not that he feared her escort's jealousy— though the drug dealer might conceivably entertain such a sentiment, Lastel no longer had the courage (or the contractual protective wardings) to dare a reprisal against a Hazard-class mage.

Of all the enchanters in wizard-ridden Sanctuary, only three were archmages, nameless adepts beyond summoning or responsibility, and this Hazard was one. In fact, he was the very strongest of those three.

When he had been young, he had had a name, but he will forget it, and everything else, quite promptly: the domed and spired estuary of venality which is Sanctuary, nadir of the empire called Ranke; the unmitigated evil he had fielded for decades from his swamp-encircled Mageguild fortress; the compromises he had made to hold sway over curmudgeon, courtesan and criminal (so audacious that even the bounds of magics and planeworlds had been eroded by his efforts, and his fellow adepts felled on occasion by demons roused from forbidden defiles to do his bidding here at the end of creation where no balance remains between logic and faith, law and nature, or heaven and hell); the disingenous methods through which his will was worked, plan by tortuous plan, upon a town so hateful and immoral that both the flaunted gods and magicians' devils agreed that its inhabitants deserved no less dastardly a fate—all of this, and more, will fade from him in the time it takes a star to burn out, falling from the sky.

Now, the First Hazard glimpses her movement, though he is close to ejaculation, sputtering with sensations that for years he has assumed he had outgrown, or forgotten how to feel. Senility creeps upon the finest flesh when a body is maintained for millenia, and into the deepest mind, through thousands of years. He does not look his age, or tend to think of it. The years are his, mandated. Only a very special kind of enemy could defeat him, and those were few and far between. Simple death, morbidity or the spells of his brothers were like gnats he kept away by the perfume of his sweat: merely the proper diet, herbs and spells and consummated will, had long ago vanquished them as far as he was concerned.

So strange to lust, to desire a particular woman; he was amused, joyous; he had not felt so good in years. A tiny thrill of caution had horripilated his nape early on, when he noticed the silvering of her nightblack hair, but this girl was not old enough to be—"Ahhhh!" Her premeditated rippling takes him over passion's edge, and he is falling, place and provenance forgotten, not a terrible adept wrenching the world about to suit his whim and comfort, but just a man.

In that instant, eyes defocused, he sees but does not note the diamond sparkle of the rods poised above him; his ears are filled with his own breathing; the song of entrapment she sings softly has him before he thinks to think, or thinks to fear, or thinks to move.

By then, the rods, their sharp fine points touching his arched throat, owned him. He could not move; not his body nor his soul responded; his mind could not control his tongue. Thinking bitterly of the indignity of being frozen like a rearing stallion, he hoped his flesh would slump once life had fled. As he felt the points enter into his skin and begin to suck at the thread binding him to life, his mortification marshaled his talents: he cleared his vision, forced his eyes to obey his mind's command. Though he was a great sorcerer, he was not omnipotent: he could not manage to make his lips frame a curse to cast upon her, just watched the free agent Cime—who had slipped, disguised, into so many mages' beds of late—sip the life from his relishingly. So slow she was about it he had time to be thankful she did not take him through his eyes. The song she sings has cost her much to learn, and the death she staves off will not be so kind as his. Could he have spoken, then, resigned to it, he would have thanked her: it is no shame to be brought down by an opponent so worthy. They paid their prices to the same host. He set about composing his exit, seeking his meadow, starshaped and evergreen, where he did his work when meditation whisked him into finer awarenesses than flesh could ever share. If he could seat himself there, in his established place of power, then his death was nothing, his flesh a fingernail, overlong and ready to be pared.

He did manage that. Cime saw to it that he had the time. It does not do to anger certain kinds of powers, the sort which, having dispensed with names, dispense with discorporation. Some awful day, she would face this one, and others whom she had guided out of life, in an afterlife which she had helped populate. Shades tended to be unforgiving.

When his chest neither rose nor fell, she slid off him and ceased singing. She licked the tips of her wands and wound them back up in her thick black hair. She soothed his body down, arranged it decorously, donned her party clothes, and kissed him once on the tip of his nose before heading, humming, back down the stairs to where Lastel and the party still waited. As she passed the bar, she snatched a piece of citrus and crushed it in her palms, dripping the juice upon her wrists, smearing it behind her ears and in the hollow of her throat. Some of these folk might be clumsy necromancers and thrice-cursed merchants with store-bought charms-to-ward-off-charms bleeding them dry of soul and purse, but there was nothing wrong with their noses.

Lastel's bald head and wrestler's shoulders, impeccable in customed silk velvet, were easy to spot. He did not even glance down at her, but continued chatting with one of the prince/governor Kadakithis's functionaries, Molin Something-or-other, Vashanka's official priest. It was New Year's holiday, and the week was bursting with festivities which the Rankan overlords must observe, and seem to sanction: since (though they had conquered and subjugated Ilsig lands and Ilsig peoples so that some Rankans dared call Ilsigs "'Wrigglies" to their faces) they had failed to suppress the worship of the god Ils and his self-begotten pantheon, word had come down from the emperor himself that Rankans must endure with grace the Wrigglies celebration of Ils's creation of the world and renewal of the year. Now, especially, with Ranke pressed into a war of attrition in the north, was no time to allow dissension to develop on her flanks from so paltry a matter as the perquisites of obscure and weakling gods.

This uprising among the buffer states upon Upper Ranke's northernmost frontier and the inflated rumors of slaughter coming back from Wizardwall's mountainous skirts all out of proportion to reasonable numbers dominated Molin's monologue: "And what say you, esteemed lady? Could it be that Nisibisi magicians have made their peace with Mygdon's barbarian lord, and found him a path through Wizardwall's fastness? You are well-traveled, it is obvious. . . . Could it be true that the border insurrection is Mygdonia's doing, and their hordes so fearsome as we have been led to believe? Or is it the Rankan treasury that is suffering, and a northern incursion the cure for our economic ills?"

Lastel flickered puffy lids down at her from ravaged cheeks and his turgid arm went around her waist. She smiled up at him reassuringly, then favored the priest: "Your Holiness, sadly I must confess that the Mygdonian threat is very real. I have studied realms and magics, in Ranke and beyond. If you wish a consultation, and Lastel permits—" she batted the thickest lashes in Sanctuary "—I shall gladly attend you, some day when we both are fit for 'solemn' discourse. But now I am too filled with wine and revel, and must interrupt you—your pardon please—that my escort bear me home to bed." She cast her glance upon the ballroom floor, demure and concentrating on her slippered feet poking out under amber skirts. "Lastel, I must have the night air, or faint away. Where is our host? We must thank him for a more complete hospitality than I had thought to find. . . ."

The habitually pompous priest was simpering with undisguised delight, causing Lastel to raise an eyebrow, though Cime tugged coquettishly at his sleeve, and inquire as to its source: "*Lord* Molin?"

"It is nothing, dear man, nothing. Just so long since I have heard court Rankene—and from the mouth of a *real* lady. . . ." The Rankan priest, knowing well that his wife's reputation bore no mitigation, chose to make sport of her, and of his town, before the foreign noblewoman did. And to make it more clear to Lastel that the joke was on them—the two Sanctuarites—and for the amusement of the voluptuous gray-eyed woman, he bowed low, and never did answer her genteel query as to the whereabouts of the First Hazard.

By the time he had promised to give their thanks and regards to the absent host when he saw him, the lady was gone, and Molin Torchholder was left wishing he knew what it was that she saw in Lastel. Certainly it was not the dogs he raised, or his fortune, which was modest, or his business . . . well, yes, it might have been just that . . . drugs. Some who knew said the best krrf—black and Caronnestamped—came from Lastel's connections. Molin sighed, hearing his wife's twitter among the crowd's buzz. Where *was* that Hazard? The damn Mageguild was getting too arrogant. No one could throw a bash as star-studded as this one and then walk away from it as if the luminaries in attendance were nonentities. He was glad he had not prevailed on the prince to come along. . . . *What* a woman! And what *was* her name? He had been told, he was sure, but just forgot. . . .

Outside, torchlit, their breath steaming white through cold-sharpened night air, waiting for their ivory-screened wagon, they giggled over the distinction between "serious" and "solemn": the First Hazard had been serious, Molin was solemn; Tempus the Hell Hound was serious, Prince Kadakithis, solemn; the destabilization campaign they were undertaking in Sanctuary under the auspices of a Mygdonian-funded Nisibisi witch (who had come to Lastel, alias One-Thumb, in the guise of a comely caravan mistress hawking Caronne drugs) was serious; the threat of northern invasion, down-country at the Empire's anus, was most solemn. As her laughter tinkled, he nuzzled her: "Did you manage to . . . ?"

"Oh, yes. I had a perfectly lovely time. What a wonderful idea of yours this was," she whispered, still speaking court Rankene, a dialect she had been using exclusively in public ever since the two of them—the Mazedweller One-Thumb and the escaped sorcerer-slayer Cime—had decided that the best cover for them was that which her magic provided: they need not do more. Her brother Tempus knew that Lastel was actually One-Thumb, *and* that she was with him, but he would hesitate to reveal them: he had given his silence, if not his blessing, to their union. Within reasonable limits, they considered themselves safe to bargain lives and information to both sides in the coming crisis. Even now, with the war barely under way, they had already started. This night's work was her pleasure and his profit. When they reached his modest east-side estate, she showed him the portion of what she had done to the First Hazard which he would like best—and most probably survive, if his heart was strong. For her service, she demanded a Rankan soldat's worth of black krrf, before the act. When he had paid her, and watched her melt it with water over a flame, cool it, and bring it to him on the bed, her fingers stirring the viscous liquid, he was glad he had not argued about her price, or about her practice of always charging one.

— *2* —

Wizard weather blew in off the sea later that night, as quickly as one of the Sanctuary whores could blow a client a kiss, or a pair of Stepsons disperse an unruly crowd. Everyone in the suddenly mist-enshrouded streets of the Maze ran for cover; adepts huddled under beds with their best warding spells wrapped tighter than blankets around shivering shoulders; east-siders bade their jesters perform and their musicians play louder; dogs howled; cats yowled; horses screamed in the palace stables and tried to batter their stallboards down.

Some unlucky ones did not make it to safety before a dry thunder roared and lightning flashed and in the streets, the mist began to glitter, thicken, chill. It rolled headhigh along byway and alley, claws of ice scrabbling at shuttered windows, barred doors. Where it found life, it shredded bodies, lacerating limbs, stealing away warmth and souls and leaving only flayed carcasses frozen in the streets.

A pair of Tempus's Stepsons was caught out in the storm, but it could not be said that the weather killed one: the team had been investigating uncorroborated reports that a warehouse conveniently situated at a juncture of three major sewers was being used by an alchemist to concoct and store incendiaries. The surviving partner guessed that his teammate must have lit a torch, despite the cautions of research: human wastes, flour, sulphur and more had gone in through those now-nonexistent doors. Though the problem the team had been dispatched to investigate was solved by a concussive fireball that threw the second Stepson—Nikodemos—through a window into an intersection, singeing his beard and brows and eyelashes, the young Sacred Band member relived the circumstances leading to his partner's death repeatedly, agonizing over the possibility that he was to blame throughout the night, alone in the pair's billet. So consumed was he with grief at the death of his mate, he did not even realize that his friend had saved his life: the fireball and ensuing conflagration had blown back the mist and made an oven of the wharfside; Wideway was freed from the vicious fog for half its length. He had ridden at a devil's pace out of Sanctuary home to the Stepsons' barracks, which once had been a slaver's estate and thus had rooms enough for Tempus to allow his hard-won mercenaries the luxury of privacy: ten pairs plus thirty single agents comprised the team's core group—until this evening past. . . .

Sun was trying to beat back the night, Niko could see it through his window. He had not even been able to return with a body. His beloved spirit-twin would be denied the honor of a hero's fiery bier. He could not cry; he simply sat, huddled, amputated, diminished and cold upon his bed, watching a sunray inch its way toward one of his sandaled feet.

Thus he did not see Tempus approaching with the first light of day haloing his just-bathed form the very image of a god's avatar. The tall, autumnal figure stooped and peered in the window, sun gilding his yarrow-honey hair and his vast bronze limbs where they were free of his army-issue woolen chiton. He wore no arms or armor, no cloak or shoes; furrows deepened on his brow, and a severe frown tightened his willful mouth. Sometimes, the expression in his long, slitted eyes grew readable: this was such a time. The pain he was about to face was a pain he had known too well, too often. It brought to features not brutal enough by half for their history or profession the slight, defensive smile which would empty out his eyes. When he could, he knocked. Hearing no reply, he called softly, "Niko?" And again. . . .

Having let himself in, he waited for the Stepson, who looked younger than the quarter-century he claimed, to raise his head. He met a gaze as blank as his own, and bared his teeth.

The youth nodded slowly, made to rise, sank back when Tempus motioned "stay" and joined him on his wood-framed cot in blessed shadow. Both sat then, silent, as day filled up the room, stealing away their hiding place. Elbows on knees, Niko thanked him for coming. Tempus suggested that under the circumstances a bier could still be made, and funerary games would not be out of order. When he got no response, the mercenary's commander sighed rattlingly and allowed that he himself would be honored to perform the rites. He knew how the Sacred Banders who had adopted the war name "Stepsons" revered him. He did not condone or encourage it, but since they had given him their love and were probably doomed to the man for it—even as their original leader, Stepson, Abarsis, had been doomed—Tempus felt responsible for them. His instructions and his curse had sent the gelded warrior-priest to his death, and such fighters as these could not offer loyalty to a lesser man, to a pompous prince or an abstracted cause. Sacred Bands were the mercenaries' elite; this one's history under the Slaughter Priest's command was nearly mythical; Abarsis had brought his men to Tempus before sacrificing his life for Tempus, leaving them as his parting gift—and as his way of ensuring that Tempus could not just walk away from Vashanka's service: Abarsis had been Vashanka's priest.

Of all the mercenaries Rankan money had enabled

Tempus to gather for Prince/Governor Kadakithis, this young recruit was the most singular. There was something remarkable about the finely made slate-haired fighter with his quiet hazel eyes and his understated manner, something that made it seem perfectly reasonable that this self-effacing youngster with his clean long limbs and his quick canny smile had been the right-side partner in a Syrese legend twice his age for nine years. Tempus would rather have been doing anything else than trying to give comfort to the bereaved Stepson Nikodemos. Choosing a language appropriate to philosophy and grief (for Niko was fluent in six tongues, ancient and modern), he asked the youth what was in his heart.

"Gloom," Niko responded in the mercenary-argot, which admitted many tongues, but only the bolder emotions: pride, anger, insult, declaratives, imperatives, absolutes.

"Gloom," Tempus agreed in the same linguistic pastiche, yet ventured: "You will survive it. We all do."

"Oh, Riddler . . . I know . . . You did, Abarsis did—twice," he took a shivering breath; "but it is not easy. I feel so naked. He was . . . always on my left, if you understand me—where you are now."

"Consider me here for the duration, then, Niko."

Niko raised too-bright eyes, slowly shaking his head. "In our spirits' place of comfort, where trees and men and life are one, he *is still there*. How can I rest, when my rest-place holds his ghost? There is no *maat* left for me . . . do you know the word?"

Tempus did: balance, equilibrium, the tendency of things to make a pattern, and that pattern to be discernible, and therefore revivifying. He thought for a moment, gravely, not about Niko's problem, but about a youthful mercenary who spoke offhandedly of adept's refreshments and archmagical medita-

tions, who routinely transported his spirit into a
mystical realm and was accustomed to meeting another spirit there. He said at last: "I do not read it ill
that your friend waits there. Why is it bad, unless
you make it so? Maat, if you have had it, you will find
again. With him, you are bound in spirit, not just in
flesh. He would be hurt to hurt you, and to see that
you are afraid of what once you loved. His spirit will
depart your place of relaxation when we put it formally to rest. Yet you must make a better peace with
him, and surmount your fear. It is well to have a
friendly soul waiting at the gate when your time
comes around. Surely, you love him still?"

That broke the young Stepson, and Tempus left
him curled upon his bed, so that his sobs need not
be silent, and he could heal upon his own.

Outside, leaning against the doorjamb, the planked
door carefully closed, Tempus put his fingers to the
bridge of his nose and rubbed his eyes. He had
surprised himself, as well as the boy, offering Niko
such far-reaching support. He was not sure he dared
to mean it, but he had said it. Niko's team had
functioned as the Stepsons' ad hoc liaisons, coordi-
nating (but more usually arbitrating disputes among)
the mercenaries and the Hell Hounds (the Rankan
Imperial Elite Guards), the Ilsig regular army and
the militia Tempus was trying to covertly make out
of some carefully-chosen street urchins, slit purses,
and sleeves—the real rulers of this overblown slum
and the only people who ever knew what was going
on in Sanctuary, a town which might just become a
strategic staging area if war did come down from the
north. As liaisons, both teammates had come to him
often for advice. Part of Niko's workload had been
the making of an adequate swordsman out of a certain Ilsig thief named Hanse. But the young backstreeter, emboldened by his easy early successes, had

proved increasingly irascible and contentious when Niko—aware that Tempus was indebted to Hanse and that Kadakithis inexplicably favored the thief—endeavored to lead him far beyond slash-and-thrust infantry tactics into the subtleties of Niko's own expertise: cavalry strategies, guerrilla tactics, western fighting forms that dispensed with weaponry by accenting surprise, precision, and meditation-honed instinct. Though the thief recognized the value of what the Stepson offered, his pride made him sneer: he could not admit his need to know, would not chance being found wanting, and hid his fear of failure behind anger. After three months of justifying the value of methods and mechanics the Stepson felt to be self-explanatory (black stomach blood, bright lung blood, or pink foam from the ears indicates a mortal strike; yarrow root shaved into a wound quells its pain; ginseng, chewed, renews stamina; mandrake in an enemy's stewpot incapacitates a company, monkshood decimates one; green or moldy hay downs every horse on your opponents' line; cheese wire, the right handhold, or a knife from behind obviates the need for passwords, protracted dissembling, or forged papers), Niko had turned to Tempus for a decision as to whether instruction must continue: Shadowspawn, called Hanse was a natural bladesman, as good as any man wishing to wield a sword for a living needed to be—on the *ground*, Niko had said. As far as horsemanship, he had added almost sadly, niceties could not be taught to a cocky novice who spent more time arguing that he would never need to master them than practicing what he was taught. Similarly, so far as tradecraft went, Hanse's fear of being labelled a Stepson-in-training or an apprentice Sacred Bander prevented him from fraternizing with the squadron during the long evenings when shoptalk and exploits flowed freely, and every man found much to learn.

Niko had shrugged, spreading his hands to indicate
an end to his report. Throughout it (the longest
speech Tempus had ever heard the Stepson make),
Tempus could not fail to mark the disgust so carefully masked, the frustration and the unwillingness to
admit defeat which had hidden in Nikodemos' lowered eyes and blank face. Tempus's decision to pro-
nounce the student Shadowspawn graduated, gift him
with a horse, and go on to new business had elicited
a subtle inclination of head—an agreement, nothing
less—from the youthful and eerily composed junior
mercenary. Since then, he had not seen him. And,
upon seeing him, he had not asked any of the things
he had gone there to find out: not one question as to
the exact circumstances of his partner's death, or the
nature of the mist which had ravaged the Maze, had
passed his lips. Tempus blew out a noisy breath,
grunted, then pushed off from where he leaned against
the whitewashed barracks wall. He would go out to
see what headway the band had made with the bier
and the games, set for sundown behind the walled
estate. He did not need to question the boy further,
only to listen to his own heart.

He was not unaware of the ominous events of the
preceding evening: sleep was never his. He had
made a midnight creep through the sewage tunnels
into Kadakithis's most private apartments, demon-
strating that the old palace was impossible to secure,
in hopes that the boy-prince would stop prattling
about "winter palace/summer palace" and move his
retinue into the new fortress Tempus had built for
him on the eminently defensible spit near the lighthouse with that very end in mind. So it was that he
had heard firsthand from the prince (who all the
while was making a valiant attempt not to bury his
nose in a scented handkerchief he was holding almost casually but had fumbled desperately to find

when first Tempus appeared, reeking of sewage, between two of his damask bedroom hangings) about the killer mist and the dozen lives it claimed. Tempus had let his silence agree that the mages must be right, such a thing was totally mystifying, though the "thunder without rain" and its results had explained itself to him quite clearly. Nothing is mysterious after three centuries and more of exploring life's riddles, except perhaps why gods allow men magic, or why sorcerers allow men gods.

Equally reticent was Tempus when Kadakithis, wringing his lacquer-nailed hands, told him of the First Hazard's unique demise, and wondered with dismal sarcasm if the adepts would again try to blame the fall of one of their number on Tempus's *alleged* sister (here he glanced sidelong up at Tempus from under his pale Imperial curls), the escaped mage-killer who, *he* was beginning to think, was a figment of sorcerers' nightmares: When they had had this "person" in the pits, awaiting trial and sentence, no two witnesses could agree on the description of the woman they saw; when she had escaped, no one saw her go. It might be that the adepts were purging their Order again, and didn't want anyone to know, didn't Tempus agree? In the face of Kadakithis's carefully thought-out policy statement, meant to protect the prince from involvement and the soldier from implication, Tempus refrained from comment.

The First Hazard's death was a welcome surprise to Tempus, who indulged in an active, if surreptitious, bloodfeud with the Mageguild. Sortilege of any nature he could not abide. He had explored and discarded it all: philosophy, systems of personal discipline such as Niko employed, magic, religion, the sort of eternal side-taking purveyed by the warrior-mages who wore the Blue Star. The man who in his youth had proclaimed that those things which could be touched and perceived were those which he preferred had not been changed by time, only hardened. Adepts and sorcery disgusted him. He had faced wizards of true power in his youth, and his sorties upon the bloody roads of life had been colored by those encounters: his hatred of them was as immortal as the curse of one of their number that he yet bore. He had thought that even should he die, his despite would live on to harass them—he hoped that it were true. For to fight with enchanters of skill, the same skills were needed, and he eschewed those arts. The price was too high. He would never acknowledge power over freedom, eternal servitude of the spirit was too great a cost for mastery in life. Yet a man could not stand alone against witchfire-hatred. To survive, he had been forced to make a pact with the Storm God, Vashanka. He had been brought to collar like a wild dog. He heeled to Vashanka, these days, at the god's command. But he did not like it.

There were compensations, if such they could be called. He lived interminably, though he could not sleep at all; he was immune to simple, nasty war-magics; he had a sword which cut through spells like cheese and glowed when the god took an interest. In battle he was more than twice as fast as a mortal man—while they moved so slowly he could do as he willed upon a crowded field which was a melee to all but him, and even extend his hyper speed to his mount, if the horse was of a certain strain and tough constitution. And wounds he took healed quickly—instantly if the god loved him that day, more slowly if they had been quarreling.

For these reasons, and many more, he had a mystique, but no charisma. Only among mercenaries could he look into eyes free from the glint of fear. He stayed much among his own, these days in Sanctu-

ary. Abarsis's death had struck home harder than he
cared to admit. It seemed, sometimes, that one more
soul laying down its life for him and one more burden laid upon him would surpass his capacity and he
would crack apart into the dessicated dust he doubtless was.

Crossing the whitewashed court, passing the stables, his Trôs horses stuck steel-gray muzzles over
their half-doors and whickered. He stopped and
stroked them, speaking soft words of comradeship
and endearment, before he left to let himself out the
back gate to the training ground, a natural amphi-
theatre between hillocks where the Stepsons drilled
the few furtive Ilsigs wishing to qualify for the militia-
reserves Kadakithis was funding.

He was thinking, as he closed the gate behind him
and squinted out over the arena (counting heads and
fitting names to them where men sat perched atop the
fence or lounged against it or raked sand or counted
off paces for sunset's funerary games), that it was a
good thing no one had been able to determine the
cause of the ranking Hazard's death. He would have
to do something about his sister Cime, and soon—
something substantive. Since she had turned up in
Sanctuary he had given her the latitude befitting a
probable sibling and childhood passion, and she had
exceeded his forbearance. He had been willing to
overlook the fact that he had been paying her debts
with his soul ever since he had been cursed on her
account, but he was not willing to ignore the fact that
she refused to abstain from taking down magicians. It
might be her right, in general, to slay sorcerers, but
it was not her right to do it here, where he was
pinned tight between law and morality, as it was.
The whole conundrum of how he might successfully
deal with Cime was something he did not want to
contemplate. So he did not, just then, only walked,

cold brown grass between his toes, to the near side of the chest-high wooden fence behind which, on happier days, his men schooled Ilsigs, and each other. Today they were making a bier there, dragging dry branches from the brake beyond Vashanka's altar, a pile of stones topping a rise, due east, where the charioteers worked their teams.

Sweat never stayed long enough to drip in the chill winter air, but breaths puffed white from noses and mouths in the taut pearly light, and grunts and taunts carried well in the crisp morning air. Tempus ducked his head and rubbed his mouth to hide his mirth as a stream of scatological invective sounded: one of the branch-draggers exhorting the loungers to get to work. Were curses soldats, the Stepsons would all be men of ease. The fence-sitters, counter-cursing the work-boss gamely, slipped to the ground; the loungers gave up their wall. In front of him, they pretended to be untouched by the ill-omen of accidental death. But he, too, was uneasy in the face of tragedy without reason, bereft of the glory of death in the field. All of them feared accident, mindless fortune's disfavor: they lived by luck, as much as by the god's favor. As the dozen men, more or less in a body, headed toward the alter and the brake beyond, Tempus felt the god rustling inside him, and took time to upbraid Vashanka for wasting an adherent. They were not on the best of terms, the man and his god. His temper was hard-held these days, and the gloom of winter quartering was making him fey—not to mention reports of the Mygdonians' foul depredations to the far north, the quelling of which he was not free to join. . . .

First, he noticed that two people sauntering casually down the altar's hillock toward him were not familiar; and then, that none of his Stepsons were moving: each was stock-still. A cold overswept him, like a wind-driven wave, and rolled on toward the barracks. Above, the pale sky clouded over; a silky dusk swallowed the day. Black clouds gathered; over Vashanka's altar two luminous, red moons appeared high up in the inky air, as if some huge night-cat lurked on a lofty perch. Watching the pair approaching (through unmoving men who did not even know they stood now in darkness), swathed in a pale nimbus which illuminated their path as the witch-cold had heralded their coming, Tempus muttered under his breath. His hand went to his hip, where no weapon lay, but only a knotted cord. Studying the strangers without looking at them straight-on, leaning back, his arms outstretched along the fencetop, he waited.

The red lights glowing above Vashanka's altar winked out. The ground shuddered; the altar stones tumbled to the ground. *Wonderful*, he thought. *Just great*. He let his eyes slide over his men, asleep between blinks, and wondered how far the spell extended, whether they were ensorceled in their bunks, or in the mess, or on their horses as they made their rounds in the country or the town.

Well, Vashanka? he tested. *It's your altar they took down*. But the god was silent.

Besides the two coming at measured pace across the ground rutted with chariot tracks, nothing moved. No bird cried or insect chittered, no Stepson so much as snored. The companion of the imposing man in the thick, fur mantle had him by the elbow. Who was helping whom, Tempus could not at first determine. He tried to think where he had seen that austere face—soul-shriveling eyes so sad, bones so fine and yet full of vitality beneath the black, silver-starred hair—and then blew out a sibilant breath when he realized what power approached over the rutted, Sanctuary ground. The companion, whose lithe musculature and bare, tanned skin were counterpointed by an enameled tunic of scale-armor and soft low boots, was either a female or the prettiest eunuch Tempus had ever seen—whichever, she/he was trouble, coming in from some nonphysical realm on the arm of the entelechy of a shadow lord, master of the once-in-a-while archipelago that bore his name: Aškelon, lord of dreams.

When they reached him, Tempus nodded carefully and said, very quietly in a noncommittal way that almost passed for deference, "Salutations, Ash. What brings you into so poor a realm?"

Aškelon's proud lips parted; the skin around them was too pale. It *was* a woman who held his arm; her health made him seem the more pallid, but when he spoke, his words were ringing basso profundo: "Life to you, Riddler. What are you called here?"

"Spare me your curses, mage." To such a power, the title alone was an insult. And the shadow lord knew it well.

Around his temples, stars of silver floated, stirred by a breeze. His colorless eyes grew darker, draining the angry clouds from the sky: "You have not answered me."

"Nor you, me."

The woman looked in disbelief upon Tempus. She opened her lips, but Aškelon touched them with a gloved hand. From the gauntlet's cuff a single drop of blood ran down his left arm to drip upon the sand. He looked at it somberly, then up at Tempus. "I seek your sister, what else? I will not harm her."

"But will you cause her to harm herself?"

The shadow lord whom Tempus had called Ash, so familiarly, rubbed the bloody trail from his elbow back up to his wrist. "Surely you do not think you can protect her from me? Have I not accomplished even this? Am I not real?" He held his gloved hands out, turned them over, let them flap abruptly down against his thighs. Niko, who had been roused from deep meditation in the barracks by the cold which had spread sleep over the waking, skidded to a halt and peered around the curve of the fence, his teeth gritted hard to stay their chatter.

"No." Tempus had replied to Aškelon's first question with that sensitive little smile which meant he was considering commencing some incredible slaughter; "Yes" to his second; "Yes, indeed" to the third.

"And would I be here," the dream lord continued, "in so ignominious a state if not for the havoc she has wrought?"

"I don't know what havoc she's wrought that could have touched you out there. But I take it that last night's deadly mist was your harbinger. Why come to me, Ash? I'm not involved with her in any way."

"You connived to release her from imprisonment, Tempus—it *is* Tempus, so the dreams of the Sanctuarities tell me. And they tell me other things, too. I am here, sleepless one, to warn you: though I cannot reach you through dreams, have no doubt: I *can* reach you. All of these, you consider yours . . ." He waved his hand to encompass the still men, frozen unknowing upon the field. "They are mine now. I can claim them any time."

"What do you want, Ash?"

"I want you to refrain from interfering with me while I am here. I will see her and settle a score with her, and if you are circumspect, when I leave, your vicious little band of cutthroats will be returned to you, unharmed, uncomprehending."

"All that, to make sure of me? I don't respond well to flattery. You will force me to a gesture by trying to prevent one. I don't care what you do about Cime— whatever you do, you will be doing me a favor. Release my people, and go about your quest."

"I cannot trust you not to interfere. By noon I shall be installed as temporary First Hazard of your local Mageguild—"

"Slumming? It's hardly your style."

"*Style?*" he thundered so that his companion shuddered and Niko started, dislodging a stone which clicked, rolled, then lay still. "*Style!* She came unto me with her evil and destroyed my peace." His other hand cradled his wrist. "I was lucky to receive a reprieve from damnation. I have only a limited dispensation: either I force her to renege on murdering me, or make her finish the job. And you of all men know what awaits a contractee such as myself when existance is over. What would you do in my place?"

"I did not know how she got here, but now it comes clearer. She went to destroy you in your place, and was spat out into this world from there? But how is it she has not succeeded?"

The Power, looking past Tempus with a squint, shrugged. "She was not certain, her will was not united with her heart. I have a chance, now, to remedy it . . . bring back restful dreaming in its place, and my domain with it. I will not let anything stop me. Be warned, my friend. You know what strengths I can bring to bear."

"Release my people, if you want her, and we will think about how to satisfy you over breakfast. From the look of you, you could use something warm to drink. You do drink, don't you? With the form come the functions, surely even here."

Aškelon sighed feelingly; his shoulders slumped. "Yes, indeed, the entire package is mine to tend and lumber about in, some little while longer . . . until after the Mageguild's fete this evening, at the very least. . . . I am surprised, not to mention pleased, that you display some disposition to compromise. It is for everyone's benefit. This is Jihan." He inclined his head toward his companion. "Greet our host."

"It is my pleasure to wish that things go exceedingly well with you," the woman said, and Niko saw Tempus shiver, a subtle thing that went over him from scalp to sandals—and almost bolted out to help, thinking some additional, debilitating spell was being cast. He was not fooled by those polite exchanges: bodies and timbres had been speaking more plainly of respectful opposition and cautious hostility. Distressed and overbalanced from long crouching without daring to lean or sit, he fell forward, catching himself too late to avoid making noise.

Niko heard Tempus remonstrate, "Let him be, Aškelon!" and felt a sudden ennui, his eyelids closing, a drift toward sleep he fought—then heard the dream lord reply: "I will take this one as my hostage, and leave Jihan with you, a fair trade. Then I will release these others, who remember nothing—for the interim. When I am done here, if you have behaved well, you may have them back permanently, free and unencumbered. We will see how good your faith can be said to be."

Niko realized he could still hear, still see, still move.

"Come here, Nikodemos," Tempus summoned him.

He obeyed. His commander's mien implored Niko to take all this in his stride, as his voice sent him to see to breakfast for three. He was about to object that only by the accident of meditation had he been untouched by the spell—which sought out waking minds and could not find his in his rest-place, and thus the cook and all the menials must be spellbound, still—when men began to stir and finish sentences begun before Aškelon's arrival, and Tempus waved him imperatively on his way. He left on the

double, ignoring the stares of those just coming out
of limbo, whistling to cover the wheeze of his fear.

— *3* —

So it was that Nikodemos accompanied Aškelon
into Sanctury on the young Stepson's two best horses,
his ears ringing with what he had heard and his eyes
aching from what he had seen and his heart clandes-
tinely taking cautious beats in a constricted chest.

Over breakfast, Aškelon had remarked to Tempus
that it must be hell for one of his temperament to
languish under curse and god. "I've gotten used to
it." "I could grant you mortality, so small a thing is
still within my power." "I'll limp along as I am,
thanks, Ash. If my curse denies me love, it gives me
freedom." "It would be good for you to have an ally."
"Not one who will unleash a killing mist merely to
make an entrance," Tempus had rejoined, his fingers
steepled before him. "Sorcery is yet beneath your
contempt? You are hardly nonaligned in the conflict
brewing." "I have my philosophy." "Oh?" And what is
that?" "A single axiom, these days, is sufficient to my
needs." "Which is?" " 'Grab reality by the balls and
squeeze.' " "We will see how well it serves you,
when you stand without your god." "Are you still
afraid of me, Ash? I have never given you cause,
never vied with you for your place." "Who do you
think to impress, Riddler? The boy? Your potential,
and dangerous proclivities, speak for themselves. I
will grant no further concessions. . . ."

Riding with the dream lord into Sanctury in broad
daylight was a relief after the tension of his commander's dining table. Being dismissed by Aškelon
before the high-walled Mageguild on the Street of
Arcana was a reprieve he had not dared to hope for,

though the entelechy of the seventh sphere decreed that Nikodemos must return to the outer gates at sundown. He watched his best horse disappear down that vine-hung way without even a twinge of regret. If he never saw that particular horse and its rider again, it would be too soon.

And he had his orders, which, when he had received them, he had despaired of successfully carrying out. When Aškelon had been absorbed in making his farewells to the woman whose fighting stature and muscle tone were so extraordinary, Tempus had bade Niko warn certain parties to spread the word that a curfew must be kept, and some others not to attend the Mageguild's fete this evening, and lastly find a way to go alone to the Vulgar Unicorn, tavern of consummate ill-repute in this scabrous town, and perform a detailed series of actions there.

Niko had never been to the Vulgar Unicorn, though he had been by it many times during his tours in the Maze. The eastside taverns like the Alekeep at the juncture of Promise Park and Governor's Walk, and the Golden Oasis, outside the Maze, were more to his liking, and he stopped at both to fortify himself for a sortie into Ilsig filth and Ilsig poverty. At the Alekeep, he managed to warn the father of a girl he knew to keep his family home this evening lest the killing mist diminish his house should it come again; at the Oasis, he found a Hell Hound and the Ilsig captain Walegrin gaming intently over a white-bladed knife (a fine prize if it were the "hard steel" the blond-braided captain claimed it was, a metal only fabled to exist), and so had gotten his message off to both the palace and the garrison in good order.

Yet, in the Maze, it seemed that his luck deserted him as precipitately as his sense of direction had fled. It should be easy to find the Serpentine—just head south by southwest . . . unless the entelechy

Aškelon had hexed him! He rode tight in his saddle under a soapy, scum-covered sky gone noncommittal, its sun nowhere to be seen, doubling back from Wideway and the gutted wharfside warehouses where serendipity had taken his partner's life as suddenly as their charred remains loomed before him out of a pearly fog so thick he could barely see his horse's ears twitch. Rolling in off the water, it was rank and fetid and his fingers slipped on his weeping reins. The chill it brought was numbing, and lest it penetrate to his very soul, he fled into a light meditation, clearing his mind and letting his body roll with his mount's gait while its hoofbeats and his own breathing grew loud and that mixed cadence lulled him.

In his expanded awareness, he could sense the folk behind their doors, just wisps of passion and subterfuge leaking out beyond the featureless mudbrick facades from inner courts and wizened hearts. When glances rested on him, he knew it, feeling the tightening of focus and disturbance of auras like roused bees or whispered insults. When his horse stopped with a disapproving snort at an intersection, he had been sensing a steady attention on him, a presence pacing him which knew better than the occasional street-denizen who turned watchful at the sight of a mercenary riding through the Maze, or the whores half-hidden in doorways with their predatory/cautious/disappointed pinwheels of assessment and dismissal. Still thoroughly disoriented, he chose the leftward fork at random, as much to see whether the familiar pattern stalking him would follow along as in hopes that some landmark would pop up out of the fog to guide him—he did not now the Maze as well as he should, and his meditation-sensitized peripheral perception could tell him only how close the nearest walls were and a bit about who lurked behind them: he was no adept, only a western-trained fighter. But, being one, he had shaken his fear and his foreboding, and waited to see if Shadowspawn, called Hanse, would announce himself: should Niko hail the thief prematurely, Hanse would almost certainly melt back into the alleys he commanded rather than own that Niko had perceived himself shadowed—and leave him lost among the hovels and the damned.

He had learned patience waiting for gods to speak to him on wind-whipped precipices while heaving tides licked about his toes in anticipation. After a time, he began to see canopied stalls and hear muted haggling, and dismounted to lead his horse among the splintered crates and rotten fruit at the bazaar's edge.

"Psst! Stealth!" Hanse called him by his war-name, and dropped, soundless as a phantom, from a shuttered balcony into his path. Startled, Niko's horse scrambled backward, hind hooves kicking crates and stanchions over so that a row ensued with the stall's enraged proprietor. When that was done, the dark slumhawk still waited, eyes glittering with unsaid words sharper than any of the secreted blades he wore, a triumphant smile fierce as his scarlet sash fading to his more customary street-hauteur as he turned figs in his fingers, pronounced them unfit for human consumption, and eased Niko's way.

"I was out there this morning," Niko heard, bent down over his horse's left hind hoof, checking for splinters caught in its shoe; "heard your team lost a member, but not who. Pissass weird weather, these days. You know something *I* should know?"

"Possibly." Niko, putting down the hoof, brushed dust from his thighs and stood up. "Once when I was wandering around the back-streets of a coastal city— never mind which one—with an arrow in my gut and afraid to seek a surgeon's help there was weather like this. A man who took me in told me to *stay* off the streets at night until the weather'd been clear a full day— something to do with dead adepts and souls to pay their way out of purgatory. Tell your friends, if you've got any. And do me a favor, fair exchange?" He gathered up his reins and took a handful of mane, about to swing up on his horse, and thus he saw Hanse's fingers flicker: *state it*. So he did, admitting that he was lost, quite baldly, and asking the thief to guide him on his way.

When they had walked far enough that Shadowspawn's laughter no longer echoed, the thief said, "What's wrong? Like I said, I was out at the barracks. I've never seen *him* scared of anything, but he's scared of that girl he's got in his room. And he's meaner than normal—told me I couldn't stable my horse out there, and not to come around—" Shadowspawn broke off, having said what he did not want to say, and kicked a melon in their path, which burst open, showing the teeming maggots within.

"Maybe he'd like to keep you out of troubles that aren't any of your business. Or maybe he estimates his debt to you is paid in full—you can't keep coming around when it suits you and still be badmouthing us like any other Ilsig—"

A spurt of profanity contained some cogent directions to the Vulgar Unicorn, and some other suggestions impossible to follow. Niko did not look up to see Hanse go. If he failed to take the warning to heart, then hurt feelings would keep him away from Niko and his commander for a while. It was enough.

Directions or no, it took him longer than it should have to find his way. Finally, when he was eyeing the sky doubtfully, trying to estimate the lateness of the hour, he spied the Unicorn's autoerotic sign creaking in the moist, stinking breeze blowing in off the harbor. Discounting Hanse, since Niko had entered the close and ramshackle despair of the shantytown he had seen not one friendly face. If he had been jeered once, he had been cursed a score of times, aloud and with spit and glare and handsign, and he had had more than his fill of Sanctuary's infamous slum.

Within the Unicorn, the clientele did not look happy to see a Stepson. A silence as thick as Rankan ale decended as he entered and took more time to disperse than he liked. He crossed to the bar, scanning the room full of local brawlers, grateful he had neglected to shave since the previous morning. Perhaps he seemed more fearsome than he felt as he turned his back to the sullen, hostile crowd just resuming their drinking and scheming and ordered a draught from the bartender. The big, overmuscled man with a balding head slapped it down before him, growling that it would be well if he drank up and left before the crowd began to thicken, or the barkeep would not be responsible for the consequences, and Niko's "master" would get a bill for any damage to the premises. The look in the big man's eyes was decidedly unfriendly. "You're the one they call Stealth, aren't you?" the barkeep accused him. "The one who told Shadowspawn that one of the best kills is a knife from behind down beside the collarbone, and with a sword, cut up between your opponent's legs, and in general the object is never to have to engage your enemy, but dispatch him before he has seen your face?"

Niko stared at him, feeling anger chase the disquiet from his limbs. "I know you Ilsigs don't like us," he said quietly, "but I haven't time now to charm you into a change of mind. Where's One-Thumb, barkeep? I have a message for him that cannot wait."

"Right here," smirked the aproned mountain, tossing his rag onto the barsink's chipped pottery rim. "What *is* it, sonny?"

"*He* wants you to take me to the lady—you know the one." Actually, Tempus had instructed Niko to tell One-Thumb about Aškelon's intention to confront Cime, and wait for word as to what the woman wanted Tempus to do. But he was resentful, and he was late. "I have to be at the Mageguild by sundown. Let's move."

"You've got the wrong One-thumb, and the wrong idea. Who's this 'he'?"

"Bartender, I leave it on your conscience—" He pushed his mug away and took a step back from the bar, then realized he could not leave without discharging his duty, and reached out to pick it up again.

The bid bartender's thumbless hand curled around his wrist and jerked him against the bar. He prayed for patience. "And *he* didn't tell you *not* to come in here, bold as brass tassels on a witch-bitch whore? *He* is getting sloppy, or he's forgotten who his friends are. Why didn't you come round the back? What do you expect me to do, leave with you in the middle of the day? I—"

"I was lucky I found your pisshole at all, Wriggly. Let me go or you're going to lose the rest of those fingers, sure as Lord Storm's anger rocks even this god-ridden garbage heap of a peninsula—"

Someone stepped up to the bar, and One-Thumb, with a wrench of wrist, went to serve him, meanwhile motioning close a girl whose breasts were mottled gray with dirt and pinkish white where she had sweated it away, saying to her that Niko was to be taken to the office.

In it, he watched the man called One-Thumb through a one-way mirror, and fidgeted. Eventually, though he saw no reason why it happened, a door he had thought to be a closet's opened behind him, and a woman stepped in, clad in Ilsig doe-skin leggings. She said, "What word did my brother send to me?"

He told her, thinking, watching her, that her eyes were gray like Aškelon's, and her hair was arrestingly black and silver, and that she did not in any way resemble Tempus. When he was finished with his story and his warning that she not, under any circumstances, go out this evening—not, upon her life, attend the Mageguild fete, she laughed, a sweet tinkle so inappropriate his spine chilled and he stiffened.

"Tell my brother not to be afraid. You must not know him well, to take his terror of the adepts so seriously." She moved close to him, and he drowned in her storm-cloud eyes while her hand went to his swordbelt and by it she pulled him close. "Have you money Stepson? And some time to spend?"

Niko beat a hasty retreat with her mocking, throaty laughter chasing him down the stairs. She called after him that she only wanted to have him give her love to Tempus. As he made the landing near the bar, he heard the door at the stair's top slam shut. He was out of there like a torqued arrow—so fast he forgot to pay for his drink, and yet, when he remembered it, on the street where his horse waited, no one had come chasing him. Looking up at the sky, he estimated he could just make the Mageguild in time, if he did not get lost again.

— *4* —

Thinking back over the last ten months, Tempus realized he should have expected something like this. Vashanka was weakening steadily: *some*thing had removed the god's name from Kadakithis's palace dome;

the state-cult's temple had proved unbuildable, its grounds defiled and its priest a defiler; the ritual of the Tenslaying had been interrupted by Cime and her fire, and he and Vashanka had begotten a male child upon the First Consort which the god did not seem to want to claim; Abarsis had been allowed to throw his life away without regard to the fact that he had been Vashanka's premier warrior-priest. Now the field altar his mercenaries had built had been tumbled to the ground before his eyes by one of Abarsis's teachers, an entelechy chosen specifically to balance the beserker influence of the god. And he, Tempus, was imprisoned in his own quarters by a Froth Daughter in an all-too-human intent on exacting from him recompense for what his sister had denied her.

Glumly he wondered if his god could be undergoing a midlife crisis, then if he, too, was, since Vashanka and he were linked by the Law of Consonance. Certainly, Jihan's proclamation of intended rape had taken him aback. He had not been taken aback by *any*thing in years. "Rapist, they call you, and with good reason," she had said, reaching up under the scale-armor corselet to wriggle out of her loinguard. "We will see how you like it, in receipt of what you're used to giving out." He could not stop her, or refrain from responding to her. Cime had interrupted Jihan's scheduled tryst with Aškelon, perhaps aborted it. The body which faced him had been chosen for a woman's retribution. Later she said to him, rubbing the imprint of her scale-armor from his loins with a high-veined hand: "Have you never heard of letting the lady win?"

"No," he replied, genuinely puzzled. "Jihan, are you saying I was unfair?"

"Only arcane, weighting the scales to your side. Love without feeling, mind-caress, spell-excitation. . . .

I am new to flesh. I hope you are well-chastised and repentant," she giggled, just briefly, before his words found her ears: "I warn you, straight-out: those who love me, die of it, and those I favor are fated to spurn me."

"You are an arrogant man. You think I care? I should have struck you more viciously." Her flat hand slapped, more than playfully, down upon his belly. "*He*—" she meant Aškelon "—cannot spare me any of his substance. I do this for him, that he not look upon me hungry for a man and know shame. You saw his wrist, where she skewered him. . . ."

"I don't fancy a gift from him, convenient or no." He was going to pull her up beside him, where he might casually get his hands around her fine, muscular throat. But she sat back and retorted. "You think *he* would suggest this? Or even know of it? I take what I choose from men, and we do not discuss it. It is all I can do for him. And *you* owe me whatever price I care to name—your own sister took from me my husband before ever his lips touched mine. When my father chose me from my sisters to be sent to ease Aškelon's loneliness, I had a choice—yea or nay—and a year to make it. I studied him, and felt love enough to come to human flesh to claim it. To become human—you concede that I am, for argument's sake?"

He did that—her spectacular body, sheathed in muscle, taut and sensuous, was too powerful and yet too shapely to be mortal, but even so, he did not critique her.

"Then," she continued, rising up, hands on her impossibly slim waist, pacing as she spoke in a rustle of armor-scales, "consider my plight. To become human for the love of a demiurge, and then not to be able to claim him. . . . It is done, I have this form, I cannot undo it until its time is up. And since I cannot collect satisfaction from her—*he* has forbidden me that pleasure—all the powers on the twelfth plane agree: I may have what I wish from you. And what I wish, I have made quite plain." Her voice was deepening. She took a step toward him.

He objected, and she laughed. "You should see your face."

"I can imagine. You are a very attractive . . . lady, and you come with impeccable credentials from an unimpeachable source. So if you are inexperienced in the ways of the world, brash and awkward and ineffective because of that, I suppose I must excuse you. Thus, I shall make allowances." His one hand raised, gestured, scooped up her loinguard and tossed it at her. "Get dressed, get out of here. Go back to your master, familiar, and tell him I do not any longer pay my sister's debts."

Then, finally, she came at him: "You mistake me. I am not asking you, I am telling you." She reached him, crouched down, thighs together, hands on her knees, knees on what had once been Jubal the Slaver's bed. "This is a real debt, in lieu of payment for which, my patron and the elementals will exact—"

He clipped her exactly behind her right ear, and she fell across him, senseless.

Other things she had said, earlier in passion, rang in his head: that should he in any way displease her, her duty would then be plain: he and Vashanka could both be disciplined by way of the child they had together begotten on one of Molin Torchholder's temple dancers.

He was not sure how he felt about that, as he was not sure how he felt about Aškelon's offer of mortality or Vashanka's cowardice, or the positives and negatives of his sister's self-endangered fate.

He gave the unconscious woman over to his Stepsons with instructions that made the three he had hailed grin widely. He could not estimate how long they would be able to hold her—however long they managed it, it had better be long enough. The Stepson who had come from seeking Niko in Sanctuary found him, garbed for business, saddling a Trôs horse in the stables.

"Stealth said," the gruff, sloe-eyed commando reported: " 'She said stay out of it, no need to fear.' He's staying with the archmage, or whatever it is. He's going to the Mageguild party and suggests you try and drop by." A feral grin stole over the mercenary's face. He knew something was up. "Need anybody on your right for this, commander?"

Tempus almost said no, but changed his mind and told the Stepson to get a fresh horse and his best panoply and meet him at the Mageguild's outer gate.

— *5* —

There was a little mist in the streets by the time Tempus headed his Trôs horse across the east side toward the Mageguild—nothing daunting yet, just a fetlock-high steaminess as if the streets were cobbled with dry ice. He had had no luck intercepting his sister at Lastel's estate: a servant shouted through a grate, over the barking of dogs, that the master had already left for the fete. He had stopped briefly at the mercenaries' hostel before going there, to burn a rag he had had for centuries in the common room's hearth: he no longer needed to be reminded not to argue with warlocks, or that love, for him, was always a losing game. With his sister's scarf, perhaps the problem of her would waft away, changed like the ancient linen to smoke upon the air.

Before the Mageguild's outer wall, an imprudent crowd had gathered to watch the luminaries arriving in the ersatz-daylight of its ensorceled grounds. Pink clouds formed a glowing canopy to the wall's edge—a godly pavilion; elsewhere, it was night. Where dark met light, the Stepson Janni waited, one leg crooked over his saddlehorn, rolling a smoke, his best helmet dangling by his knee and his full-length dress-mantle draped over his horse's croup, while around his hips the ragged crowd thronged and his horse, ears flattened, snapped at Ilsigs who came too near.

Tempus's gray rumbled a greeting to the bay; the curly-headed mercenary straightened up in his saddle and saluted, grinning through his beard.

He wasn't smiling when the Mageguild's ponderous doors enfolded them, and three junior functionaries escorted them to the "changing rooms" within the outer wall where they were expected to strip and hand over their armaments to the solicitously smirking mages-in-training before donning proferred "fete-clothes" (gray silk chitons and summer sandals) the wizards had thoughtfully provided. Aškelon wasn't taking any chances, Tempus thought but did not say, though Janni wondered aloud what use there was in checking their paltry swords and daggers when enchanters could not be made to check their spells.

Inside the Mageguild's outer walls, it was summer. In its gardens—transformed from their usual dank fetidness by artful conjure into a wonderland of orchids and eucalyptus and willows weeping where before moss-hung swamp-giants had held sway over quickmires—Tempus saw Kadakithis, resolutely imperious in a black robe oversewn with gems into a map of Ranke-caught-in-the-web-of-the-world. The prince/governor's pregnant wife, a red gift-gown splendid over her child-belly, leaned heavily on his arm. Kittycat's approving glance was laced with commiseration: yes, he, too, found it hard to smile here, but both of them knew it prudent to observe the forms, especially with wizards. . . .

Tempus nodded and walked away.

Then he saw her, holding Lastel's hand, to which the prosthetic thumb of his disguise was firmly attached. A signal bade Janni await him; he did not have to look back to know that the Stepson obeyed.

Cime was blond, tonight, and golden-eyed, tall in her adept-chosen robe of iridescent green, but he saw through the illusion to her familiar self. And she knew it. "You come here without your beloved armaments or even the god's amulet? The man I used to know would have pulled rank and held on to his weapons."

"Nothing's going to happen here," he murmured, staring off over her head into the crowd looking for Niko; "unless the message I received was in error and we do have a problem?"

"*We* have no problem—" glowed Lastel/One-Thumb.

"One-Thumb, disappear, or I'll have Janni, over there, teach you how to imitate your bar's sign." With a reproachful look that Tempus would utter his alias here, the man who did not like to be called One-Thumb outside the Maze lumbered off.

Then he had to look at her. Under the golden-eyed illusion, her char-and-smoke gaze accused him, as it had chased him across the centuries and made him content to be accursed and constrained from other loves. *God*, he thought, *I will never get through this without error*. It was the closest he had come to *asking* Vashanka to help him for ages. In the back of his skull, a distant whisper exhorted him to take his sister while he could . . . that bush on his right would be bower enough. But more than advice the god could not give: "*I have my own troubles, mortal, for which you are partly responsible*." With the echo of Vashanka's last word, Tempus knew the god was gone.

"Is Lastel telling the truth, Cime? Are you content to face Aškelon's wrath, and your peril, alone? Tell me how you came to *half*-kill a personage of that magnitude, and assure me that you can rectify your mistake without my help."

She reached up and touched his throat, running her finger along his jaw until it found his mouth. "Ssh, ssh. You are a bad liar, who proclaims he does not still love me. Have you not enough at risk, presently? Yes, I erred with Aškelon. He tricked me. I shall solve it, one way or the other. My heart saw him, and I could not then be the one who stood there watching him die. His world beguiled me, his form enthralled me. You know what punishment love could bring me. . . . He begged me leave him to die alone. And I *believed* him . . . because I feared for my life, should while he died I come to love him. We each bear our proper curse, that is sure."

"You think this disguise will fool him?"

She shook her head. "I need not; he will want a meeting. This," she ran her hands down over her illusory youth and beauty, "was for the magelings, those children at the gates. As for you, stay clear of this matter, my brother. There is no time for quailing or philosophical debates, now. You never were competent to simply *act*, unencumbered by judgment or conscience. Don't try to change, on my account. I will deal with the entelechy, and then I will drink even his name dry of meaning. Like that!" She snapped her fingers, twirled on her heel, and flounced off in a good imitation of a young woman offended by a forward soldier.

While he watched, Aškelon appeared from the crowd to bar her path, a golden coin held out before him like a wand or a warding charm.

That fast did he have her, too fast for Tempus to get between them, simply by the mechanism of invoking her curse: for pay, she must give herself to any comer. He watched them flicker out of being with his stomach rolling and an ache in his throat. It was some little while before he saw anything external, and then he saw Nikodemos showing off his gift-cuirass to Janni.

The two came up to him wondering why it was, when everyone else's armaments had been taken from them, Niko, who had arrived in shabby duty-gear, had been given better than ever he could afford. Tempus drew slowly into his present, noting Molin Torchholder's over-gaudy figure nearby, and a kohl-eyed lady who might easily be an infiltrator from the Mygdonian Alliance talking to Lastel.

He asked his Stepsons to make her acquaintance: "She might just be smuggling drugs into Sanctuary with Lastel's help, but do not arrest her for trifles. If she is a spy, perhaps she will try to recruit a Stepson disaffected enough with his lot. Either of you—a single agent or half a broken pair—could fit that description."

"At the least, we must plumb her body's secrets. Stealth," Janni rumbled to Niko as the two strutted her way, looking virile and predatory.

With a scowl of concern for the Stepson to whom he was bound by ill-considered words, he sought out Torchholder, recalling, as he slid with murmured greetings and apologies through socialites and Hazard-class adepts, Niko's blank and steady eyes: the boy knew his danger, and trusted Tempus, as a Sacred Bander must, to see him through it. No remonstrance or doubt had shown in the fighter called Stealth's open countenance, that Tempus would come here against Aškelon's wishes, and risk a Stepson's life. It was war, the boy's calm said, what they both did and what they both knew. Later, perhaps there would be explanations—or not. Tempus knew that Niko, should he survive, would never broach the subject.

"Torchholder, I think you ought to go see to the First Consort's baby," he said as his hand came down heavily on the palace-priest's bebaubled shoulder. Torchholder was already pulling on his beard, his mouth curled with anger, when he turned. Assessing Tempus's demeanor, his face did a dance which ended in a mien of knowing caution. "Ah, yes, I did mean to look in on Seylalha and her babe. Thank you for reminding me, Hell Hound."

"*Stay with her,*" Tempus whispered sotto voce as Molin sought to brush by him, "*or get them both to a safer place—*"

"We *got* your message, this afternoon, Hound," the privy priest hissed, and he was gone.

Tempest was just thinking that it was well Fete Week only came once yearly, when above him, in the pink, tented clouds, winter gloom began to spread; and beside him, a hand closed upon his left arm with a numbingly painful grip: Jihan had arrived.

— 6 —

Aškelon of Meridian, entelechy of the seventh sphere, lord of dream and shadow, faced his would-be assassin little strengthened. The Hazards of Sanctuary had given what they could of power to him, but mortal strength and mortals' magic could not replace what he had lost. His compassionate eyes had sunken deep under lined and arching brows; his skin was pallid; his cheeks hosted deep hollows like his colossus's where it guarded an unknown sea, so fierce that folk there who had never heard of Sanctuary swore that in those stony caverns demons raised their broods.

It had cost him much to take flesh and make chase. It cost him more to remove Cime to the Mageguild's innermost sanctum before the disturbance broke out above the celebrants on the lawn. But he had done it.

He said to her, "Your intention, free agent, was not clear. Your resolve was not firm. I am neither dead nor alive, because of you. Release me from this torture. I saw in your eyes you did not truly wish my demise, nor the madness that must come upon the world entire from the destruction of the place of salving dreams. You have lived awhile, now, in a world where dreams cannot solve problems, or be used to chart the future, or to heal or renew. What say you? You can charge it, bring sanity back among the planes, and love to your aching heart. I will make you lady of Meridian. Our quays will once again rise crystal, streets will glitter gold, and my people will finish the welcoming paean they were singing when you shattered my heart." As he spoke, he pulled from his vestments a kerchief and held it out, unfolded, in his right hand. There on snowy linen glittered the shards of the Heart of Aškelon, the obsidian talisman which her rods had destroyed when he wore it on his wrist.

She had them out by then, taken down from her hair, and she twirled them, blue-white and ominous, in her fingers.

He did not shrink from her, nor eye her weapons. He met her glance with his, and held, willing to take either outcome—anything but go on the way he was.

Then he heard the hardness of her laugh, and prepared himself to face the tithe-collectors who held the mortgage on his soul.

Her aspect of blond youthfulness fell away with

her laughter, and she stepped near him, saying, "Love, you offer me? You know my curse, do you not?"

"I can lift it, if you but spend one year with me."

"*You can lift it?* Why should I believe you, father of magic? Not even gods must tell the truth, and you, I own, are beyond even the constraints of right and wrong which gods obey."

"Will you not help me, and help yourself? Your beauty will not fade; I can give youth unending, and heal your heart, if you but heal mine." His hand, outstretched to her, quivered. His eyes sparkled with unshed tears. "Shall you spend eternity as a murderer and a whore, *for no reason?* Take salvation, now it is offered. Take it for us both. Neither of us could claim such a boon from eternity again."

Cime shrugged, and the woman's eyes so much older than the three decades her body showed impaled him. "Some kill politicians, some generals, foot soldiers in the field. As for me, I think the mages are the problem, twisting times and worlds about like children play with string. And as for help, what makes you think either you or I deserve it? How many have you aided, without commensurate gain? When old Four-Eyes-Spitting-Fire-And-Four-Mouths-Spitting-Curses came after me, *no* one did *anything*, not my parents, or our priests or seers. They all just looked at their feet, as if the key to my salvation was written in Azehur's sand. *But it was not!* And oh, did I learn from *my* wizard! More than he thought to teach me, since he crumbled into dust on my account, and that is sure."

Yet, she stopped the rods twirling, and she did not start to sing.

They stared a time longer at each other, and while they saw themselves in one another, Cime began to cry, who had not wept in thrice a hundred years.

And in time she turned her rods about, and butts first, she touched them to the shards of the obsidian he held in a trembling palm.

When the rods made contact, a blinding flare of blue commenced to shine in his hand, and she heard him say, "I will make things right with us," as the room in which they stood began to fade away, and she heard a lapping sea and singing children and finger cymbals tinkling while lutes were strummed and pipes began to play.

— *7* —

All hell breaking loose could not have caused more pandemonium than Jihan's father's blood-red orbs peering down through shredded clouds upon the Mageguild's grounds. The fury of the father of a jilted bride was met by Vashanka in his full manifestation, so that folk thrown to the ground lay silent, staring up at the battle in the sky with their fingers dug deep into chilling, spongy earth.

Vashanka's two feet were widespread, one upon his temple, due west, one upon the Mageguild's wall. His lightning bolts rocked the heavens, his golden locks whipped by his adversary's black winds. Howls from the foreign Stormbringer's cloudy throat pummeled eardrums; people rolled to their stomachs and buried their heads in their arms as the inconceivable cloud creature enveloped their god, and blackness reigned. Thunder bellowed; the black cloud pulsed spasmodically, lit from within.

In the tempest, Tempus shouted to Jihan, grabbed her arms in his hands: "Stop this; you can do it. Your pride, and his, are not worth so many lives." A lightning bolt struck earth beside his foot, so close a blue sparkling aftercharge nuzzled his leg.

She jerked away, palmed her hair back, stood glaring at him with red flecks in her eyes. She shouted something back, her lips curled in a flash of light, but the gods' roaring blotted out her words. Then she merely turned her back to him, raised her arms to heaven, and perhaps began to pray.

He had no more time for her; the god's war was his; he felt the claw-cold blows Stormbringer landed, felt Vashanka's substance leeching away. Yet he set off running, dodging cowerers upon the ground, adepts and nobles with their cloaks wrapped about their heads, seeking his Stepsons: he knew what he must do.

He did not stop for arms or horses, when he found Niko and Janni, but set off through the raging din toward the Avenue of Temples, where the child the man and god had begotten upon the First Consort was kept.

Handsigns got them through until speech was useful, when they had run west through the lawns and alleys, coming to Vashanka's temple grounds from the back. Inside the shrine's chancery, it was quieter, shielded from the sky that heaved with light and dark.

Niko shared his weapons, those Aškelon had given him: a dirk to Tempus, the sword to Janni. "But you have nothing left," Janni protested in the urgent undertone they were all employing in the shadowed corridors of their embattled god's earthly home. "I have this," Niko replied, and tapped his armored chest.

Whether he meant the cuirass Aškelon had given him, the heart underneath, or his mental skills, Tempus did not ask, just tossed the dirk contemptuously back, and dashed out into the murky temple hall.

They smelled sorcery before they saw the sick green light or felt the curdling cold. Outside the

door under which wizardsign leaked like sulphur
from a yellow spring, Janni muttered blackly. Niko's
lips were drawn back in a grin: "After you, commander?"

Tempus wrenched the doors apart, once Janni had
cut the leather strap where it had been drawn within
to secure the latch, and beheld Molin Torchholder in
the midst of witchfire, wrestling with more than
Tempus would have thought he could handle, and
holding his own.

On the floor in the corner a honey-haired northern
dancer hugged a man-child to her breast, her mouth
an "ooh" of relief, as if now that Tempus was here,
she was surely saved.

He took time to grimace politely at the girl, who
insisted on mistaking him for his god—his senses
were speeding much faster than even the green,
stinking whirlwind in the middle of the room. He was
not so sure that anything was salvageable, here, or
even if he cared if girl or priest or child or town . . .
or *god* . . . were to be saved. But then he looked
behind him, and saw his Stepsons, Niko on the left
and Janni with sword drawn, both ready to advance
on hell itself, would he but bid them, and he raised a
hand and led them into the lightfight, eyes squinted
nearly shut and all his body tingling as his preternatural abilities came into play.

Molin's ouster was uppermost in his mind: he
picked the glareblind priest up bodily and threw
him, wrenching the god's golden icon from his frozen
fist. He heard a grunt, a snapping-in of breath, behind, but did not look around to see reality fade
away. He was fighting by himself, now, in a higher,
colder place full of day held at bay and Vashanka's
potent breath in his right ear. *"It is well you have
come, manchild; I can use your help this day."* The
left is the place of attack in team battle; a shield-

holding line drifts right, each trying to protect his open side. He had Vashanka on his right, to support him, and a shield, full-length and awful, came to be upon his own left arm. The thing he fought here, the Stormbringer's shape, was part cat, part manlike, and its sword cut as hard as an avalanche. Its claws chilled his breath away. Behind, black and gray was split with sunrise colors, Vashanka's blazon snapping on a flag of sky. He thrust at the clouds and was parried with cold that ran up his sword and seared the skin of his palm so that his sweat froze to ice and layers of his flesh bonded to a sharkskin hilt. . . . That gave him pause, for it was his own sword, come from wherever the mages secreted it, which moved in his hand. Pink glowed that blade, as always when his god sanctified His servant's labor. His right was untenanted, suddenly, but Vashanka's strength was in him, and it must be enough.

He fought it unto exhaustion, he fought it to a draw. The adversaries stood in clouds, typhoon-breaths rasping, both seeking strength to fight on. And then he had to say it: "Let this slight go, Stormbringer. Vengeance is disappointing, always. You soil yourself, having to care. Let her stay where she is, Weather-Gods' Father; a mortal sojourn will do her good. The parent is not responsible for the errors of the child. Nor the child for the parent." And deliberately, he put down the shield the god had given him and peeled the sticky swordhilt from a skinless palm, laying his weapon atop the shield. "Or surmount me, and have done with it. I will not die of exhaustion for a god too craven to fight by my side. And I will not stand aside and let you have the babe. You see, it is me you must punish, not my god. I led Aškelon to Cime, and disposed her toward him. It is my transgression, not Vashanka's. And I am not going to make it easy for you: you will have to slaughter me, which

I would much prefer to being the puppet of yet another omnipotent force."

And with a growl that was long and seared his inner ear and set his teeth on edge, the clouds began to dissolve around him, and the darkness to fade away.

He blinked, and rubbed his eyes, which were smarting with underworld cold, and when he took his hands away he found himself standing in a seared circle of stinking fumes with two coughing Stepsons, both of whom were breathing heavily, but neither of whom looked to have suffered any enduring harm. Janni was supporting Niko, who had discarded the gift-cuirass, and it glowed as if cooling from a forger's heat between his feet. The dirk and sword, too, lay on the smudged flagstones, and Tempus's sword atop the heap.

There passed an interval of soft exchanges, which did not explain either where Tempus had disappeared to, or why Niko's gear had turned white-hot against the Stormbringer's whirlpool cold, and of assessing damages (none, beyond frost-bite, blisters, scrapes and Tempus's flayed swordhand) and suggestions as to where they might recoup their strength.

The tearful First Consort was calmed, and Torchholder's people (no one could locate the priest) told to watch her well.

Outside the temple, they saw that the mist had let go of the streets; an easy night lay chill and brisk upon the town. The three walked back to the Mageguild at a leisurely pace, to reclaim their panoplies and their horses. When they got there they found that the Second and Third Hazards had claimed the evening's confrontation to be of their making, a cosmological morality play, their most humbly offered entertainment which the guests had taken too much to heart. Did not Vashanka triumph? Was not

the cloud of evil vanquished? Had not the wondrous
tent of pink-and-lemon summer sky returned to illu-
minate the Mageguild's fete?

Janni snarled and flushed with rage at the adepts'
dissembling, threatening to go turn Torchholder (who
had preceded them back among the celebrants, di-
sheveled, loudmouthed, but none the worse for wear)
upside down to see if any truth might fall out, but
Niko cautioned him to let fools believe what fools
believe, and to make his farewells brief and polite—
whatever they felt about the mages, they had to live
with them.

When at last they rode out of the Street of Arcana
toward the Alekeep, to quench their well-earned
thirsts where Niko could check on the faring of a girl
who mattered to him, he was ponying the extra
horse he had lent Aškelon, since neither the dream
lord nor his companion Jihan had been anywhere to
be found among guests trying grimly to recapture at
least a semblance of revelry.

For Niko, the slow ride through mercifully dark
streets was a godsend, the deep midnight sky a mask
he desperately needed to keep between him and the
world awhile. In its cover, he could afford to let his
composure, slipping away inexorably of its own weight,
fall from him altogether. As it happened, because of
the riderless horse, he was bringing up the rear.
That, too, suited him, as did their tortuous progress
through the ways and intersections thronging inter-
mittently with upper-class (if there was such a distinction to be made here) Ilsigs ushering in the new
year. Personally, he did not like the start of it: the
events of the last twenty-four hours he considered
somewhat less than auspicious. He fingered the enameled cuirass with its twining snakes and glyphs
which the entelechy Aškelon had given him, touched
the dirk at his waist, the matching sword slung at his

hip. The hilts of both were worked as befitted weapons bound for a son of the armies, with the lightning and the lions and the bulls which were, the world over, the signatures of its Storm Gods, the god of war and death. But the workmanship was foreign, and the raised demons on both scabbards belonged to the primal deities of an earlier age, whose sway was misty, everywhere but among the western islands where Niko had gone to strive for initiation into his chosen mystery and mastery over body and soul. The most appropriate legends graced these opulent arms that a shadow lord had given him; in the old ways and the elder gods and in the disciplines of transcendent perception, Niko sought perfection, a mystic calm. And the weapons were perfect, save for two blemishes: they were fashioned from precious metals, and made nearly priceless by the antiquity of their style; they were charmed, warm to the touch, capable of meeting infernal forces and doing damage upon icy whirlwinds sent from unnamed gods. Nikodemos favored unarmed kills, minimal effort, precision. He judged himself sloppy should it become necessary to parry an opponent's stroke more than once. The temple-dancing exhibitions of proud swordsmen who "tested each other's mettle" and had time to indulge in style and disputatious dialogue repelled him: one got in, made the kill, and got out, hopefully leaving the enemy unknowing; if not, confused.

He no more coveted blades that would bring acquisitive men down upon him hoping to acquire them in combat than he looked forward to needing ensorceled swords for battles that could not be joined in the way he liked. The cuirass he wore kept off supernal evil— should it prove impregnable to mortal arms, that knowledge would eat away at his self-discipline, perhaps erode his control, make him careless. In the lightfight, when Tempus had flickered out of being as completely as a doused torch, he had felt an inexplicable elation, leading point into Chaos with Janni steady on his right hand. He had imagined he was indomitable, fated, chosen by the gods and thus inviolate. The steadying fear that should have been there, in his mind, assessive and balancing, was missing . . . his *maat*, as he had told Tempus in that moment of discomfitting candor, was gone from him. No trick panoply could replace it, no arrogance or battle-lust could substitute for it. Without equilibrium, the quiet heart he strove for could never be his. He was not like Tempus, preternatural, twice a man, living forever in extended anguish to which he had become accustomed. He did not aspire to more than what his studies whispered a man had right to claim. Seeing Tempus in action, he now believed what before, though he had heard the tales, he had discounted. He thought hard about the Riddler, and the offer he had made him, and wondered if he was bound by it, and the weapons Aškelon had given him no more than omens fit for days to come. And he shivered, upon his horse, wishing his partner were there up ahead instead of Janni, and that his maat was within him, and that they rode Syrese byways or the Azehuran plain, where magic did not vie with gods for mortal allegiance, or take souls in tithe.

When they dismounted at the Alekeep, he had come to a negotiated settlement within himself: he would wait to see if what Tempus said was true, if his maat would return to him once his teammate's spirit ascended to heaven on a pillar of flame. He was not unaware of the rhythmic nature of enlightenment through the procession of events. He had come to Ranke with his partner at Abarsis's urging; he remembered the Slaughter Priest from his early days of ritual and war, and had made his own decision, not followed blindly because his left-side leader wished to teach Rankans the glory of his name. When the elder fighter had put it to him, his friend had said that it might be time for Nikodemos to lead his own team—after Ranke, without doubt, the older man would lay down his sword. He had been dreaming, he had said, of mother's milk and waving crops and snot-nosed brats with wooden shields, a sure sign a man is done with damp camps and bloody dead stripped in the field.

So it would have happened, this year, or the next, that he would be alone. He must come to terms with it; not whine silently like an abandoned child, or seek a new and stronger arm to lean on. Meditation should have helped him, though he recalled a parchment grin and a toothless mouth instructing him that what is needed is never to be had without price.

The price of the thick brown ale in which the Alekeep specialized was doubled for the holiday's night-long vigil, but they paid not one coin, drinking, instead, in a private room in back where the grateful owner led them: he had heard about the manifestation at the Mageguild, and had been glad he had taken Niko's advice and kept his girls inside. "Can I let them out, then?" he said with a twinkling eye. "Now that you are here? Would the Lord Marshal and his distinguished Stepsons care for some gentle companionship this jolly eve?"

Tempus, flexing his open hand on which the clear serum glistened as it thickened into scabby skin, told him to keep his children locked up until dawn, and sent him away so brusquely Janni eyed Niko askance.

Their commander sat with his back against the wall opposite the door through which the tavern's owner had disappeared. "We were followed here. I'd like to think you both realized it on your own."

The placement of their seats, backs generously offered to any who might enter, spoke so clearly of their failure that neither said a word, only moved their chairs to the single table's narrow sides. When next the door swung open, One-Thumb, not their host, stood there, and Tempus chuckled hoarsely in the hulking wrestler's face. "Only you, Lastel? I own you had me worried."

"Where is she, Tempus? What have you done with her?" Lastel stomped forward, put both ham-hands flat upon the table, his thick neck thrust forward, bulging with veins.

"Are you tired of living, One-Thumb? Go back to you hidey-hole. Maybe she's there, maybe not. If not . . . easy come, easy go."

Lastel's face purpled; his words rode on a froth of spray so that Janni reached for his dagger and Niko had to kick him.

"Your sister's disappeared and you don't *care?*"

"I let Cime snuggle up with you in your thieves' shanty. If I had 'cared,' would I have done that? And *did* I care, I would have to say to you that you aspire beyond your station, with her. Stick to whoremistresses and street urchins, in future. Or go talk to the Mageguild, or your gods if you have the ears of any. Perhaps you can reclaim her for some well-bartered treachery or a block of Caronne krrf. Meanwhile, you who are about to become 'No-thumbs,' mark these two—" He gestured to either side, to Niko and Janni. "They'll be around to see you in the next few days, and I caution you to treat them with the utmost deference. They can be very temperamental. As for myself, I have had easier days, and so am willing to estimate for you your chances of walking out of here with all appendages yet attached and in working order, though your odds are lessening with every breath I have to watch you take. . . ."

Tempus was rising as he spoke. Lastel gave back, his flushed face paling visibly as Tempus proposed a new repository for his prosthetic thumb, then retreated with surprising alacrity toward the half-open door in which the tavern's owner now stood uncertainly, now disappeared.

But Lastel was not fast enough; Tempus had him by the throat. Holding him off the ground, he made One-Thumb mouth civil farewells to both the Stepsons before he dropped him and let him dash away.

— *8* —

At sundown the next day (a perfectly natural sundown without a hint of wizard weather about it), Niko's partner's long-delayed funeral was held before the replied stones of Vashanka's field altar, out behind the arena where once had been a slaver's girl-run. A hawk heading home flew over, right to left, most auspicious of bird omina, and when it had gone, the men swore, Abarsis's ghost materialized to guide the fallen mercenary's spirit up to heaven. These two favorable omens were attributed by most to the fact that Niko had sacrificed the enchanted cuirass Aškelon had given him to the fire of his left-man's bier.

Then Niko released Tempus from his offered vow of pairbond, demurring that Nikodemos himself had never accepted, explaining that it was time for him to be a left-side fighter, which, with Tempus, he could never be. And Janni stood closeby, looking uncomfortable and sheepish, not realizing that in this way Tempus was freed from worrying that harm might come to Niko on account of Tempus's curse.

Seeing Abarsis's shade, wizard-haired and wise, tawny skin quite translucent yet upswept eyes the same, smiling out love upon the Stepsons and their commander, Tempus almost wept. Instead he raised his hand in greeting, and the elegant ghost blew him a kiss.

Once the ceremony was done, he sent Niko and Janni into Sanctuary to make it clear to One-Thumb that the only way to protect his dual identity was to make himself very helpful in the increasingly difficult task of keeping track of Mygdonia's Nisibisi spies. As an immediate show of good faith, he was to begin helping Niko and Janni infiltrate them.

Long after the last of the men had wandered off to game or drink or duty, he lingered by the shrine, considering Vashanka and the god's habit of leaving him to fight both their battles as best he could.

So it was that he heard a soft sound, half hiccough and half sniffle, from the altar's far side, as the dusk cloaked him close.

When he went to see what it was, he saw Jihan, sitting slumped against a rough-hewn plinth, tearing brown grasses to shreds between her fingers. He squatted down there, to determine whether a Froth Daughter could shed human tears.

Dusk was his favorite time, when the sun had fled and the night was luminous with memory. Sometimes, his thoughts would follow the light, fading, and the man who never slept would find himself dozing, at rest.

This evening, it was not sleep he sought to chase in his private witching hour: he touched her scaled, enameled armor, its gray/green/copper pattern just dappled shadow in the deepening dark. "This does come off?" he asked her.

"Oh, yes. Like so."

"Come to think of it," he remarked after a strenuous but rewarding interval, "it is not so bad that you are stranded here. Your father's pique will ease eventually. Meanwhile, I have an extra Trŏs horse. Having two of them to tend has been hard on me. You could take over the care of one. And, too, if you are going to wait the year out as a mortal, perhaps you would consider staying on in Sanctuary. We are sore in need of fighting women this season."

She clutched his arm; he winced. "Do not offer me a sinecure," she said. "And, consider: I will have you, too, should I stay."

Promise or threat, he was not certain, but he was reasonably sure that he could deal with her, either way.

BEGINNER'S LUCK

"I didn't understand anything then, I was just a boy." Niko's voice was choked with emotion. The palm before him, wavering with its curled fingers and then descending into the aged adept's bony lap, was like an enemy, a tattler, a betrayer.

If Niko had seen all this, relived it, did that mean the adept had seen it too? All Niko's anguish, his shame, his loss? His partner, his first left-side leader . . .

And the first time he'd spurned Tempus, denied the Riddler, played games with the latitude of his oath and pairbond. He was ashamed. His head hung.

Thus he did not see the adept's face as the old one said, "You were a man then, as the World determines such things. Always take responsibility for your past. It is your only collateral in life. Unless you despise yourself now, you cannot despise yourself then. Everything you did is a part of the process that brought you here. All your past is as alive and real as your so-called 'present'; this experience should teach you that."

"And you see it too—all that I'm seeing?" Into

others' minds? he wanted to add, but did not. Was this not magic as foul as that which he and Tempus were sworn to fight—as foul as any in Sanctuary, or on Wizardwall, or beyond?

He looked up then, and a movement beyond the adept's shoulder, past the meadow where the forest began, caught his eye.

Movement in Niko's rest-place was unusual, at any time. Now, it would be a sign of disturbance—his own, or some force from outside. He hoped the adept knew what forces had battled here, what personages had walked here in the past. It would be hubristic to warn an ancient, a teacher and a master, to be careful of what he wrought, so Niko didn't.

He just stared for a moment at the brushing of branches in the wood and murmured, "Someone's coming, but then you know that."

And the adept replied only, "Then we must hurry. Your lessons are almost done."

With that, the old one's hand opened once more and once more Niko was drawn into another world by the mechanism of that lined and callused flesh.

Only in this case, Niko knew what time and place it was, and struggled against the force that drew him, as soon as he realized what he was heading for . . .

HIGH MOON

— 1 —

Just south of Caravan Square and the bridge over the White Foal River, the Nisibisi witch had settled in. She had leased the isolated complex—one three-storied "manor house" and its outbuildings—as much because its grounds extended to the White Foal's edge (rivers covered a multitude of disposal problems) as for its proximity to her business interests in the Wideway warehouse district and its convenience to her caravan master, who must visit the Square at all hours.

The caravan disguised their operations. The drugs they'd smuggled in were no more pertinent to her purposes than the dilapidated manor at the end of the bridge's south-running cart track or the goods her men bought and stored in Wideway's most pilferproof holds, though they lubricated her dealings with the locals and eased her troubled nights. It was all subterfuge, a web of lies, plausible lesser evils to which she could own if the Rankan army caught her or Tempus's Stepsons rousted her minions and flunkies or even brought her up on charges.

Lately, a pair of Stepsons had been her particular

concern. And Jagat—her first lieutenant in espionage—
was no less worried. Even their Ilsig contact, the
unflappable Lastel who had lived a dozen years in
the cesspool of Sanctuary without being discovered,
was distressed by the attentions the pair of Stepsons
were paying her.

She had thought her allies overcautious at first,
when it seemed she would be here only long enough
to see to the "death" of the Rankan war god, Vashanka.
Discrediting the state-cult's power icon was the purpose for which the Nisibisi witch, Roxane, had come
down from Wizardwall's fastness, down from her
shrouded keep of black marble on its unscalable peak,
down among the mortal and the damned. They were
all in this together: the mages of Nisibis; Lacan Ajami
(warlord of Mygdon and the known world north of
Wizardwall) with whom they had made pact; and the
whole Mygdonian Alliance which he controlled.

Or so her lord and lover had explained it when he
decreed that Roxane must come. She had not argued—
one pays one's way among sorcerers; she had not
worked hard for a decade nor faced danger in twice
as long. And if *one* did not serve Mygdon— *only
one*—all would suffer. The Alliance was too strong to
thwart. So she was here, drawn here with others fit
for better, as if some power more than magical was
whipping up a tropical storm to cleanse the land and
using them to gild its eye.

She should have been home by now; she would
have been, but for the hundred ships from Beysib
which had come to port and skewed all plans. Word
had come from Mygdon, capital of Mygdonia, through
the Nisibisi network, that she must stay.

And so it had become crucial that the Stepsons
who sniffed round her skirts be kept at bay—or
ensnared, or bought, or enslaved. Or, if not, destroyed. But carefully, so carefully. For Tempus fought

like the gods themselves, like an entelechy from a higher sphere—and even had friends among those powers not corporeal or vulnerable to sortilege of the quotidian sort a human might employ.

And now it was being decreed in Mygdonia's tents that he must be removed from the field—taken out of play in this southern theater, maneuvered north where the warlocks could neutralize him. Such was the word her lover/lord had sent her: move him north, or make him impotent where he stayed. The god he served here had been easier to rout. But she doubted that would incapacitate him; there were other Storm Gods, and Tempus, who under a score of names had fought in more dimensions than she had ever visited, knew them all. Vashanka's denoument might scare the Rankans and give the Ilsigs hope, but more than rumors and manipulation of theomachy by even the finest witch would be needed to make Tempus fold his hand or bow his head. To make him run, then, was an impossibility. To *lure* him north, she hoped, was not. For this was no place for Roxane. Her nose was offended by the stench which blew east from Downwind and north from Fisherman's Row and west from the Maze and south from either the slaughterhouses or the palace—she'd not decided which.

So she had called a meeting, itself an audacious move, with her kind where they dwelled on Wizardwall's high peaks. When it was done, she was much weakened—it is no small feat to project one's soul so far—and unsatisfied. But she had submitted her strategy and gotten approval, after a fashion, though it pained her to have to ask.

Having gotten it, she was about to set her plan in motion. To begin it, she had called upon Lastel/One-Thumb and cried foul: "Tempus's sister, Cime the free agent, was part of our bargain, Ilsig. If you cannot produce her, then she cannot aid me, and I am paying you far too much for a third-rate criminals' paltry talents."

The huge wrestler adjusted his deceptively soft gut. His east side house was commodious; dogs barked in their pens and favorite curs lounged about their feet, under the samovar, upon riotous silk prayer rugs, in the embrace of comely krrf-drugged slaves—not her idea of entertainment, but Lastel's, his sweating forehead and heavy breathing proclaimed as he watched the bestial event a dozen other guests found fetching.

The dusky Ilsigs saw nothing wrong in enslaving their own race. Nisibisi had more pride. It was well that these were comfortable with slavery—they would know it far more intimately, by and by.

But her words had jogged her host, and Lastel came up on one elbow, his cushions suddenly askew. He, too, had been partaking of krrf—not smoking it, as was the Ilsig custom, but mixing it with other drugs which made it sink into the blood directly through the skin. The effects were greater, and less predictable.

As she had hoped, her words had the power of krrf behind them. Fear showed in the jowled mountain's eyes. He knew what she was; the fear was her due. Any of these were helpless before her, should she decide a withered soul or two might amuse her. Their essences could lighten her load as krrf lightened theirs.

The gross man spoke quickly, a whine of excuses: the woman had "disappeared . . . taken by Aškelon, the very lord of dreams. All at the Mageguild's fete where the god was vanquished saw it. You need not take my word—witnesses are legion."

She fixed him with her pale stare. Ilsigs were called Wrigglies, and Lastel's craven self was a good example why. She felt disgust and stared longer.

The man before her dropped his eyes, mumbling that their agreement had not hinged on the mage-killer Cime, that he was doing more than his share as it was, for little enough profit, that the risks were too high.

And to prove to her he was still her creature, he warned her again of the Stepsons: "That pair of Whore-sons Tempus sicced on you should concern us, not money—which neither of us will be alive to spend if—" One of the slaves cried out, whether in pleasure or pain Roxane could not be certain; Lastel did not even look up, but continued: ". . . Tempus finds out we've thirty stone of krrf in—"

She interrupted him, not letting him name the hiding place. "Then do this that I ask of you, without question. We will be rid of the problem they cause, thereafter, and have our own sources who'll tell us what Tempus does and does not know."

A slave serving mulled wine approached, and both took electrum goblets. For Roxane, the liquor was an advantage: looking into its depths, she could see what few cogent thoughts ran through the fat drug dealer's mind.

He thought of her, and she saw her own beauty: wizard hair like ebony and wavy; her sanguine skin like velvet: he dreamed her naked, with his dogs. She cast a curse without word or effort, reflexively, giving him a social disease no Sanctuary mage or barber-surgeon could cure, complete with running sores upon lips and member, and a virus in control of it which buried itself in the brainstem and came out when it chose. She hardly took note of it; it was a small show of temper, like for like: let him exhibit the condition of his soul, she had decreed.

To banish her leggy nakedness from the surface of her wine, she said straight out: "You know the other bar owners. The Alekeep's proprietor has a girl about

to graduate from school. Arrange to host her party,
let it be known that you will sell those children
krrf—Tamzen is the child I mean. Then have your
flunky lead her down to Shambles Cross. Leave them
there—up to half a dozen youngsters, it may be—
lost in the drug and the slum."

"*That* will tame two vicious Stepsons? You *do* know
the men I mean? Janni? And Stealth? They bugger each
other, Stepsons. Girls are beside the point. And
Stealth—he's a *fuzz*buster—I've seen him with no
woman old enough for breasts. Surely—"

"Surely," she cut in smoothly, "you do not want to
know more than that—in case it goes awry. Protection in these matters lies in ignorance." She would
not tell him more—not that Stealth, called Nikodemos,
had come out of Azehur, where he'd earned his war
name and worked his way toward Syr in search of a
Trôs horse via Mygdonia, hiring on as a caravan
guard and general roustabout, or that a dispute over
a consignment lost to mountain bandits had made
him bondservant for a year to a Nisibisi mage—her
lover-lord. There was a string on Nikodemos, ready
to be pulled.

And when he felt it, it would be too late, and she
would be at the end of it.

— 2 —

Tempus had allowed Niko to breed his sorrel mare
to his own Trôs stallion to quell mutters among knowledgeable Stepsons that assigning Niko and Janni to
hazardous duty in the town was their commander's
way of punishing the slate-haired fighter who had
declined Tempus's offered pairbond in favor of Janni's
and subsequently quit their ranks.

Now the mare was pregnant and Tempus was curious as to what kind of foal the union might produce, but rumors of foul play still abounded.

Critias, Tempus's second in command, had paused in his dour report and now stirred his posset of cooling wine and barley and goat's cheese with a finger, then wiped the finger on his bossed cuirass, burnished from years of use. They were meeting in the mercenaries' guild hostel, in its common room dark as congealing blood and safe as a grave, where Tempus had bade the veteran mercenary lodge—an operations officer charged with secret actions could be no part of the Stepsons' barracks cohort. They met covertly, on occasion; most times, coded messages brought by unwitting couriers were enough.

Crit, too, it seemed, thought Tempus wrong in sending Janni, a guileless cavalryman, and Niko, the youngest of the Stepsons, to spy upon the witch: clandestine schemes were Crit's province, and Tempus had usurped, overstepped the bounds of their agreement. Tempus had allowed that Crit might take over management of the fielded team and Crit had grunted wryly, saying he'd run them but not take the blame if they lost both men to the witch's wiles.

Tempus had agreed with the pleasant-looking Syrese agent and they had gone on to other business: Prince/ Governor Kadakithis was insistent upon contacting Jubal, the slaver whose estate the Stepsons sacked and made their home. "But when we had the black bastard, you said to let him crawl away."

"Kadakithis expressed no interest." Tempus shrugged. "He has changed his mind, perhaps in light of the appearance of these mysterious death squads your people haven't been able to identify or apprehend. If your teams can't deliver Jubal or turn up a hawkmask who is in contact with him, I'll find another way."

"Ischade, the vampire woman who lives in Shambles Cross, is still our best hope. We've sent slave-bait to her and lost it. Like a canny carp, she takes the bait and leaves the hook." Crit's lips were pursed as if his wine had turned to vinegar; his patrician nose drew down with his frown. He ran a hand through his short, feathery hair. "And our joint venture with the Rankan garrison is impeding rather than aiding success. Army Intelligence is a contradiction in terms, like the Mygdonian Alliance or the Sanctuary pacification program. The cutthroats I've got on our payroll are sure the god is dead and all the Rankans soon to follow. The witch—or *some* witch—floats rumors of Mygdonian liberators and Ilsig freedom and the gullible believe. That snotty thief you befriended is either an enemy agent or a pawn of Nisibisi propaganda—telling everyone that *he's* been told by the Ilsig gods themselves that Vashanka was routed . . . I'd like to silence him permanently." Crit's eyes met Tempus's then, and held.

"No," he replied, to all of it, then added: "Gods don't die; men die. Boys die in multitudes. The thief, Shadowspawn, is no threat to us, just misguided, semiliterate, and vain, like all boys. Bring me a conduit to Jubal, or the slaver himself. Contact Niko and have him report—if the witch needs a lesson, I myself will undertake to teach it. And keep your watch upon the fish-eyed folk from the ships—I'm not sure yet that they're as harmless as they seem."

Having given Crit enough to do to keep his mind off the rumors of the god Vashanka's troubles—and hence, his own—he rose to leave: "Some results, by week's end, would be welcome."

The officer toasted him cynically as Tempus walked away.

Outside, his Trôs horse whinnied joyfully. He stroked its mist-dappled neck and felt the sweat there.

The weather was close, an early heatwave as unwelcome as the late frosts which had frozen the winter crops a week before their harvest and killed the young sets just planted in anticipation of a bounteous fall.

He mounted up and headed south by the granaries toward the palace's north wall where a gate nowhere as peopled or public as the Gate of the Gods was set into the wall by the cisterns. He would talk to Prince Kittycat, then tour the Maze on his way home to the barracks.

But the prince wasn't receiving, and Tempus's mood was ill—just as well; he had been going to confront the young popinjay, as once or twice a month he was sure he must do, without courtesy or appropriate deference. If Kadakithis was holed up in conference with the blond-haired, fish-eyed folk from the ships and had not called upon him to join them, then it was not surprising: since the gods had battled in the sky above the Mageguild, all things had become confused, worse had come to worst, and Tempus's curse had fallen on him once again with its full force.

Perhaps the god *was* dead—certainly, Vashanka's voice in his ear was absent. He'd gone out raping once or twice to see if the Lord of Pillage could be roused to take part in His favorite spot. But the god had not rustled around in his head since New Year's day; the resultant fear of harm to those who loved him by the curse that denied him love had made a solitary man withdraw even further into himself; only the Froth Daughter Jihan, hardly human, though woman in form, kept him company now.

And that, as much as anything, irked the Stepsons. Theirs was a closed fraternity, open only to the paired lovers of the Sacred Band and distinguished single mercenaries culled from a score of nations and di-

verted, by Tempus's service and Kittycat's gold from
the northern insurrection they'd drifted through Sanctuary en route to join.

He, too, ached to war, to fight a declared enemy,
to lead his cohort north. But he had vowed to do his
best for Kitty, and there was this thrice-cursed fleet
of merchant warriors come to harbor talking "peace-
ful trade" while their vessels rode too low in the
water to be filled with grain or cloth or spices—if not
barter, his instinct told him, the Burek faction of
Beysib would settle for conquest.

He was past caring; things in Sanctuary were too
confuted for one man, even one near-immortal, god-
ridden avatar of a man, to set aright. He would take
Jihan and go north, with or without the Stepsons—
his accursed presence among them and the love they
bore him would kill them if he let it continue: if the
god was truly gone, then he must follow. Beyond
Sanctuary's borders, other Storm Gods held sway,
other names were hallowed. The primal Lord Storm
(Enlil) whom Niko venerated had heard a petition
from Tempus for a clearing of his path and his heart:
he wanted to know what status his life, his course,
and his god-bond had, these days. He awaited only a
sign.

Once, long ago, when he went abroad as a philospher and sought a calmer life in a calmer world, he
had said that to gods all things are beautiful and good
and just, but men have supposed some things to be
unjust, others just. If the god had died, or been
banished, though it didn't seem that this could be so,
then it was meet that this occurred. But those who
thought it so did not realize that one could not
escape the intelligible light: the notice of that which
never sets: the apprehension of the elder gods. So he
had asked, and so he waited.

He had no doubt that the answer would be forthcoming, as he had no doubt that he would not mistake it when it came.

On his way to the Maze he brooded over his curse, which kept him unloved by the living and spurned by any he favored if they be mortal. In heaven he had a brace of lovers, ghosts like the original Stepson, Abarsis. But to heaven he could not repair: his flesh regenerated itself immemorially; to make sure this was still the case, last night he had gone to the river and slit both wrists. By the time he'd counted to fifty the blood had ceased to flow and healing had begun. That gift of healing—if gift it was— still remained his, and since it was god-given, some power more than mortal "loved" him still.

It was whim that made him stop by the weapons shop the mercenaries favored. Three horses tethered out front were known to him; one was Niko's stallion, a big black with points like rust and a jughead on thickening neck perpetually sweatbanded with sheepskin to keep its jowls modest. The horse, as mean as it was ugly, snorted a challenge to Tempus's Trôs—the black resented that the Trôs had climbed Niko's mare.

He tethered it at the far end of the line and went inside, among the crossbows, the flying wings, the steel and wooden quarrels and the swords.

Only a woman sat behind the counter, pulchritudinous and vain, her neck hung with a wealth of baubles, her flesh perfumed. She knew him, and in seconds his nose detected acrid, nervous sweat and the defensive musk a woman can exude.

"Marc's out with the boys in back, sighting-in the high-torque bows. Shall I get him, Lord Marshal? Or may I help you? What's here's yours, my lord, on trial or as our gift—" Her arm spread wide, bangles tinkling, indicating the racked weapons.

"I'll take a look out back, madam, don't disturb yourself."

She settled back, not calm, but bidden to remain and obedient.

In the ochre-walled yard ten men were gathered behind the log fence that marked the range; a hundred yards away three oxhides had been fastened to the encircling wall, targets painted red upon them; between the hides, three cuirasses of four-ply hardened leather armored with bronze plates were propped and filled with straw.

The smith was down on his knees, a crossbow fixed in a vise with its owner hovering close by. The smith hammered the sights twice more, put down his file, grunted and said, "You try it, Straton; it should shoot true. I got a handbreadth group with it this morning; it's your eye I've got to match . . ."

The large-headed, raw-boned smith sporting a beard which evened a rough complexion rose with exaggerated effort and turned to another customer, just stepping up to the firing line. "No, Stealth, not like that, or, if you must, I'll change the tension—" Marc moved in, telling Niko to throw the bow up to his shoulder and fire from there, then saw Tempus and left the group, hands spreading on his apron.

Bolts spat and thunked from five shooters when the morning's range officer hollered "Clear" and "Fire," then "Hold," so that all could go to the wall to check their aim and the depths to which the shafts had sunk.

Shaking his head, the smith confided: "Straton's got a problem I can't solve. I've had it truly sighted—perfect for me—three times, but when he shoots, it's as if he's aiming two feet low."

"For the bow, the name is life, but the work is death. In combat it will shoot true for him; here, he's worried how they judge his prowess. He's not thinking enough of his weapon, too much of his friends."

The smith's keen eyes shifted; he rubbed his smile

with a greasy hand. "Aye, and that's the truth. And for you, Lord Tempus? We've the new hard-steel, though why they're all so hot to pay twice the price when men're soft as clay and even wood will pierce the boldest belly, I can't say."

"No steel, just a case of iron-tipped short flights, when you can."

"I'll select them myself. Come and watch them, now? We'll see what their nerve's like, if you call score . . ."

"A moment or two, Marc. Go back to your work, I'll sniff around on my own."

And so he approached Niko, on pretense of admiring the Stepson's new bow, and saw the shadowed eyes, blank as ever but veiled like the beginning beard that masked his jaw: "How goes it, Niko? Has your *maat* returned to you?"

"Not likely," the young fighter, cranking the spring and lever so a bolt notched, said and triggered the quarrel which whispered straight and true to center his target. "Did Crit send you? I'm fine, commander. He worries too much. We can handle her, no matter how it seems. It's just time we need . . . she's suspicious, wants but to prove our faith. Shall I, by whatever means?"

"Another week on this is all I can give you. Use discretion, your judgment's fine with me. What you think she's worth, she's worth. If Critias questions that, your orders came from me and you may tell him so."

"I will, and with pleasure. I'm not his to wetnurse; he can't keep that in his head."

"And Janni?"

"It's hard on him, pretending to be . . . what we're pretending to be. The men talk to him about coming back out to the barracks, about forgetting what's past and resuming his duties. But we'll weather it. He's man enough."

Niko's hazel eyes flicked back and forth, judging the other men: who watched; who pretended he did not, but listened hard. He loosed another bolt, a third, and said quietly that he had to collect his flights. Tempus eased away, heard the range officer call "Clear" and watched Niko go retrieve his grouped quarrels.

If this one could not breach the witch's defenses, then she was unbreachable.

Content, he left then, and found Jihan, his de facto right-side partner, waiting astride his other Trôs horse, her more than human strength and beauty brightening Smith Street's ramshackle facade as if real gold lay beside fool's gold in a dusty pan.

Though one of the matters estranging him from his Stepsons was his pairing with his foreign "woman," only Niko knew her to be the daughter of a power who spawned all contentious gods and even the concept of divinity; he felt the cool her flesh gave off, cutting the midday heat like wind from a snowcapped peak.

"Life to you, Tempus." Her voice was thick as ale, and he realized he was thirsty. Promise Park and the Alekeep, an east side establishment considered upper class by those who could tell classes of Ilsigs, were right around the corner, a block up the Street of Gold from where they met. He proposed to take her there for lunch. She was delighted—all things mortal were new to her; the whole business of being in flesh and attending to it was yet novel. A novice at life, Jihan was hungry for the whole of it.

For him, she served a special purpose: her loveplay was rough and her constitution hardier than his Trôs horses—he could not couple gently and she was born of violence inchoate and savored what would kill or cripple mortals.

At the Alekeep, they were welcome. They talked

in a back and private room of the god's absence and what could be made of it and the owner served them himself, an avuncular sort still grateful that Tempus's men had kept his daughters safe when wizard weather roamed the streets. "My girl's graduating school today, Lord Marshal—my youngest. We've a fete set and you and your companion would be most welcome guests."

Jihan touched his arm as he began to decline, her stormy eyes flecked red and glowing.

". . . ah, perhaps we will drop by, then, if business permits."

But they didn't, having found pressing matters of lust to attend to, and all things that happened then might have been avoided if they hadn't been out of touch with the Stepsons, unreachable down by the creek that ran north of the barracks when sorcery met machination and all things went awry.

— 3 —

On their way to work, Niko and Janni stopped at the Vulgar Unicorn to wait for the moon to rise. The moon would be full this evening, a blessing since anonymous death squads roamed the town—whether they were Rankan army regulars, Jubal's scattered hawkmasks, fish-eyed Beysib spoilers, or Nisibisi assassins, none could say.

The one thing that could be said of them for certain was that they weren't Stepsons or Sacred Banders or nonaligned mercenaries from the guild hostel. But there was no convincing the terrorized populace of that.

And Niko and Janni—under the guise of disaffected mercenaries who had quit the Stepsons, been thrown out of the guild hostel for unspeakable acts,

and were currently degenerating Santuary-style in
the filthy streets of the town—thought that they
were close to identifying the death squads' leader.
Hopefully, this evening or the next, they would be
asked to join the murderers in their squalid sport.

Not that murder was uncommon in Sanctuary, or
squalor. The Maze, now that Niko knew it like his
horses' needs or Janni's limits, was not the town's
true nadir, only the multi-tiered slum's upper eche-
lon. Worse than the Maze was Shambles Cross, filled
with the weak and the meek; worse than the Shambles was Downwind, where nothing moved in the
light of day and at night hellish sounds rode the
stench on the prevailing east wind across the White
Foal. A tri-level hell, then, filled with murderers,
sold souls and succubi, began here in the Maze.

If the death squads had confined themselves to
Maze, Shambles, and Downwind, no one would have
known about them. Bodies in those streets were
nothing new; neither Stepsons nor Rankan soldiers
bothered counting them; near the slaughter-houses
cheap crematoriums flourished; for those too poor
even for that, there was the White Foal, taking am-
biguous dross to the sea without complaint. But the
squads ventured uptown, to the east side and the
center of Sanctuary itself where the palace hiero-
phants and the merchants lived and looked away
from downtown, scented pomanders to their noses.

The Unicorn crowd no longer turned quiet when
Niko and Janni entered; their scruffy faces and shabby
gear and bleary eyes proclaimed them no threat to
the mendicants or the whores. Competition, they
were now considered, and it had been hard to float
the legend, harder to live it. Or to live it down, since
none of the Stepsons but their task force leader, Crit
(who himself had never moved among the barracks
ranks, proud and shining with oil and fine weapons

and finer ideals) knew that they had not quit but only
worked shrouded in subterfuge on Tempus's orders
to flush the Nisibisi witch.

But the emergence of the death squads had raised
the pitch, the note, given the matter a new urgency.
Some said it was because Shadowspawn, the thief,
was right: the god Vashanka had died and the Rankans
would suffer their due. Their due or not, traders,
politicians, and moneyleaders—the "oppressors," were
nightly dragged out into the streets, whole families
slaughtered or burned alive in their houses, or hacked
to pieces in their festooned wagons.

The agents ordered draughts from One-Thumb's
new girl and she came back, cowering but determined, saying that One-Thumb must see their money
first. They had started this venture with the barman's help; he knew their provenance; they knew his
secret.

"Let's kill the swillmonger, Stealth," Janni growled.
They had little cash—a few soldats and some Machadi
coppers—and couldn't draw their pay until their work
was done.

"Steady, Janni. I'll talk to him. Girl, fetch two
Rankan ales or you won't be able to close your legs
for a week."

He pushed back his bench and strode to the bar,
aware that he was only half joking, that Sanctuary
was rubbing him raw. *Was* the god dead? *Was* Tempus in thrall to the Froth Daughter who kept his
company? *Was* Sanctuary the honeypot of chaos? A
hell from which no man emerged? He pushed a
threesome of young puds aside and whistled pierc-
ingly when he reached the bar. The big bartender
looked around elaborately, raised a scar-crossed eyebrow, and ignored him. Stealth counted to ten and
then methodically began emptying other patrons'
drinks onto the counter. Men were few here; approx-

imations cursed him and backed away; one went for a beltknife but Stealth had a dirk in hand that gave him pause. Niko's gear was dirty, but better than any of these had. And he was ready to clean his soiled blade in any one of them. They sensed it; his peripheral perception read their moods though he could not read their minds. Where his *maat*—his balance—once had been was a cold, sick anger. In Sanctuary he had learned despair and futility, and these had introduced him to fury. Options he once had considered last resorts, off the battlefield, came easily to mind now. Son of the armies, he was learning a different kind of war in Sanctuary, and learning to love the havoc his own right arm could wreak. It was not a substitute for the equilibrium he'd lost when his left-side leader died down by the docks, but if his partner needed souls to buy a better place in heaven, Niko would gladly send him double his comfort's price.

The ploy brought One-Thumb down to stop him. "Stealth, I've had enough of you." One-Thumb's mouth was swollen, his upper lip crusted with sores, but his ponderous bulk loomed large; from the corner of his eye Niko could see the Unicorn's bouncer leave his post and Janni intercept him.

Niko reached out and grabbed One-Thumb by the throat, even as the man's paw reached under the bar, where a weapon might lie. He pulled him close: "What you've had isn't even a shadow of what you're going to get, Tum-Tum, if you don't mind your tongue. Turn back into the well-mannered little troll we both know and love, or you won't *have* a bar to hide behind by morning." Then, sotto voce: "What's up?"

"*She* wants you," the barkeep gasped, his face purpling, "to go to her place by the White Foal at high noon. If it's convenient, of course, my *lord*."

Niko let him go before his eyes popped out of his head. "You'll put this on our tab?"

"Just this one more time, beggar boy. Your Whoreson bugger-buddies won't lift a leg to help you; your threats are as empty as your purse."

"Care to bet on it?"

They carried on a bit more, for the crowd's benefit, Janni and the bouncer engaged in a staring match the while. "Call your cur off, then, and we'll forget about this—this once." Niko turned, neck aprickle, and headed back toward his seat, hoping that it wouldn't go any further. Not one of the four—bouncer, bar owner, Stepsons—was entirely playing to the crowd.

When he'd reached his door-facing table, Lastel/One-Thumb called his bruiser off and Janni backed toward Niko, white-faced and trembling with eagerness: "Let me geld one of them, Stealth. It'll do our reputations no end of good."

"Save it for the witch-bitch."

Janni brightened, straddling his seat, both arms on the table, digging fiercely with his dirk into the wood: "You've got a rendezvous?"

"Tonight, high moon. Don't drink too much."

It wasn't the drink that skewed them, but the krrf they snorted, little piles poured into clenched fists where thumb muscles made a well. Still, the drug would keep them alert: it was a long time until high moon, and they had to patrol for marauders while seeming to be marauding themselves. It was almost more than Niko could bear. He'd infiltrated a score of camps, lines and palaces on reconnaissance sorties with his deceased partner, but those were cleaner, quicker actions than this protracted infiltration of Sanctuary, bunghole of the known world. If this evening made an end to it and he could wash and shave and stable his horses better, he'd make a sacrifice to Enlil which the god would not soon forget.

An hour later, mounted, they set off on their tour

of the Maze, Niko thinking that not since the affair with the archmage Aškelon and Tempus's sister Cime had his gut rolled up into a ball with this feeling of unmitigated dread. The Nisibisi witch might know him—she might have known him all along. He'd been interrogated by Nisibisi before, and he would fall upon his sword rather than endure it again now, when his dead teammate's ghost still haunted his mental refuge and meditation could not offer him shelter as it once had.

A boy came running up calling his name and his jughead black tossed its rust nose high and snorted, ears back, waiting for a command to kill or maim.

"By Vashanka's sulfurous balls, what now?" Janni wondered.

They sat their mounts in the narrow street; the moon was just rising over the shantytops; people slammed their shutters tight and bolted their doors. Niko could catch wisps of fear and loathing from behind the houses' facades; two mounted men in these streets meant trouble, no matter whose they were.

The youth trotted up, breathing hard. "Niko! Niko! The master's so upset. Thank Ils I've found you . . ." The delicate eunuch's lisp identified him: a servant of the Alekeep's owner, one of the few men Niko thought of as a friend here.

"What's wrong, then?" He leaned down in his saddle.

The boy raised a hand and the black snaked his head round fast to bite it. Niko clouted the horse between the ears as the boy scrambled back out of range. "Come on, come here. He won't try it again. Now, what's your master's message?"

"Tamzen! Tamzen's gone out without her body-guard, with—" The boy named six of the richest Sanctuary families' fast-living youngsters. "They said

they'd be right back, but they didn't come. It's *her*
party she's missing. The master's beside himself. He
said if you can't help him, he'll have to call the Hell
Hounds—the palace guard, or go to the Stepsons'
barracks. But there's no time, no time!" the frail
eunuch wailed.

"Calm down, pud. We'll find her. Tell her father
to send word to Tempus anyway, it can't hurt to alert
the authorities. And say exactly this: that I'll help if I
can, but he knows I'm not empowered to do more
than any citizen. Say it back, now."

Once the eunuch had repeated the words and run
off, Janni said: "How're you going to be in two places
at once, Stealth? Why'd you tell him that? It's a job
for the regulars, not for us. We can't miss this meet,
not after all the bedbugs I've let chomp on me for
this . . ."

"*Seh!*" The word meant offal in the Nisi tongue.
"We'll round her and her friends up in short order.
They're just blowing off steam—it's the heat and
school's end. Come on, let's start at Promise Park."

When they got there, the moon showed round and
preternaturally large above the palace and the wind
had died. Thoughts of the witch he must meet still
troubled Niko, and Janni's grousing buzzed in his
ears: ". . . we should check in with Crit, let the girl
meet her fate—ours will be worse if we're snared by
enchantment and no backup alerted to where or
how."

"We'll send word or stop by the Shambles drop,
stop worrying." But Janni was not about to stop, and
Niko's attempts to calm himself, to find transcendent
perception in his rest-place and pick up the girl's
trail by the heat-track she'd left and the things she'd
said and done here were made more difficult by
Janni's worries, which jarred him back to concerns
he must put aside, and Janni's words, which startled

him, over-loud and disruptive, every time he got himself calmed enough to sense Tamzen's energy trail among so many others like red/yellow/pink yarn twined among chiaroscuro trees.

Tamzen, thirteen and beautiful, pure and full of fun, who loved him with all her heart and had made him promise to "wait" for her: He'd had her, a thing he'd never meant to do, and had her with her father's knowledge, confronted by the concerned man one night when Niko, arm around the girl's waist, had walked her through the park. "Is this how you repay a friend's kindness, Stealth?" the father'd asked. "Better me than any of this trash, my friend. I'll do it right. She's ready, and it wouldn't be long, in any case," he'd replied while the girl looked between the soldier, twelve years older, and her father, with uncomprehending eyes. He had to find her.

Janni, as if in receipt of the perceptive spirit Niko tried now to reclaim, swore and said that Niko'd had no business getting involved with her, a child.

The silence come between them then gave Stealth his chance to find the girl's red time-shadow, a hot ghost-trial to follow southwest through the Maze . . .

As the moon climbed high its light shone brighter, giving Maze and then Shambles shape and teasing light; color was almost present among the streets, so bright it shone a reddish cast like blood upon its face, so that when common Sanctuary horrors lay revealed at intersections, they seemed worse even than they were. Janni saw two whores fight for a client; he saw blood run black in gutters from thugs and just incautious folk. Their horses' hoofbeats cleared their path, though, and Maze was left behind, as willing to let them go as they to leave it, although Janni muttered at every vile encounter their presence interrupted, wishing they could intervene.

Once he thought they'd glimpsed a death squad,

and urged Stealth to come alert, but the strange young fighter shook his head and hushed him, slouched loose upon his horse as if entranced, following some trail that neither Janni nor any mortal man with God's good fear of magic should have seen. Janni's heart was troubled by this boy who was too good at craft, who had a charmed sword and dagger given him by the entelechy of dreams, yet left them in the barracks, decrying magic's price. But what was this, if not sorcery? Janni watched Niko watch the night and take them deep into shadowed alleys with all the confidence a mage would flout. The youth had offered to teach him "controls" of mind, to take him "up though the planes and get your guide and your twelfth-plane name." But Janni was no connoisseur of witchcraft; like boy-loving, he left it to the Sacred Banders and the priests. He'd gotten into this with Niko for worldly advantage; the youth ten years his junior was pure genius in a fight; he'd seen him work at Jubal's and marveled even in the melee of the sack. Niko's reputation for prowess in the field was matched only by Stratus's, and the stories told of Niko's past. The boy had trained among Successors, the Nisibisi's bane, wild guerrillas, mountain commandos who let none through Wizardwall's defiles without gold or life in tithe, who'd sworn to reclaim their mountains from the mages and the warlocks and held out, outlaws, countering sorcery with swords. In a campaign such as the northern one coming, Niko's skills and languages and friends might prove invaluable. Janni, from Machad, had no love for Rankans, but it was said Niko served despite the blood hatred: Rankans had sacked his town nameless; his father had died fighting Rankan expansion when the boy was five. Yet he'd come south on Abarsis's venture, and stayed when Tempus inherited the band.

When they crossed the Street of Shingles and headed

into Shambles Cross, the pragmatic Janni spoke a soldier's safe-conduct prayer and touched his warding charm. A confusion of turns within the ways high-grown with hovels which cut off view and sky, they heard commotion, shouting men and running feet.

They spurred their horses and careened round corners, forgetful of their pose as independent reavers, for they'd heard Stepsons calling maneuver codes. So it was that they came, sliding their horses down on haunches so hard sparks flew from iron-shod hooves, cutting off the retreat of three running on foot from Stepsons and vaulted down to the cobbles to lend a hand.

Niko's horse, itself, took it in its mind to help, and charged past them, reins dragging, head held high, to back a fugitive against a mudbrick wall. "*Seh!* Run, Vis!" they heard, and more in a tongue Janni thought might be Nisi, for the exclamation was.

By then Niko had one by the collar and two quarrels shot by close to Janni's ear. He hollered out his identity and called to the shooters to cease their fire before he was skewered like the second fugitive, pinned by two bolts against the wall. The third quarry struggled now between the two on-duty Stepsons, one of whom called out to Janni to hold the second. It was Straton's voice, Janni realized, and Straton's quarrels pinning the indigent by cape and crotch against the wall. Lucky for the delinquent it had been: Straton's bolts had pierced no vital spot, just clothing.

It was not till then that Janni realized that Niko was talking to the first fugitive, the one his horse had pinned, in Nisi, and the other answering back, fast and low, his eyes upon the vicious horse, quivering and covered with phosphorescent froth, who stood watchful by his master, hoping still that Niko would let him pound the quarry into gory mud.

Straton and his partner, dragging the third unfortunate between them, came up, full of thanks and victory: ". . . finally got one, alive. Janni, how's yours?"

The one he held at crossbow-point was quiet, submissive, a Sanctuarite, he thought, until Straton lit a torch. Then they saw a slave's face, dark and arch like Nisibisi's were, and Straton's partner spoke for the first time: "That's Haught, the slave-bait." Critias moved forward, torch in hand. "Hello, pretty. We'd thought you'd run or died. We've lots to ask you, puppy, and nothing we'd rather do tonight. . . ." As Crit moved in and Janni stepped back, Janni was conscious that Niko and his prisoner had fallen silent.

Then the slave, amazingly, straightened up and raised its head, reaching within its jerkin. Janni levered his bow, but the hand came out with a crumpled paper in it, and this he held forth, saying: "She freed me. She said this says so. Please . . . I know nothing, but that she's freed me. . . ."

Crit snatched the feathered parchment from him, held it squinting in the torch's light. "That's right, that's what it says here." He rubbed his jaw, then stepped forward. The slave flinched, his handsome face turned away. Crit pulled out the bolts that held him pinned, grunting; no blood followed; the slave crouched down, unscatched but incapacitated by his fear. "Come as a free man, then, and talk to us. We won't hurt you, boy. Talk and you can go."

Niko, then, intruded, his prisoner beside him, his horse following close behind. "Let them go, Crit."

"*What?* Niko, forget the game, tonight. They'll not live to tell you helped us. We've been needing this advantage too long—"

"Let them go, Crit." Beside him his prisoner cursed or hissed or intoned a spell, but did not break to run. Niko stepped close to his task force leader, whispering: "This one's an ex-commando, a fighter from

Wizardwall come upon hard times. Do him a service, as I must, for services done."

"Nisibisi? More's the reason, then, to take them and break them—"

"No. He's on the other side from warlocks; he'll do us more good free in the streets. Won't you, Vis?"

The foreign-looking ruffian agreed, his voice thick with an accent detectable even in his three clipped syllables.

Niko nodded. "See, Crit? This is Vis. Vis, this is Crit. I'll be the contact for his reports. Go on, now. You, too, freedman, go. Run!"

And the two, taking Niko at his word, dashed away before Crit could object.

The third, in Straton's grasp, writhed wildly. This was a failed hawkmask, very likely, in Straton's estimation, the prize of the three and one no word from Niko could make the mercenary loose.

Niko agreed that he'd not try to save any of Jubal's minons, and that was that . . . almost. They had to keep their meeting brief; any could be peeking out from windowsill or shadowed door, but as they mounted up to ride away, Janni saw a cowled figure rising from a pool of darkness occluding the intersection. It stood, full up momentarily, and moonrays struck its face. Janni shuddered; it was a face with hellish eyes, too far to be so big or so frightening, yet their met glance shocked him like icy water and made his limbs to shake.

"Stealth! Did you see that?"

"What?" Niko snapped, defensive over interfering in Crit's operation. "See what?"

"That—thing . . ." Nothing was there, where he had seen it. "Nothing . . . I'm seeing things." Crit and Straton had reached their horses; they heard hoofbeats receding in the night.

"Show me where, and tell me what."

Janni swung up on his mount and led the way; when they got there they found a crumpled body, a youth with bloated tongue outstuck and rolled up eyes as if a fit had taken him, dead as Abarsis in the street. "Oh, no . . ." Niko, dismounted, rolled the corpse. "It's one of Tamzen's friends." The silk-and-linened body came clearer as Janni's eyes accustomed themselves to moonlight after the glare of the torch. They heaved the corpse up upon Janni's horse who snorted to bear a dead thing but forebore to refuse outright. "Let's take it somewhere, Stealth. We can't carry it about all night." Only then did Janni remember they'd failed to report to Crit their evening's plan.

At his insistence, Niko agreed to ride by the Shambles Cross safe haven, caulked and shuttered in iron, where Stepsons and street men and Ilsig/Rankan garrison personnel, engaged in chasing hawkmasks and other covert enterprises, made their slum reports *in situ*.

They managed to leave the body there, but not to alert the task force leader; Crit had taken the hawkmask wherever he thought the catch would serve them best; nothing was in the room but the interrogation wheel and bags of lime to tie on unlucky noses and truncheons of sailcloth filled with gravel and iron filngs to change the most steadfast heart. They left a note, carefully coded, and hurried back onto the street. Niko's brow was furrowed, and Janni, too, was in a hurry to see if they might find Tamzen and her friends as a living group, not one by one, cold corpses in the gutter.

— 4 —

The witch Roxane had house snakes, a pair brought down from Nisibis, green and six feet long, each one.

She brought them into her study and set their baskets by the hearth. Then, bowl of water by her side, she spoke the words that turned them into men. The facsimiles aped a pair of Stepsons; she got them clothes and sent them off. Then she took the water bowl and stirred it with her finger until a whirlpool sucked and writhed. This she spoke over, and out to sea beyond the harbor a like disturbance began to rage. She took from her table six carven ships with Beysib sails, small and filled with wax miniatures of men. These she launched into the basin with its whirlpool and spun and spun her finger round until the flagships of the fleet floundered, then were sunk and sucked to lie at last, upon the bottom of the bowl. Even after she withdrew her finger the water raged awhile. The witch looked calmly into her maelstrom and nodded once, content. The diversion would be timely; the moon, outside her window, was nearly high, scant hours from its zenith.

Then it was time to take Jagat's report and send the death squads—or dead squads, for none of those who served in them had life of their own to lead—into town.

— 5 —

Tamzen's heart was pounding, her mouth dry and her lungs burning. They had run a long way. They were lost and all six knew it; Phryne was weeping and her sister was shaking and crying she couldn't run, her knees wouldn't hold her; the three boys left were talking loud and telling all how they'd get home if they just stayed in a group—the girls had no need to fear. More krrf was shared, though it made things worse, not better, so that a toothless crone who tapped her stick and smacked her gums sent them flying through the streets.

No one talked about Mehta's fate; they'd seen him with the dark-clad whore, seen him mesmerized, seen him take her hand. They'd hid until the pair walked on, then followed—the group had sworn to stay together, wicked adventure on their minds; all were officially adults now; none could keep them from the forbidden pleasures of men and women—to see if Mehta would really lay the whore, thinking they'd regroup right after, and find out what fun he'd had.

They'd seen him fall, and gag, and die once he'd raised her skirts and had her, his buttocks thrusting hard as he pinned her to the alley wall. They'd seen her bend down over him and raise her head and the glowing twin hells there had sent them pall-mall, fleeing what they knew was no human whore.

Now they'd calmed, but they were deep in the Shambles, near its end where Caraven Square began. There was light there, from midnight merchants engaged in double dealing; it was not safe there, one of the boys said: slaves were made this way: children taken, sold north and never seen again.

"It's safe *here*, then?" Tamzen blurted, her teeth chattering but the krrf making her bold and angry. She strode ahead, not waiting to see them follow; they would; she knew this bunch better than their mothers. The thing to do, she was sure, was to stride bravely on until they came upon the Square and found the streets home, or came upon some Hell Hounds, palace soldiers, or Stepsons. Niko's friends would ride them home on horseback if they found some; Tamzen's acquaintance among the men of steel was her fondest prize.

Niko . . . If *he* were here, she'd have no fear, nor need to pretend to valor. . . . Her eyes filled with tears, thinking what he'd say when he heard. She was never going to convince him she was grown if all her attempts to do so made her seem the more a child. A *child's* error, this, for sure . . . and one dead on her account. Her father would beat her rump to blue and he'd keep her in her room for a month. She began to fret—the krrf's doing, though she was too far gone in the drug's sway to tell—and saw an alley from which torchlight shone. She took it; the others followed, she heard them close behind. They had money aplenty; they would hire an escort, perhaps with a wagon, to take them home. All taverns had men looking for hire in them; if they chanced Caravan Square, and fell afoul of slavers, she'd never see her poppa or Niko or her room filled with stuffed toys and ruffles again.

The inn was called the Sow's Ear, and it was foul. In its doorway, one of the boys, panting, caught her arm and jerked her back. "Show money in that place, and you'll get all our throats slit quick."

He was right. They huddled in the street and sniffed more krrf and shook and argued. Phryne began to wail aloud and her sister stopped her mouth with a clapped hand. Just as the two girls, terrified and defeated, crouched down in the street and one of the boys, his bladder loosed by fear, sought a corner wall, a woman appeared before them, her hood thrown back, her face hidden by a trick of light. But the voice was a gentlewoman's voice and the words were compassionate. "Lost, children? There, there, it's all right now, just come with me. We'll have mulled wine and pastries and I'll have my man form an escort to see you home. You're the Alekeep owner's daughter, if I'm right? Ah, good, then; your father's a friend of my husband . . . surely you remember me?"

She gave a name and Tamzen, her sense swimming in drugs and her heart filled with relief and the sweet taste of salvation, lied and said she did. All six went along with the woman, skirting the square until they came to a curious house behind a high gate, well lit and gardened and full of chaotic splendor. At its rear, the rush of the White Foal could be heard.

"Now sit, sit, little one. Who needs to wash off the street grime? Who needs a pot?" The rooms were shadowed, no longer well lit; the woman's eyes were comforting, calming like sedative draughts for sleepless nights. They sat among the silks and the carven chairs and they drank what she offered and began to giggle. Phryne went and washed, and her sister and Tamzen followed. When they came back, the boys were nowhere in sight. Tamzen was just going to ask about that when the woman offered fruit, and somehow she forgot the words on her tongue-tip, and even that the boys had been there at all, so fine was the krrf the woman smoked with them. She knew she'd remember in a bit, though, whatever it was she'd forgot. . . .

— *6* —

When Crit and Straton arrived with the hawkmask they'd captured at the Foalside home of Ischade, the vampire woman, all its lights were on, it seemed, yet little of that radiance cut the gloom.

"By the god's four mouths, Crit, I still don't understand why you let those others go. And for Niko. What—?"

"Don't ask me, Straton, what his reasons are; I don't know. Something about the one being of that Successors band, revolutionaries who want Wizardwall back from the Nisibisi mages—there's more to Nisibis than the warlocks. If that Vis *was* one, then he's an outlaw as far as Nisibisi law goes, and maybe a fighter. So we let him go, do him a favor, see if maybe he'll come to us, do us a service in his turn. But as for the other—you saw Ischade's writ of freedom—we gave him to her and she let him go. If we want to use her . . . if she'll *ever* help us find Jubal—and she *does* know where he is; this freeing of the slave was a message: she's telling us we've got to up the ante— we've got to honor her wishes as far as this slave-bait goes."

"But this . . . coming here *ourselves?* You know what she can do to a man . . ."

"Maybe we'll like it; maybe it's time to die. I don't know. I *do* know we can't leave it to the garrison— every time they find us a hawkmask he's too damaged to tell us anything. We'll never recruit what's left of them if the army keeps killing them slowly and we take the blame. And also," Crit paused, dismounted his horse, pulled the trussed and gagged hawkmask he had slung over his saddle like a haunch of meat down after him, so that the prisoner fell heavily to the ground, "we've been told by the garrison's intelligence liaison that the army thinks Stepsons fear this woman."

"Anybody with a dram of common sense would." Straton, rubbing his eyes, dismounted also, notched crossbow held at the ready as soon as his feet touched the ground.

"They don't mean that. You know what they mean; they can't tell a Sacred Bander from a straight mercenary. They think we're all sodomizers and sneer at us for that."

"Let 'em. I'd rather be alive and misunderstood than dead and respected." Straton blinked, trying to clear his blurred vision. It was remarkable that Critias would undertake this action on his own; he wasn't supposed to take part in field actions, but command them. Tempus had been to see him, though, and since then the task force leader had been more taciturn and even more impatient than usual. Straton knew there was no use in arguing with Critias, but he was one of the few who could claim the privilege of voicing his opinion to the leader, even when they disagreed.

They'd interrogated the hawkmask briefly; it didn't take long; Straton was a specialist in exactly that. He was a pretty one, and substantively undamaged. The vampire was discerning, loved beauty; she'd take to this one, the few bruises on him might well make him more attractive to a creature such as she: not only would she have him in her power but it would be in her power to save him from a much worse death than that she'd give. By the look of the tall, lithe hawkmask, by his clothes and his pinched face in which sensitive, liquid eyes roamed furtively, a pleasant death would be welcome. His ilk were hunted by more factions in Sanctuary than any but Nisibisi spies.

Crit said, "Ready, Strat?"

"I own I'm not, but I'll pretend if you do. If you get through this and I don't, my horses are yours."

"And mine, yours." Crit bared his teeth. "But I don't expect that to happen. She's reasonable, I'm wagering. She couldn't have turned that slave loose that way if she wasn't in control of her lust. And she's smart—smarter than Kadakithis's so-called 'intelligence staff,' or Hell Hounds, we've seen that for a fact."

So, despite sane cautions, they unlatched the gate, their horses drop-tied behind them, cut the hawkmask's ankle bonds and walked him to the door. His eyes went wide above his gag, pupils gigantic in the torchlight on her threshold, then squeezed shut as Ischade herself came to greet them when, after knocking thrice and waiting long, they were about to turn away, convinced she wasn't home after all.

She looked them up and down, her eyes half-lidded. Straton, for once, was grateful for the shimmer in his vision, the blur he couldn't blink away. The hawkmask shivered and lurched backward in their grasp as Crit spoke first:

"Good evening, madam. We thought the time had come to meet, face to face. We've brought you this gift, a token of our good will." He spoke blandly, matter-of-factly, letting her know they knew all about her and didn't really care what she did to the unwary or the unfortunate. Straton's mouth dried and his tongue stuck to the roof of it. None was colder than Crit, or more tenacious when work was under way.

The woman, Ischade, dusky-skinned but not the ruddy tone of Nisibis, an olive cast that made the whites of her teeth and eyes very bright, bade them enter. "Bring him in, then, and we'll see what can be seen."

"No, no. We'll leave him—an article of faith. We'd like to know what you hear of Jubal, or his band—whereabouts, that sort of thing. If you come to think of any such information, you can find me at the mercenaries' hostel."

"Or in your hidey-hole in Shambles Cross?"

"Sometimes." Crit stood firm. Straton, his relief a flood, now that he knew they weren't going *in* there, gave the hawkmask a shove. "Go on, boy, go to your mistress."

"A slave, then, is this one?" she asked Strat and that glance chilled his soul when it fixed on him. He'd seen butchers look at sheep like that. He half expected her to reach out and tweak his biceps.

He said: "What you wish, he is."

She said: And you?"

Crit said: "Forbearance has its limits."

She replied: "Yours, perhaps, not mine. Take him with you; I want him not. What you Stepsons think of me, I shall not even ask. But cheap, I shall never come."

Crit loosed his hold on the youth, who wriggled then, but Straton held him, thinking that Ischade was without doubt the most beautiful woman he'd ever seen, and the hawkmask was luckier than most. If death was the gateway to heaven, she was the sort of gatekeep he'd like to admit him, when his time came.

She remarked, though he had not spoke aloud, that such could easily be arranged.

Crit, at that, looked between them, then shook his head. "Go wait with the horses, Straton. I thought I heard them, just now."

So Straton never did find out exactly what was—or was not— arranged between his task force leader and the vampire woman, but when he reached the horses, he had his hands full calming them, as if his own had scented Niko's black, whom his gray detested above all other studs. When they'd both been stalled in the same barn, the din had been terrible, and stallboards shattered as regularly as stalls were mucked, from those two trying to get at each other. Horses, like men, love and hate, and those two stallions wanted a piece of each other the way Strat wanted a chance at the garrison commander or Vashanaka at the Wrigglies' Ils.

Soon after, Crit came sauntering down the walk, unscathed, alone, and silent.

Straton wanted to ask, but did not, what had been arranged: his leader's sour expression warned him off. And an hour later, at the Shambles Cross safe haven, when one of the street men came running in saying there was a disturbance and Tempus could not be found, so Crit would have to come, it was too late.

What they could do about waterspouts and whirlpools in the harbor was unclear.

— 7 —

When Straton and Crit had ridden away, Niko
eased his black out from hiding. The spirit-track he'd
followed had led them here; Tamzen and the others
were inside. The spoor met up with the pale blue
traces of the house's owner near the Sow's Ear and
did not separate thereafter. Blue was no human's
color, unless that human was an enchanter, a witch,
accursed or charmed. Both Niko and Janni knew
whose house this was, but what Crit and Straton
were doing here, neither wanted to guess or say.

"We can't rush the place, Stealth. You know what
she is."

"I know."

"Why didn't you let me hail them? Four would be
better than two, for this problem's solving."

"Whatever they're doing here, I don't want to
know about. And we've broken cover as it is tonight." Niko crooked a leg over his horse's neck,
cavalry style. Janni rolled a smoke and offered him
one; he took it and lit it with a flint from his belt
pouch just as two men with a wagon came driving up
from Downwind, wheels and hooves thundering across
the White Foal's bridge.

"Too much traffic," Janni muttered, as they pulled
their horses back into shadows and watched the men
stop their team before the odd home's door; the
wagon was screened and curtained; if someone was
within, it was impossible to tell.

The men went in and when they came out they
had three smallish people with them swathed in
robes and hooded. These were put into the carriage
and it then drove away, turning onto the cart-track
leading south from the bridge—there was nothing

down there but swamp, and wasteland, and at the
end of it, Fisherman's Row and the sea . . . nothing,
that is, but the witch Roxane's fortified estate.

"Do you think—Stealth, was that them?"

"Quiet, curse you; I'm trying to tell." It might
have been; his heart was far from quiet, and the
passengers he sensed were drugged and nearly som-
nambulent.

But from the house, he could no longer sense the
girlish trails which had been there, among the blue/
archmagical/anguished ones of its owner and those of
men. Boys' auras still remained there, he thought,
but quiet, weaker, perhaps dying, maybe dead. It
could be the fellow Crit had left there, and not the
young scions of east side homes.

The moon, above Niko's head, was near at zenith.
Seeing him look up, Janni anticipated what he was
going to say: "Well, Stealth, we've got to go down
there anyway; let's follow the wagon. Mayhap we'll
catch it. Perchance we'll find out whom they've got
there, if we do. And we've little time to lose—girls
or no, we've a witch to attend to."

"Aye." Niko reined his horse around and sat it at a
lope after the wagon, not fast enough to catch it too
soon, but fast enough to keep it in earshot. When
Janni's horse came up beside his, the other mercenary
called: "Convenience of this magnitude makes me nervous; you'd think the witch sent that wagon, even
snared those children, to be sure we'd have to come."

Janni was right; Niko said nothing; they were committed; there was nothing to do but follow; whatever
was going to happen was well upon them, now.

— *8* —

A dozen riders materialized out of the wasteland

near the swamp and surrounded the two Stepsons;
none had faces; all had glowing pure-white eyes.
They fought as best they could with mortal weapons,
but ropes of spitting power came round them and
blue sparks bit them and their flesh sizzled through
their linen chitons and, unhorsed, they were dragged
along behind the riders until they no longer knew
where they were or what was happening to them or
even felt the pain. The last thing Niko remembered,
before he awoke bound to a tree in some featureless
grove, was the wagon ahead, stopping, and his horse,
on its own trying to win the day. The big black had
climbed the mount of the rider who dragged Niko on
a tether, and he'd seen the valiant beast's thick jowls
pierced through by arrows glowing blue with magic,
seen his horse falter, jaws gaping, then fall as he was
dragged away.

Now he struggled, helpless in his bonds, trying to
clear his vision and will his pain away.

Before him he saw figures, a bonfire limning silhouettes. Among them, as consciousness came full upon
him and he began to wish he'd never waked, was
Tamzen, struggling in grisly embraces and wailing
out his name, and the other girls, and Janni, spreadeagled, staked out on the ground, his mouth open,
screaming at the sky.

"Ah," he heard, "Nikodemos. So kind of you to
join us."

Then a woman's face swam before him, beautiful,
though that just made it worse. It was the Nisibisi
witch and she was smiling, itself an awful sign. A
score of minions ringed her, creatures roused from
graves, and two with ophidian eyes and lipless mouths
whose skins had a greenish cast.

She began to tell him softly the things she wished
to know. For a time he only shook his head and
closed his ears and tried to flee his flesh. If he could

retire his mind to his rest-place, he could ignore it all; the pain, the screams which split the night; he would know none of what occurred here, and die without the shame of capitulation: she'd kill him anyway, when she was done. So he counted determinedly backward, eyes squeezed shut, envisioning the runes which would save him. But Tamzen's screams, her sobs to him for help, and Janni's animal anguish, kept interfering, and he could not reach the quiet place and stay: he kept being dragged back by the sounds.

Still, when she asked him questions he only stared back at her in silence: Tempus's plans and state of mind were things he knew little of; he couldn't have stopped this if he'd wanted to; he didn't know enough. But when at length, knowing it, he closed his eyes again, she came up close and pried them open, impaling his lids with wooden splinters so that he would see what made Janni cry.

They had staked the Stepson over a wild creature's burrow—a badger, he later saw, when it had gnawed and clawed its way to freedom—and were smoking the rodent out by setting fire to its tunnel. When Janni's stomach began to show the outline of the animal within, Niko, capitulating, told all he knew and made up more besides.

By then the girls had long since been silenced.

All he heard was the witch's voice; all he remembered was the horror of her eyes and the message she bade him give to Tempus, and that when he had repeated it, she pulled the splinters from his lids. . . . The darkness she allowed him became complete, and he found a danker rest-place than meditation's quiet cave.

— 9 —

In Roxane's "manor house" commotion raged;

slaves went running and men cried orders, and in the court the caravan was being readied to make away.

She herself sat petulant and wroth, among the brocades of her study and the implements of her craft: water and fire and earth and air, and minerals and plants, and a globe sculpted from high peaks clay with precious stones inset.

A wave of hand would serve to load these in her wagon. The house spells' undoing would take much less than that—a finger's wave, a word unsaid, and all would be no more than it appeared: rickety and threadbare. But the evening's errors and all the work she'd done to amend them had drained her strength.

She sat, and Niko, in a corner, propped up but not awake, breathed raspingly: another error—those damn snakes took everything too literally, as well as being incapable of following simple orders to their completion.

The snakes she'd sent out, charmed to look like Stepsons, should have found the children in the streets; as Niko and Janni, their disguises were complete. But that vampire bitch had chanced upon the quarry and taken it home. Then she'd had to change all plans and make the wagon and send the snakes to retrieve the bait—the girls alone, the boys were expendable—and snakes were not up to fooling women grown and knowledgeable of spells. Ischade had given up her female prizes, rather than confront Nisibisi magic, pretending that she believed the "Stepsons" who came to claim Tamzen and her friends.

So she took the snakes out once more from their baskets and held their heads up to her face. Tongues darted out and reptilian eyes pled mercy, but Roxane had forgotten mercy long ago. And strength was what she needed, which in part these had helped to drain away. Holding them high she picked herself up and speaking words of power took them both and cast them in the blazing hearth. The flames roared up and snakes writhed in agony, and roasted. When they were done she fetched them out with silver tongs and ate their tails and heads.

Thus fortified, she turned to Niko, still hiding mind and soul in his precious mental refuge, a version of it she'd altered when her magic saw it. This place of peace and perfect relaxation, a cave behind the meadow of his mind, had a ghost in it, a friend who loved him. In its guise she'd spoken long to him and gained his spirit's trust. He was hers, now, as her lover-lord had promised; all things he learned she'd know as soon as he. None of it he'd remember, just go about his business of war and death. Through him she'd herd Tempus whither she willed and through him she'd know the Riddler's every plan.

For Nikodemos, the Nisibisi bondservant, had never shed his brand or slipped his chains: though her lover had freed his body, deep within his soul a string was tied. Any time, her lord could pull it; and she, too, now, had it twined around her pinky.

He remembered none of what occurred after his interrogation in the grove; he recalled just what she pleased and nothing more. Oh, he'd think he'd dreamed delirious nightmares, as he sweated now to feel her touch.

She woke him with a tap upon his eyes and told him what he was: her pawn, her tool, even that he would not recall their little talk or coming here. And she warned him of undeads, and shriveled his soul when she showed him, in her mirror-eyes, what Tamzen and her friends could be, should he even remember what passed between them here.

Then she put her pleasure by and touched the bruised and battered face: one more thing she took from him, to show his spirit who was slave and who was master. She had him service her and took strength from his swollen mouth and then, with a laugh, made him forget it all.

Then she sent her servant forth, unwitting, the extra satisfaction—gleaned from knowing that his spirit knew, and deep within him cried and struggled—giving the whole endeavor spice.

Jagat's men would see him to the road out near the Stepsons' barracks; they took his sagging weight in brawny arms.

And Roxane, for a time, was free to quit this scrofulous town and wend her way northward: she might be back, but for the nonce the journey to her lord's embrace was all she craved. They'd leave a trail well marked in place and plane for Tempus; she'd lie in high peak splendor, with her lover-lord well pleased by what she'd brought him: some Stepsons, and a Froth Daughter, and a man the gods immortalized.

— *10* —

It took until nearly dawn to calm the fish-faces who'd lost their five best ships; "lucky" for everyone that the Burek faction's nobility had been enjoying Kadakithis's hospitality, ensconced in the summer palace on the lighthouse spit and not aboard when the ships snapped anchor and headed like creatures with wills of their own toward the maelstrom that had opened at the harbor's mouth

Crit, through all, was taciturn; he was not supposed to surface; Tempus, when found, would not be pleased. But Kadakithis needed counsel badly; the young prince would give away his Imperial curls for "harmonious relations with our fellows from across the sea."

Nobody could prove that this was other than a

natural disaster; an "act of gods" was the unfortunate turn of phrase.

When at last Crit and Strat had done with the dicey process of standing around looking inconsequential while in fact, by handsign and courier, they mitigated Kadakithis's bent to compromise (for which there was no need except in the Beysib matriarch's mind) they retired from the dockside.

Crit wanted to get drunk, as drunk as humanly possible: helping the Mageguild defend its innocence, when like as not some mage or other had called the storm, was more than distasteful; it was counterproductive. As far as Critias was concerned, the newly elected First Hazard ought to step forward and take responsibility for his guild's malevolent mischief. When frogs fell from the sky, Straton prognosticated, such would be the case.

They'd done some good there: they'd conscripted Wrigglies and deputized fishermen and bullied the garrison duty officer into sending some of his men out with the long boats and Beysib dinghies and slave-powered tenders which searched shoals and coastline for survivors. But with the confusion of healers and thrill-seeking civilians and boat owners and Beysibs on the docks, they'd had to call in all the Stepsons and troops from road patrols and country posts in case the Beysibs took their loss too much to heart and turned upon the townsfolk.

On every corner, now, a mounted pair stood watch; beyond, the roads were desolate, unguarded. Crit worried that if diversion was some culprit's purpose, it had worked all too well: an army headed south would be upon them with no warning. If he'd not known that yesterday there'd been no sign of southward troop movement, he confided to Straton, he'd be sure some such evil was afoot.

To make things worse, when they found an open

bar it was the Alekeep, and its owner was wringing his hands in a corner with five other upscale fathers. Their sons and daughters had been out all night; word to Tempus at the Stepsons' barracks had brought no answer; the skeleton crew at the garrison had more urgent things to do than attend to demands for search parties when manpower was suddenly at a premium; the fathers sat awaiting their own men's return and thus had kept the Alekeep's graveyard shift from closing.

They got out of there as soon as politic, weary as their horses and squinting in the lightening dark.

The only place where peace and quiet could be had now that the town was waking, Crit said sourly, was the Shambles drop. They rode there and fastened the iron shutters down against the dawn, thinking to get an hour or so of sleep, and found Niko's coded note.

"Why wouldn't the old barkeep have told us that he'd set them on his daughter's trail?" Strat sighed, rubbing his eyes with his palms.

"Niko's legend says he's defected to the slums, remember?" Crit was shrugging into his chiton, which he'd just tugged off and thrown upon the floor.

"We're not going back out."

"I am."

"To look for *Niko? Where?*

"Niko and *Janni*. And I don't *know* where. But if that pair hasn't turned up those youngsters yet, it's no simple adolescent prank or graduation romp. Let's hope it's just that their meet with Roxane took precedence and it's inopportune for them to leave her." Crit stood.

Straton didn't.

"Coming?" Crit asked.

"Somebody should be where authority is expected to be found. You should be here or at that hostel, not chasing after someone who might be chasing after you."

So in the end, Straton won that battle and they went up to the hostel, stopping, since the sun had risen, at Marc's to pick up Straton's case of flights along the way.

The shop's door was ajar, though the opening hour painted on it hadn't come yet. Inside, the smith was hunched over a mug of tea, a crossbow's trigger mechanism dismantled before him on a split of suede, scowling at the crossbow's guts spread upon his counter as if at a recalcitrant child.

He looked up when they entered, wished them a better morning than he'd had so far this day, and went to get Straton's case of flights.

Behind the counter an assortment of high-torque bows was hung.

When Marc returned with the wooden case, Straton pointed: "That's Niko's, isn't it—or are my eyes that bad?"

"I'm holding it for him, until he pays," explained the smith with the unflinching gaze.

"We'll pay for it now and he can pick it up from me," Crit said.

"I don't know if he'd . . ." Marc, half into someone else's business, stepped back out of it with a nod of head: "All right, then, if you want. I'll tell him you've got it. That's four soldats, three . . I've done a lot of work on it for him. Shall I tell him to seek you at the guild hostel?"

"Thereabouts."

Taking it down from the wall, the smith wound and levered, then dry-fired the crossbow, its mechanism to his ear. A smile came over his face at what he heard. "Good enough, then," he declared and wrapped it in its case of padded hide.

This way, Straton realized, Niko would come direct to Crit and report when Marc told him what they'd done.

— 11 —

By the time dawn had cracked the world's egg, Tempus as well as Jihan was sated, even tired. For a man who chased sleep like other men chased power or women, it was wondrous that this was so. For the daughter of an elemental who had only recently become a woman, it was a triumph. They walked back toward the Stepsons' barracks, following the creekbed, all pink and gold in sunrise, content and even playful, his chuckle and her occasional laugh startling sleepy squirrels and flushing birds from their nests.

He'd been morose, but she'd cured it, convincing him that life might take a better turn, if he'd just let it. They'd spoken of her father, called Stormbringer in lieu of name, and arcane matters of their joint preoccupation: whether humanity had inherent value, whether gods could die or merely lie, whether Vashanka was hiding out somewhere, petulant in godhead, only waiting for generous sacrifices and heartfelt prayers to coax him back among his Rankan people—or, twelfth plane powers forfend, really "dead."

He'd spoken openly to her of his affliction, reminding her that those who loved him died by violence and those he loved were bound to spurn him, and what that could mean in the case of his Stepsons, and herself, if Vashanka's power did not return to mitigate his curse. He'd told her of his plea to Enlil, ancient deity of universal scope, and that he awaited godsign.

She'd been relieved at that, afraid, she admitted,

that the lord of dreams might tempt him from her side. After all, Jihan had been there when Aškelon, had come to lure Cime off to his metaphysical kingdom of delights, had offered her brother the boon of mortality in return for acquiescence. Now that she'd just found him, Jihan had added throatily, she could not bear it if he chose to die.

And she'd spent that evening proving to Tempus that it might be well to stay alive with her who loved life the more for having only just begun it, and yet could not succumb to mortal death or be placed in mortal danger by his curse, his strength, or whatever he might do.

The high moon had laved them and her legs had embraced him and her red-glowing eyes like her father's had transfixed him while her cool flesh enflamed him. Yes, with Jihan beside him, he'd swallow his pride and his pique and give even Sanctuary's Kadakithis the benefit of the doubt—he'd stay though his heart tugged him northward, although he'd thought, when he took her to their creekbed bower, to chase her away.

When they'd slipped into his barracks quarters from the back, he was no longer so certain. He heard from a lieutenant all about the waterspouts and whirlpools, thinking while the man talked that this was his godsign, however obscure its meaning, and then he regretted having made an accommodation with the Froth Daughter: all his angst came back upon him, and he wished he'd hugged his resolve firmly to his breast and driven Jihan hence.

But when the disturbance at the outer gates penetrated to the slaver's old apartments which he had made his own, rousting them out to seek its cause, he was glad enough she'd remained.

The two of them had to shoulder their way through the gathered crowd of Stepsons, astir with bitter mutters; no one made way for them; none had come to their commander's billet with news of what had been brought up to the gatehouse in the dawn.

He heard a harsh whisper from a Stepson too angry to be careful, wondering if Tempus had sent Janni's team deliberately to destruction because Stealth had rejected the Riddler's offered pairbond.

One who knew better answered sagely that this was a Mygdonian message, a Nisibisi warning of some antiquity, and *he* had heard it straight from Stealth's broken lips.

"What *did* that ?" Jihan moaned, bending low over Janni's remains. "Tempus did not answer her but said generally: "And Niko?" and followed a man who headed off toward the whitewashed barracks, hearing as he went a voice choked with grief explaining to Jihan what happens when you tie a man spreadeagled over an animal's burrow and smoke the creature out.

The Stepson guiding him to where Niko lay said that the man who'd brought them wished to speak to Tempus. "Let him wait for his reward," Tempus snapped, and questioned the mercenary about the samaritan who'd delivered the two Stepsons home. But the Sacred Bander had gotten nothing from the stranger who'd rapped upon the gates and braved the angry sentries who almost killed him when they saw what burden he'd brought in. The stranger would say only that he must wait for Tempus.

The Stepsons' commander stood around helplessly with three others, friends of Niko's, until the barber-surgeon had finished with needle and gut, then chased them all away, shuttering windows, barring doors. Cup in hand, then, he gave the battered, beaten youth his painkilling draught in silence, only sitting and letting Niko sip while he assessed the Stepson's injuries and made black guesses as to how the boy had come by green and purple blood-filled bruises, rope burns at wrist and neck, and a face like doom.

Quite soon he heard from Nikodemos, concisely but through a slur that comes when teeth have been loosed or broken in a dislocated jaw, what had transpired: they had gone seeking the Alekeep owner's daughter, deep into Shambles where drug dens and cheap whores promise dreamless nights, found them at Ischade's, seen them hustled into a wagon and driven away toward Roxane's. Following, for they were due to see the witch at high noon in her lair in any case, they'd been accosted, surprised by a death squad armed with magic and visaged like the dead, roped and dragged from their horses. The next lucid interval Niko recalled was one of being propped against dense trees, tied to one while the Nisibisi witch used children's plights and spells and finally Janni's tortured drawn-out death to extract from him what little he knew of Tempus's intentions and Rankan strategies of defense for the lower land. "Was I wrong to try not to tell them?" Niko asked, eyes swollen half-shut but filled with hurt. "I thought they'd kill us all, whatever. Then I thought I could hold out . . . Tamzen and the other girls were past help . . . but Janni—" He shook his head. "Then they . . . thought I was lying, when I couldn't answer . . . questions they should have asked of *you*—Then I did lie, to please them, but she . . . the witch knew. . . ."

"Never mind. Was One-Thumb a party to this?"

A twitch of lips meant "no" or "I don't know."

Then Niko found the strength to add: "If I hadn't tried to keep my silence—I've been interrogated before by Nisibisi. . . . I hid in my rest-place . . . until Janni—They killed him to get to me."

Tempus saw bright tears threatening to spill and changed the subject: "Your rest-place? So your *maat* returned to you?"

He whispered, "After a fashion. . . . I don't care about that now. Going to need all my anger . . . no time for balance anymore."

Tempus blew out a breath and set down Niko's cup and looked between his legs at the packed clay floor. "I'm going north, tomorrow. I'll leave sortie assignments and schedules with Critias—he'll be in command here—and a rendezvous for those who want to join in the settling up. Did you recognize any Ilsigs in her company? A servant, a menial, anyone at all?"

"No, they all look alike. . . . Someone found us, got us to the gates. Some trainees of ours, maybe—they knew my name. The witch said come ahead and die upcountry. Each reprisal of ours, they'll match fourfold."

"Are you telling me not to go?"

Niko struggled to sit up, cursed, fell back with blood oozing from between his teeth. Tempus made no move to help him. They stared at each other until Stealth said, "It will seem that you've been driven from Sanctuary, that you've failed here. . . ."

"Let it seem so, it may well be true."

"Wait, then, until I can accompany—"

"You know better. I will leave instructions for you." He got up and left quickly, before his temper got the best of him where the boy could see.

The samaritan who had brought their wounded and their dead was waiting outside Tempus's quarters. His name was Vis and though he looked Nisibisi he claimed he had a message from Jubal. Because of his skin and his accent Tempus almost took him prisoner, thinking to give him to Straton, for whom all manner of men bared their souls, but he marshaled his anger and sent the young man away with a pocket full of soldats and instructions to convey Jubal's message to Critias. Crit would be in charge of the

Stepsons henceforth; what Jubal and Crit might arrange was up to them. The reward was for bringing home the casualties, dead and living, a favor cheap at the price.

Then Tempus went to find Jihan. When he did, he asked her to put him in touch with Aškelon, dream lord, if she could.

"So that you can punish yourself with mortality? This is not your fault."

"A kind, if unsound, opinion. Mortality will break the curse. Can you help me?"

"I will not, not now, when you are like this," she replied, concern knitting her brows in the harsh morning light. "But I will accompany you north. Perhaps another day, when you are calmer . . ."

He cursed her for acting like a woman and set about scheduling sorties and sketching maps, so that each of his men would have worked out his debt to Kadakithis and be in good standing with the mercenaries' guild when and if they joined him in Tyse, at the very foot of Wizardwall.

It took no longer to draft his resignation and Critias's appointment in his stead and send them off to Kadakithis than it took to clear his actions with the Rankan representatives of the mercenaries' guild: his task here of assessing Kadakithis for a Rankan faction desirous of a change in emperors was accomplished; he could honestly say that neither town nor townspeople nor effete prince was worth struggling to ennoble. For good measure he was willing to throw into the stewpot of disgust boiling in him both Vashanka and the child he had co-fathered with the god, by means of whom certain interests thought to hold him here: he disliked children, as a class, and even Vashanka had turned his back on this one.

Still, there were things he had to do. He went and found Crit in the guild hostel's common room and told him all that had transpired. If Crit had refused the appointment outright, Tempus would have had to tarry, but Critias only smiled cynically, saying that he'd be along with his best fighters as soon as matters here allowed. He left One-Thumb's case in Critias's hands; they both knew that Straton could determine the degree of the barkeep's complicity quickly enough.

Crit asked, as Tempus was leaving the dark and comforting common room for the last time, whether any children's bodies had been found—three girls and boys still were missing; one young corpse had turned up cold in Shambles Cross.

"No," Tempus said, and thought no more about it. "Life to you, Critias."

"And to you, Riddler. And everlasting glory."

Outside, Jihan was waiting on one Trôs horse, the other's reins in her hand.

They went first southwest to see if perhaps the witch or her agents might be found at home, but the manor house and its surrounds were deserted, the yard crisscrossed with cart-tracks from heavily laden wagons' wheels.

The caravan's track was easy to follow.

Riding north without a backward glance on his Trôs horse, Jihan swaying in her saddle on his right, he had one last impulse: he ripped the problematical Storm God's amulet from around his throat, dropped it into a quaggy marsh.

When he was sure he had successfully cast it aside, and the god's voice had not come ringing with awful laughter in his ear (for all gods are tricksters, and war gods worst of any), he relaxed in his saddle. The omens for this venture were good: they'd completed their preparations in half the time he'd anticipated, so that he could start it while the day was young.

— *12* —

Crit sat long at his customary table in the common room after Tempus had gone. By rights it should have been Straton or some Sacred Band pair who succeeded Tempus, someone . . . anyone but him. After a time he pulled out his pouch and emptied its contents onto the plank table: three tiny metal figures, a fishhook made from an eagle's claw and abalone shell, a single die, an old field decoration won in Azehur while the Slaughter Priest still led the original Sacred Band.

He scooped them up and threw them as a man might throw in wager: the little gold Storm God fell beneath the lead figurine of a fighter, propping the man upright; the fishhook embraced the die, which came to rest with one dot facing up—Strat's war name was Ace. The third figure, a silver rider mounted, sat square atop the field star—Abarsis had slipped it over his head so long ago the ribbon had crumbled away.

Content with the omens his private prognosticators gave, he collected them and put them away. He'd wanted Tempus to ask him to join him, not hand him fifty men's lives to yea or nay. He took such work too much to heart; it lay heavy on him, worse than the task force's weight had been, and he'd only just begun. But that was why Tempus picked him—he was conscientious to a fault.

He sighed and rose and quit the hostel, riding aimlessly through the fetid streets. Damned town was a pit, a buboe, a sore that wouldn't heal. He couldn't trust his task force to some subordinate, though how he was going to run them while stomping around vainly trying to fill Tempus's sandals, he couldn't say.

His horse, picking his route, took him by the Vulgar Unicorn where Staton would soon be "discussing sensitive matters" with One-Thumb.

By rights he should go up to the palace, pay a call on Kadakithis, "make nice" (as Straton said) to Vashanka's priest-of-record Molin, visit the Mageguild. . . . He shook his head and spat over his horse's shoulder. He hated politics.

And what Tempus had told him about Niko's misfortune and Janni's death still rankled. He remembered the foreign fighter Niko had made him turn loose—Vis. Vis, who'd come to Tempus, bearing hurt and slain, with a message from Jubal. That, and what Straton had gotten from the hawkmask they'd given Ischade, plus the vampire woman's own hints, allowed him to triangulate Jubal's position like a sailor navigating by the stars. Vis was supposed to come to him, though. He'd wait. If his hunch was right, he could put Jubal and his hawkmasks to work for Kadakithis without either knowing—or at least having to admit—that was the case.

If so, he'd be free to take the band north—what they wanted, expected, and would now fret to do with Tempus gone. Only Tempus's mystique had kept them this long; Crit would have a mutiny, or empty barracks, if he couldn't meet their expectation of war to come. They weren't baby sitters, slum police, or palace praetorians; they collected exploits, not soldats. He began to form a plan, shape up a scenario, answer questions sure to be asked him later, rehearsing replies in his mind.

Unguided, his horse led him slumward—a barnrat, it was taking the quickest, straightest way home. When he looked up and out, rather than down and in, he was almost through the Shambles, near White Foal Bridge and the vampire's house, quiet now, unprepossessing in the light of day. Did she sleep in the day? He didn't think she was that kind of vampire; there had been no bloodloss, no punctures on the boy stiff against the drop's back door when one of the street men found it. But what did she do, then, to her victims? He thought of Straton, the way he'd looked at the vampire, the exchange between the two he'd overheard and partly understood. He'd have to keep those two quite separate, even if Ischade was putatively willing to work with, rather than against, them. He spurred his horse on by.

Across the bridge, he rode southwest, skirting the thick of Downwind. When he sighted the Stepsons' barracks, he still didn't know if he could succeed in leading Stepsons. He rehearsed it wryly in his mind: "Life to all. Most of you don't know me but by reputation, but I'm here to ask you to bet your lives on me, not once, but as a matter of course over the next months. . . ."

Still, someone had to do it. And he'd have no trouble with the Sacred Band teams, who knew him in the old days, when he'd had a right-side partner, before that vulnerability was made painfully clear, and he gave up loving the death-seekers—or anything else which could disappoint him.

It mattered not a whit, he decided, if he won or if he lost, if they let him advise them or deserted post and duty to follow Tempus north, as he would have done if the sly old soldier hadn't bound him here with promise and responsibility.

He'd brought Niko's bow. The first thing he did—after leaving the stables, where he saw to his horse and checked on Niko's pregnant mare—was seek the wounded fighter.

The young officer peered at him through swollen, blackened eyes, saw the bow and nodded, unlaced its case and stroked the wood recurve when Critias laid it on the bed. Half a dozen men were there when he'd knocked and entered—three teams who'd come with Niko and his partner down to Ranke on Sacred Band business. They left, warning softly that Crit mustn't tire him—they'd just got him back.

"He's left me the command," Crit said, though he'd thought to talk of hawkmasks and death squads and Nisibisi—a witch and one named Vis.

"Gilgamesh sat by Enkidu seven days, until a maggot fell from his nose." It was the oldest legend the fighters shared, one from Enlil's time when the Lord Storm and Enki (Lord Earth) ruled the world, and a fighter and his friend roamed far.

Crit shrugged and ran a spread hand through feathery hair. "Enkidu was dead; you're not. Tempus has just gone ahead to prepare our way."

Niko rolled his head, propped against the whitewashed wall, until he could see Crit clearly: "He followed godsign; I know that look."

"Or witchsign." Crit squinted, though the light was good, three windows wide and afternoon sun raying the room. "Are you all right—beyond the obvious, I mean?"

"I lost two partners, too close in time. I'll mend."

Let's hope, Crit thought but didn't say, watching Niko's expressionless eyes. "I saw to your mare."

"My thanks. And for the bow. Janni's bier is set for morning. Will you help me with it? Say the words?"

Crit rose; the operator in him still couldn't bear to officiate in public, yet if he didn't, he'd never hold these men. "With pleasure. Life to you, Stepson."

"And to you, commander."

And that was that. His first test, passed; Niko and Tempus had shared a special bond.

That night, he called them out behind the barracks, ordering a feast to be served on the training field, a wooden amphitheater of sorts. By then Straton had come out to join him, and Strat wasn't bashful with the mess staff or the hired help.

Maybe it would work out; maybe together they could make half a Tempus, which was the least this endeavor needed, though Crit would never pair again . . .

He put it to them when all were well disposed from wine and roasted pig and lamb, standing and flatly telling them Tempus had left, putting them in his charge. There fell a silence and in it he could hear his heart pound. He'd been calmer ringed with Tyse hillmen, or alone, his partner slain, against a Rankan squadron.

"Now, we've got each other, and for good and fair, I say to you, the quicker we quit this cesspool for the clean air of high peaks war, the happier I'll be."

He could hardly see their faces in the dark with the torches snapping right before his face. But it didn't matter; they had to see him, not he them. Crit heard a raucous growl from fifty throats become assent, and then a cheer and laughter, and Strat, beside and off a bit, gave him a soldier's sign: all's well.

He raised a hand, and they fell quiet; it was a power he'd never tried before: "But the only way to leave with honor is to work your tours out." They grumbled. He continued: "The Riddler's left busy-work sorties enough—hazardous duty actions, by guild book rules; I'll post a list—that we can work off our debt to Kittycat in a month or so."

Someone nay'd that. Someone else called: "Let him finish, then we'll have our say."

"It means naught to me, who deserts to follow. But to *us*, to cadre honor, it's a slur. So I've thought about it, since I'm not to leave myself, and here's what I propose. All stay, or go. You take your vote. I'll wait. But Tempus wants no man on his right at Wizardwall who hasn't left in good standing with the guild."

When they'd voted, with Straton overseeing the

count, to abide by the rules they'd lived to enforce, he said honestly that he was glad about the choice they'd made. "Now I'm going to split you into units, and each unit has a choice: find a person, a mercenary not among us now, a warm body trained enough to hold a sword and fill your bed, and call him 'brother'—long enough to induct him in your stead. Then we'll leave the town yet guarded by 'Stepsons' and that name's enough, with what we've done here, to keep the peace. The guild has provisions for man-steading; we'll collect from each to fill a pot to hire them; they'll billet here, and we'll ride north a unit at a time and meet up in Tyse, next high moon, and surprise the Riddler."

So he put it to them, and so they agreed.

BLOOD AND HONOR

"No more," Niko gasped when the palm closed upon itself.

And as if his words were commands, the palm descended, the fingers uncurled, and a mere hand lay limply in the Bandaran master's lap.

"As you wish, Nikodemos. I think we've done enough. It remains to see whether we've done it soon enough."

Niko wanted to smash the ancient one against the rocks by his stream. He wanted to pummel the old man into stringy meat. He wanted to eradicate this creature who played with his soul and knew his innermost shame. All his tortures at the hands of the witch; Janni's death; his ignominy—these should not be brought back whole to Bandara.

It was one thing to tell your exploits into the record. It was another for the record to contain your every move, all that was forgettable, every fearful thought and bargain made with extremity.

"I survive," he said defiantly. "I survived it all and I'll survive the rest of it. Without your help. Without your prying. I want no more of this and I want you to promise you'll never call up these ghosts again."

Ghosts. So many of them. Ghosts that followed him everywhere. Ghosts that wanted rest; ghosts that could never find it.

He'd put the ghosts of Tamzen and her friends to rest, finally. The ghost of Janni couldn't rest, and had found a way to return to some sort of life, to hunt and haunt and claim a semblance of vengeance, if not peace.

Later he'd laid countless unknown ghosts to rest, once he'd met Tempus at the foot of Wizardwall, and stood shoulder to shoulder with the Riddler against the maw of Hell itself.

Stood against Aškelon, lord of dreams, who (if these adepts could be believed) pursued him still.

The adept before him shifted, and got slowly to his feet. "I'll leave you now, Nikodemos, to think on what you've seen. And what you've learned. I hope it will be enough."

"Enough?" Niko rose too. Over the shoulder of the Bandaran master, still far across the meadow, he could see a shape skulking. He knew what it meant. He didn't want the adept to see it. Niko had already learned something from what had happened to him here: he could fight his battles on his own. He always had. He always could.

The adept moved off, in the opposite direction from the motion Niko could see only as a flicker, and Niko followed, turning his back on an uninvited guest. His mind said, *Seek me in the real world, if you must seek me.*

And something answered, deep inside his head: "As you wish."

None of this the adept heard, or seemed to hear, for he was walking away and with every step his form was becoming less substantial. Pacing him, Niko said only, "Back at the cabin, then?" Not thanks or any ritual phrases. For this intrusion, no thanks were necessary. For such teaching, the student does not thank the instructor, only himself.

Turning on his heel as he become just grainy dust and then a lingering, disembodied smile, the adept said, "Fare well, Niko. For all our sakes, fare well." And disappeared.

In Niko's cabin, on his pallet, his body was tingling as if he'd been too long in the summer sun.

Every muscle felt rubbery and yet refreshed. His breathing was deep and slow, and the air his lungs took in was full of nourishment.

Coming out of so long a trance, oft-repeated formulae took over. He told himself that when he woke he would be totally refreshed, and remember everything valuable that had transpired. He told himself that he would be stronger, quicker in body and mind, than he had been before he ventured to his rest-place. He told himself that only good would come of what he'd learned there.

Then he counted to three, opened his eyes, and sat up abruptly.

There before him, nothing had changed except shadows. These had grown shorter, then long again, as he and the adept had labored. The sun, outside his cabin's window, was setting. The air smelled of dusk and night-blooming flowers, and carried the sounds of nocturnal insects.

For an instant he thought he was alone, that the adept had disappeared. But then he heard the old man's voice wispy and somehow weaker than it had been in his rest-place.

And saw the old one clearly, where he had not seen the man before. Still in a cross-legged position, the adept said: "Niko, my legs have fallen to sleep. Can you help me?"

It was a touch the teacher was asking for—not Death Touch, but Life Touch. Niko had not used such a touch since his early training. But he did now. He swung his own legs off his pallet and knelt before the old man. He held his own palm out, toward the other's body, and slowly extended it until he felt heat, and a current, a tide as if he had touched the sea.

He let his mind go blank, then, and allowed his hand to be drawn to the place of affliction. As he did this, the heat became stronger, and the sense of moving currents more intense. His palm massaged the currents, and then stopped.

He had found a "still" spot, one where the currents were not flowing properly. Slowly he let his hand rub along the air, perhaps six inches from the afflicted area, until the sense of a cohesive tide returned to this still spot, and then his palm moved on, massaging gently, though never touching the patient.

Finally, his hand was drawn as if by a lodestone to the instructor's right knee, where it touched the flesh, and Niko's tongue murmured, "Let the affliction be gone."

He knew that it was, by the way the flesh cooled under his hand, before the adept nodded as if nothing unusual had happened, said, "Thank you, Nikodemos," and rose lithely to his feet.

Niko rose also. "What now? Are you not going to explain all this to me—what you did?"

"What *you* did, my son," said the adept. "No. The weapons are there—those of perception, those of realization. The choices to come are yours. Your guest will come to Ennina. We pray you will let him venture no farther into Bandara. There will be a cost. The choice is yours. Choose well." The adept held out his hand and Nikodemos took it, shook it, let it drop.

Without another word, the teacher left, moving down the circuitous path into the dusk and out of sight. He seemed again to float, in no way slowed in his progress by the difficult path along the cliffside. The dusk swallowed him and Niko was again alone.

Niko went, not back into the cabin, but to a small overhanging jut of rock. And there he sat, swinging his legs over the air and the drop to the sea, looking out to the horizon long after darkness fell.

Thus he was there to see the barque with its dolphin prow and its gilded lions materialize in the inner harbor, where Ennina meets the sea.

When the figure came up the path, Niko knew its identity before he heard its tread. His maat was restless and his mind had gone questing.

At first he was afraid but then he remembered all the adept had shown him: fears he had withstood; doubts over which he'd triumphed; losses he had sustained. And he remembered how it had felt to look upon the world as Tempus did, and even as the dark lord who approached did.

Sadness preceded Aškelon of Meridian up the cliffside like a west wind. When he was fifteen feet behind Niko, who still sat with his legs dangling over the cliffside, the dream lord said, "Nikodemos, I have come to strike a bargain with you."

Niko didn't turn; he didn't hesitate. He said, "Hello, Ash," the way Tempus might have. "I sensed you in my rest-place. Thank you for coming in person. I don't want you there. Here . . . it's only the Bandaran adepts who fear you. Go no farther than this cabin, and you and I have no quarrel."

"Agreed," said Aškelon as casually as if they'd decided upon suitable fare for dinner. And came to sit beside him, on the rock jutting out over the sea. "Are you not curious as to what I want of you?"

"Your name venerated, your intentions understood—as you wanted before, I assume. I failed you once, trying to be what I'm not. I'm just a fighter. I haven't more in my heart."

"That's all any of us are, Niko; each in his own way. I want to teach you—what these cannot teach you."

"I am teaching myself, now," said the Sacred Bander.

"Here. In the World, you will need help."

"In the World, there is Tempus. And the Stormgods to whom all fighters are sworn." Niko turned slightly, enough to see the glint of ageless eyes and the infinite hollows of Aškelon's cheeks. His gray-starred hair blew in a gentle breeze.

"Adventurer," Aškelon said softly, "accept my patronage. I can help you in your quest. Tempus's sister Cime has left my domain—her year is up. She is free upon the earth. For his sake, accept the help of one who loves you both."

Niko had thought that, if Ash pulled any tricks to ensnare him, he would simply throw himself into the sea. A quick trip to heaven wasn't the worst way out. There Abarsis waited to escort him, and his first partner would be glad to see him. It was his soul's freedom that was in question. And that question was whether freedom was worth the price when it meant shirking the responsibilities of honor. "Do you think, Ash, that there is such a thing as personal freedom when some men remain unfree?"

Now he turned accusatory eyes on the dream lord, whom Cime had almost destroyed for the wrong reason. And there he saw no malignancy, no treachery, no horror. But he saw clearly, even in darkness, through the gift of maat.

Aškelon wanted for the World what the best in the

World wanted, and what the worst in the World would always fight to destroy. Aškelon was not asking for worship from Niko, as the gods did, but only for a student.

And this time, on the heels of all he'd faced in his rest-place, Niko was not afraid to learn.

But when, after hours of talk and tutoring, Aškelon returned to the unanswered question Niko had asked him, that question about freedom that still hung between them, Niko's blood ran cold.

"You asked me," Ash reminded him with a voice like a sharp blade on velvet, "whether there could be personal freedom when some men remain unfree. And what answer there is to that resides in your own memories. Are you ready to seek it?"

"I . . ." *I don't know*, he wanted to say. "Yes," he said. He squared his shoulders; he flexed his aching knees, so long folded into his cross-legged squat. He looked into the tidal eyes for Aškelon and said, "Bring it on, dream lord. Do your best—or your worst. I came here to make an end to the hiding, to the running. There's nothing in my memories I'm afraid of."

But there was, and both of them knew that. There was the witch who'd loved him—there was Roxane.

And he knew even before Aškelon reached over to grasp his hand what form this lesson would take. There were no memories within him he shunned like those of the Nisibisi witch. Therefore, the answers of which Aškelon spoke resided within those recollections.

The dream lord had Niko's right hand in his. He was sitting across from the student so close their knees nearly brushed. He said, "Niko, I will lift your hand and drop it in your lap. Each time I do so, you will reach a deeper level of relaxation. I will do this ten times. The tenth time I drop your hand, you will be completely relaxed. You will listen only to my voice and see what I must show you . . ."

Even as the dream lord droned on, he was gently dropping Niko's unresisting hand and the outside world, full of night sounds and sea smells, was fading . . .

HELL TO PAY

At night, down in Sanctuary on a perpetually dank street called Mageway, in a tower of the citadel of magic, Randal the Tysian Hazard woke in his Mage-guild bed, strangling in his own sheets.

The slight mage went pale beneath his freckles—pale to his prodigious ears, as the sheets, pure and innocent linen as far as anyone knew, bound him tighter. If he ever got out of this alive, he'd have to have a talk with his treacherous bedclothes—they had no right to treat him this way. Had his mouth not been stopped by their grasp, he could have shouted counterspells or cursed his inanimate bedclothes, come alive. But Randal's mouth, as well as his hands and feet, was bound by hostile magic.

His eyes, alas, were not. Randal stared into a darkness which lightened perceptibly before the bed on which he struggled, helpless, as the Nisibisi witch Roxane coalesced from nimbus, a sensuous smile upon her face.

Roxane the Nisibisi witch was Randal's nemesis, a hated enemy, a worrisome foe.

The young mage writhed within the person of his

sheets and wordless exhortations came from his gagged mouth. Roxane, whom he'd fought on Wizardwall, had sworn to kill him—not just for what he'd done to help Tempus's Stepsons and Bashir's guerrilla fighters reclaim their homeland, Wizardwall, from Nisibisi wizards, but because Randal had once been the rightside partner of Stealth.

Sweating freely, Randal tried to wriggle off his mageguild bed as Roxane's form lost its wraithlike quality and became palpably present. He succeeded only in banging his head against the wall, and cowered there, wishing this particular witch couldn't slit mageguild wards like butter, wishing he'd never fought with Stepsons or claimed a Nisi warlock's globe of power, wishing he'd never heard of Nikodemos or inherited Niko's panoply, armor forged by the entelechy of dream.

"Umn hmn, nnh nohnu, rrgorhrrr!" Randal shouted at the witch who now had human form, even down to perfumed flesh whose scent mixed with his own acrid, fearful sweat: *Go away, you horror, evermore!*

Roxane only laughed, a tinkling laugh, not horrid, and minced over to his bedside with exaggerated care: "Say you what, little mageling? Say again?" She leaned close, smiling broadly, her lovely sanguine face no older than a marriageable girl's. Her fearsome faith, behind those eyes which supped on fear and now were feasting on Randal's anguish, was older than the mageguild in which she stood—stood against reason, against nature, against the best magic Rankantrained adepts and even Randal, who'd learned Nisi ways to counter the warring warlocks from the high peaks, could field.

"Whhd whd drr whdd? Whr hheh?" Randal said from behind his sopping, choking gag of sheets: *What do you want? Why me?*

And the Nisibisi witch stretched elegantly, leaned close, and answered. "Want? Why, Witchy-Ears, your soul, of course. Now, now, don't thrash around so. Don't waste your strength, such as it is. You've got 'til winter's shortest day to anticipate its loss. Unless, of course . . ." The luminous eyes that had been the last sight of too many great adepts and doomed warriors came close to his, and widened. "Unless you can prevail on Stealth, called Nikodemos, to help you save it. But then, we both know it's not likely he'd put his person in jeopardy for yours. . . . Sacred Band oath or not, Niko's left you, deserted you as he's deserted me. Isn't that so, little maladroit nonadept? Or do you think honor and glory and an abrogated bond could bring your one-time partner down to Sanctuary to save you from a long and painful stint as one of my . . . servants?" Teeth gleamed above Randal in the dark, as all of Roxane's manifestation gleamed with an unholy and inhuman light.

The Tysian Hazard-class adept lay unmoving, listening to his breathing rasp—unwilling to answer, to hope, or to even long for Niko's presence. For that was what the witch wanted, he finally realized. Not his magic globe of power, bound with the most deadly protections years of fighting Roxane's kind had taught mages of lesser power to devise; not the Aškelonian panoply without which, should he somehow survive this evening, Randal would never sleep again because that panoply was protection against such magics as Roxane's sort could weave about a simple Hazard-class enchanter. Not any of these did the witch crave, but Niko—Niko back in Sanctuary, in the flesh.

And Randal, who loved Niko better than he loved himself, who revered Niko in his heart with all the loyalty a rightman was sworn to give his left-side

leader even though Niko had formally dissolved their
pairbond long before, would gladly have given up his
soul to Roxane right then and there to prevent a call
going out on ethereal waves to summon Niko into
Roxane's foul embrace.

He would have, if his mind had been able to
control his fear. But it could not: Roxane was fear's
drover, mistress of terror, the very fount from which
the death squads plaguing Sanctuary sprang.

She began to make arcane and convoluted passes
with her red-nailed hands over Randal's immobi-
lized body and Randal began to quake. His mouth
dried up, his heart beat fast, his pulse sought to rip
right through his throat. Panicked, he lost all sense
of logic; unable to think, his mind was hers to mold
and to command.

As she wove her web of terror, Randal's mage's
talent screamed silently for help.

It screamed so well and so loudly, with every atom
of his imperiled being, that far away to the West, in
his cabin before a pool of gravel neatly raked, high
on a cliffside overlooking the misty seascape of the
Bandaran Islands' chain, Nikodemos paused in his
meditation and rubbed gooseflesh rising suddenly on
his arms.

And rose, and sought the cliffside, and stared out
to sea awhile before he bent, picked up a fist-sized
stone, and cast it into the waves before he began
making preparations to leave—to forsake his mystical
retreat once more for the World, and for the World's
buttocks, the town called Sanctuary, where of all places
in the Rankan Empire Niko, follower of *maat*—the
mystery of Balance and Transcendent Perception—
and son of the armies, least wanted to go.

Even for Niko's sable stallion, the trek from Bandara
to Sanctuary had been long and hard. Not as long or

hard as it would have been for Niko on a lesser horse, but long enough and hard enough that when Niko arrived in town, bearded and white with trail dirt, he checked into the mercenaries' guild north of the Palace and went immediately to sleep.

When he woke, he washed his face with water from an ice-crusted bedside pot, scratched his two-month's growth of beard and decided not to shave it, then went down to the common room to eat and get a brief.

The guild hostel's common room was unchanged—wine-dark even in morning, quiet all and every day. On its sideboard stood steaming bowls of mulled wine and goat's blood and, beside, cheese and barley and nuts for men who needed possets in the morning to brace them for hard work to come.

These days, in Sanctuary, the mercs were eating better—a function, Niko determined from the talk around him as he filled a bowl, of their new regard and esteem in a town coming apart at its seams, a town where personal protection was a commodity at an all–time high. There was lamb on the sideboard this morning, a whole pig with an apple in its mouth, and fish stuffed with savory. It hadn't been this way when last Niko'd worked here—then the mercs were tolerated, but not sent goodies from the palace and from the fisherfolk or from the merchants.

It hadn't been this way, before. . . . He ate his fill and got his brief from the dispatching agent, who sketched a map of faction lines which divided up the town.

"Look here, Stealth, I'll only tell you once," the dispatching agent said intently. "The Green Line runs along Palace Park; above it are your patrons—the Palace types, the merchant class, and the Beysibs . . . don't tell me what you think of that. The Maze's surrounded by Jubal's Blue Line, you'll need this pass to get in there." The dispatcher, who'd lost one eye before Niko had ever set foot in Sanctuary, pulled an armband from his hip pocket and handed it to Niko.

The band was sewn from parallel strips of colored cloth: green, red, black, blue, and yellow. Niko fingered it, said, "Fine, just don't call me Stealth in here—or anywhere. I need to sniff around before I make my presence known," and tied it on his upper arm before he looked questioningly at the dispatcher.

The old soldier in patched off-duty gear said, "You're on call to the Green Liners, remember, no matter what name you choose. The red's for the Blood Line: that's Zip's PFLS—Popular Front for the Liberation of Sanctuary. Third Commando's backing that lot, so unless you've friends there, be careful in Ratfall, and in all of Downwind—that's their turf. The Blue Line follows the White Foal—those two witches down there, Ischade and the Nisibisi witch-bitch, have death squads to enforce their will, and Shambles Cross is theirs. The Black Line's round the Mageguild— the quays and harbors, down to the sea; the Yellow Line, your own Stepsons threw up out west of Downwind and Shambles. You need any help, son, take my name in vain."

Niko nodded, said, "My thanks, sir. Life to you, and—"

"Your commander? Tempus? Will he follow? Is he here?" The eagerness in the dispatcher's voice gave Niko pause. Stealth's caution must have showed in his face, for the rough-hewn, one-eyed merc continued: "Strat's reclaimed the barracks for the Stepsons, but it was bloodier than a weekend pass to Hell. We'd like to see the Riddler—nobody lesser's going to straighten this season's mess out."

"Maybe," Niko said carefully, "after the weather breaks—it's snow to your horse's belly upcountry by now." He wasn't empowered to say more. But he could ask his own question now. "And Randal? The Tysian Hazard that came downcountry with the advance force? Seen him?"

"Randal?" The bristling jaw worked and Niko knew that he wasn't going to like what he was about to hear. "Strat was asking for him, three, four times. Seems he was spirited right out of the Mageguild—or left on his own. You never know with wizards, do ya, son? I mean, maybe he up and left. It was right after the sack of Jubal's old—of the Stepsons' barracks, and it was so bad Strat took to sleeping here until they got the place cleaned up."

"Randal wouldn't have left willingly," Niko said under his breath, rising to his feet.

"What's that, soldier?"

"Nothing. Thanks for the work—and the advance." The mercenary, who was nearing thirty but looked younger, even with a beard to point up hard-won scars, patted the purse hanging from his swordbelt. "I'll see you after a while."

Stealth needed to get out of there, ride perimeters, make sense of the worsened Chaos in a town which had been as bad, last time he'd been here, as Niko would have thought a town could be.

And that got him to thinking, as he tacked up his horse and led it snorting into the sulky air of a late dawn only a week shy of the year's shortest day, about the last tour he'd done here.

Two winters ago, the man he'd partnered with for better than a decade had been killed here. It had hurt like nothing since his childhood servitude on Wizardwall had hurt; it had happened down on Wideway, in a wharfside warehouse. Return to Sanctuary was bringing back too many memories, unlaid ghosts and hidden pain. The following spring he'd lost his second partner to the Nisibisi witch, Roxane, Death's Queen. He'd left then, quit Sanctuary for cleaner wars, he'd thought, up north.

In the north he'd found the wars no cleaner—he'd fought Datan, lord archmage of Wizardwall and Roxane on Tyse's slopes and up on the high peaks where he'd spent his youth as one of the fierce guerrillas called Successors, led now by his boyhood friend, Bashir. Then Niko had fought beside Bashir and Tempus, his commander, against the Mygdonians, venturing beyond Wizardwall to see what no man could see—Mygdonian might allied with renegade magic so that all the defenders Tempus arrayed against them were, by default, pawns in a war of magic against the gods.

After that campaign, he'd taken part in the change of Emperors that occurred during the Festival of Man and then, tired to his bones of war and restless in his spirit and his heart, he'd taken a youth—a refugee child half Mygdonian and half a wizard—far west to the Bandaran isles of mist and mysticism where Niko himself had learned to rever the elder gods and the elder wisdoms of the secular adepts, who saw gods in men and men in gods and had no truck with such young and warring dieties as Ilsigi and Rankan alike brought alive with prayers and sacrifice.

Yet all the blood he'd spilled and honors he'd won and tears he'd shed, far from Sanctuary, fell away from him as soon as he'd saddled his sable stallion in the stable behind the mercenaries' guildhall and gone venturing in the town. For there was one thread of continuity, one sameness Niko's *maat* sensed in Sanctuary that had been with him since last he'd served here as one of Tempus's Stepsons and—with the exception of his time in far Bandara—had been with him ever since as it was with him still: Roxane, the Nisibisi witch.

Silding through the upscale crowd in the Alekeep to find the owner, who had a right to know that his daughter's shade had finally been put to rest by his own hand, the fighter Stealth, called Nikodemus, was suddenly so aware of Roxane that he fancied he could smell her musk upon the beerhall's air.

She was here, somewhere. Close at hand. His *maat* told him so—he could glimpse the cobalt-shining trails of Roxane's magic out of the corner of his inner eye. Just as some lesser man might glimpse a stalker's shadow in his peripheral vision, Niko's soul had its own peripheral vision in the discipline of trancendent perception, a skill which let him track a person or sense a presence or gather the gist of emotions aimed his way, though he could not eavesdrop on specific thoughts.

The Alekeep was freshly whitewashed and full of determined revelers, men and women whose position in the town demanded that they show themselves at business as usual, undisturbed by PFLS rebels or Beysib interlopers or Nisibisi wizardry. Here Rankan mageguild functionaries in robes that made them look like badly-set tables hobnobbed with caravanners and Palace heirophants all intent on the same end: safety for their business transactions from the interference of warring factions; safety for their persons and their kin from undeads and less numinous terrorists; safety—it was the most sought after commodity in Sanctuary these days.

Safety, so far as Niko was concerned whenever he came out of Bandara into the World, was beside the point. In his cabin on its cliff he could be safe, but then his gifts of *maat* and his deep perceptions were turned inward, useful only to the student, not, as they were meant, carried by him abroad in the World to turn a fate or two or stem a tide gone too far in any one direction.

Maat forced its bearer out, among its opposite, Chaos, to set whatever imbalances he could to rights. It always hurt, it always cost, and he always longed for Bandara when his strength was spent. But, when he was home, he always grew restless, strong and able, and so he'd come out again, even into Sanctuary, where Balance was just an abstract, where everything was always wrong, and where nothing any man—or even demigod like Niko's commander Tempus—could do would bring even an intimation of lasting peace.

But peace, Niko's teacher had said, was death. He would have it by and by.

The witch, Roxane, was death, also. He hoped she couldn't sense him as clearly as he could her. Though he'd been at pains to keep his visit here a secret from those who'd use him if they could, Niko was drawn to Roxane like a Sanctuary whore to a well-heeled drunk or, if rumor could be believed, like Prince Kadakithis to the Beysib Shupansea.

Not even Bandara's gravel ponds or deep seaside meditation had cleansed his soul of its longing for the flesh of the witch who loved him.

He'd come down again to Sanctuary in answer to Randal's involuntary summons. But now that he was here, it was Roxane he'd come to see. And touch. And talk to.

For Niko had to exorcise her, take her talons from his soul, cleanse his heart of her. He'd admitted it to himself this season in Bandara. At least that was a start. The lore of his mystery whispered that any problem, named and known, was soluable. But since the name of Niko's problem was Roxane, Stealth wasn't sure that it was so.

Thus, he must confront her. Here, somewhere. Make her let him go.

But he didn't find her in the Alekeep, just a fat old man with a wispy pate who'd aged too much in the passing seasons, who had a winter in his eyes with more bite to it than any Sanctuary ever blew in off the endless sea.

The old man, when Niko told him of his daughter's fate, simply nodded, chin on fist, and said to Niko, "You did your best, son. As we're all doing now. It seems so long ago, and we've such troubles here. . . ." He paused, and sighed a quavery sigh, and wiped red eyes with his sleeve then, so Niko knew that the father's hurt was still fresh and sharp.

Niko got up from the marble table where he'd found the father, alone with the night's receipts, and looked down: "If there's ever anything I can do, sir—anything at all. I'm at the mercenaries' guild-hall, will be for a week or two."

The old barkeep blew his nose on the leather of his chiton's hem, then craned his neck: "Do? Leave my other daughters be, is all."

Niko held the barkeep's feisty gaze until the man relented. "Sorry, son. We all know none's to blame for undeads but their makers. Luck go with you, Stealth. What is it your brothers of the sword say? Ah, I've got it: Life to you, and everlasting glory." There was too much bitterness in the father's voice for Niko to have misunderstood what remained unsaid.

But he had to ask. "Sir, I need a favor—don't call me that here, or anywhere. Tell no one I'm in town. I came to you only because . . . I had to. For Tamzen's sake." That was the first time either man had used the name of the girl who'd been daughter to the elder and lover to the younger, a girl now safe and peacefully dead, who hadn't been for far too long while Roxane had made use of her, and other children she'd added to her crew of zombies, children now buried on the slopes of Wizardwall.

He got out of there as soon as the old man shielded his eyes with his hand and muttered something like assent. He shouldn't have come. It had done the Alekeep's owner harm, not good. But he'd had to do it, for himself. Because the girl had been used by the witch against him, because he'd had to kill a child to save a childish soul. He wondered whether he'd expected the old man to absolve him, as if anyone could. Then he wondered where he'd go as he stepped out into the Green Zone streets and saw torches flaring Mazeward—tiny at this distance, but a warning that there was trouble in the lower quarter of the town.

Niko didn't want to mix in any of Sanctuary's internecine disputes, to be recruited by any side— even Strat's—or even know specifics of who was right and wrong. Probably everyone was equally culpable and innocent; wars had a way of blotting out absolutes; and civil wars, or wars of liberation, were the worst.

He wandered better streets, his hand upon his scabbard, until he came to an intersection where a corner estate had an open gate and, beyond, a beggar was crouched. A beggar this far uptown was unlikely.

Niko was just about to turn away, reminding himself that he was no longer policing Sanctuary as a Stepson on covert business, but here on his own recognizance, when he heard a voice he thought he knew.

"*Seh,*" said a shadow separating itself out from shadows across from where the beggar sat. The curse was Nisi; the voice was, too.

He stepped closer and the shadows became two, and they were arguing as they came abreast of the beggar, who stood right up and demanded where they'd been so long.

"He's drunk, can't you see?" said the first voice and Niko's gift gave him a different kind of light to place the face and find the name he'd known long since.

The first speaker was a Nisi renegade named Vis, a man who owed Niko at least one favor, and might know the answer to the question Niko most wanted to ask: the whereabouts of the Nisibisi witch.

The second shadow spoke, as the drunken beggar clawed at its clothes and Niko's sight grew sharper, showing him bluish sparks swirling round the taller of the two shadows solidifying despite the moonless dark. "Mor-am, you idiot! Get up! What's Moria going to say? Fool, and worse! There's death out here. Don't get too cocky . . ." The rest was a hostile hiss from a lowered voice, but Niko had placed this man easier than the first: the deeply accented voice, the velvet tones, had made him know the other speaker was an ex-slave named Haught.

This Haught was a freedman. The witch Ischade had freed him. And Niko had saved him from interrogation, long ago, at Straton's hands. Strat, the Stepsons' chief inquisitor, was no man to cross and one who was so good at what he did that his mere reputation loosened tongues and bowels.

So it was not that these were strangers, or even that they picked the beggar up between them and carried him toward the open gate beyond which lights blazed in skin-covered windows, that gave Niko pause. It was that Haught, who'd been little more than a frightened whelp, the slave's collar bound round his very soul, when last Niko had chanced across him, was giving orders with assurance and had, by the way his aura glittered blue, magical attributes to back him up.

There was nothing magical about Vis's aura, just the red and pink of distress and passion held in check—and fear, the spice of it tingling Niko's nerves as he moved to intercept them at the gate, sword drawn and warming as it always did when in proximity to magic.

"Vis, he's got a weap—"

"Remember me, puds?" Niko said, halting all three in a practiced interception. "Don't move; I just want to talk."

Vis's hand was on his hip and a naked blade would surely follow; Niko let his attention dwell on Vis, though Haught ought to have been his first concern.

And yet Haught didn't push the beggar (moaning, "Whaddya mean, Haught, 's nothin' wrong with a little fresh air . . .") at Niko or cast a spell, just said, "Years ago—the northern fighter, isn't it? Oh yes, I remember you. And so does someone else, I'd bet—"

Vis—too taut, planning something—interrupted: "What is it, soldier? Money? We'll give you money. And work for an idle blade if . . . Remember you?" Vis took a step forward and Niko felt, rather than saw, eyes narrow: "Right, that's right. I know who you are. We owe you one, is that it? For saving us from Tempus's covert actors downtown. Well, come on in. We'll talk about it indoors."

"If," Haught put in on that silken tongue that made Niko wonder what he might be walking into, "you'll sheath that blade and treat our invitation as what it is . . . a luxury. If you want to fight, we'll not be using bronze or steel in any case."

Niko looked between the two, still holding up their beggar friend, and sheathed his blade. "I don't want your hospitality, just some information. I'm looking for Roxane—and don't tell me you don't know who I mean."

It was Haught's laughter that made Niko know he'd found more than he'd bargained for: it sent chills screeching up and down his spine, so self-assured it was and so full of taunt and anticipation. "Of course I know—me and *my* mistress, both know. But don't you think, fighter, that by now Roxane's looking for you? Come in, don't come, wait here, go your way—whatever choice, she'll find you."

My mistress, Haught had said. Someone else, then, had taught him what Niko saw there—enough magic for it to be an attribute, not an affectation; real magic, not the prestidigitator's tricks that abounded in Sanctuary's Mageguild, gone from second to third rate since Cime's depredations.

Niko shook his head and his hand of its own accord found his sword's pommel and rested there as he retreated a pace.

By then Vis was saying, "It's not a thing I'd seek, soldier, were I you. But we'll give you what we can to help you on your way to her. Yes, by all that's unholy, we'll surely give you that."

When Roxane, in her Foalside haunt, an old manor house refurbished from velvet hangings to weeds head-high in her "garden" heard a footstep belonging not to an undead or to one of her snakes dressed in human form outside her window, she went personally to see who her uninvited guest might be.

It was a Nisi type, a youth she'd never noticed, some local denizen with a trace of Nisibisi blood.

His soul was smooth and unctuous over customary evil; he was some familiar of another power here. He said, far back in the dark with wards springing up between them: "I've brought you something, Madame. You're going to like him. A gift from Haught, in case things go your way in the end."

Then there was a soft "pop" and the presence was gone, if it had ever been there. Haught. She'd remember.

Just as she was turning, a pebble skittered, a soft whicker cut the night. She blinked—twice in one night, her best wards violated, slit like cobwebs? She'd have to make the rounds tomorrow, set up new protections.

And then she concentrated on what was there: a horse, for certain; and a person on it, a person drugged and tied to its saddle.

A present from this Haught. She'd have to thank him. She went out into her garden of thornbush and nightshade, down to where the water mandrake threw poisonous tubers high along the White Foal's edge.

And there, in the luminous spill from the polluted river's waves, she glimpsed him.

Niko, drugged to a stupor, or drunk—the same.

Her heart wrenched, she ran three steps, then calmed herself. He was here but not of his own will.

Fingers working a soft and silken spell she half-danced toward him. Niko was her beloved sole decency in her universe of wickedness, and yet her undoing lay within him. Seeing him was more the proof: she wanted to take him, cut his bonds away, heal him and caress him. Not the proper reaction for a witch. Not the proper motivation for Death's Queen. She'd sent for him, used Randal the mageling to lure him, but she dared not take him now, not use him thus. Not when this Haught was obviously tempting her.

Not when Roxane had a war on her hands, a war of power with the necromant Ischade, a creature of night who might just have orchestrated this untimely meeting.

So, while Niko, bent over his horse's neck, slept on, she came up to the horse, which flattened its ears but did not move away, cut the bonds that held the fighter to his saddle, and said, before sending him away: "Not now, my love. Not yet. Your partner Janni, your beloved Sacred Band brother, is the thrall of the necromant Ischade—he lies in unpeaceful earth, is rousted out to do her foul bidding and wear her awful collar at night. You must free him from unnatural servitude, beloved, and then we will be together. Do you understand me, Niko?"

Niko's ashen head raised and he opened his eyes— eyes still asleep, yet registering all they saw. Roxane's heart leaped; she loved the touch of his gaze, the feel of his breath, the smell of his suffering.

Her fingers spelled his fate: he would remember this moment as a true dream—a dream that, his *maat* would understand, bore all he needed to know.

She stepped forward and kissed him, and a moan escaped his lips. It was hardly more than a sigh, but enough of a sign to Roxane, who could read his heart, that Niko had come to her at last—of his own free will, to the extent that free will was possessed by mere men.

"Go to Ischade. Free Janni's spirit. Then get you both here to me, and I shall succor you."

She touched his forehead and he sat up straight. His free hands reined the horse around and he rode away—ensorceled, knowing and yet unknowing, back to his hostel where he could sleep undisturbed.

And tomorrow, he would do evil unto evil for her sake, and then, as he had never truly been, Nikodemos would be hers.

In the meantime, Roxane had preparations to make. She quit the Foalside, went inside, and looked in upon the Hazard Randal. Her prisoner was playing cards with her two snakes—snakes which she'd given human form to guard him. Or sort of human form— their eyes were still ophidian, their mouths lipless, their skin bore an ineradicable cast of green.

The mage, his torso bound to his chair with blue pythons of power, had both hands free and just enough free will left to give her a friendly wave: she had him tranquilized, waiting out the time until his death day—the week's end, come Ilsday, if Niko did not return by then.

A little saddened at the realization that, if Niko did come back, she'd have to free the mage—her word was good; it had to be; she dealt with too many arbiters of souls—Roxane waved a hand to lift the calming spell from Randal.

If she had to free him, she'd not keep him comfy, safe and warm, 'til then. She'd let him suffer, help him feel as much pain as his slender body could. After all, she was Death's Queen. Perhaps if she scared him long enough and well enough, the Tysian magician would take his own life, trying to escape, or die from terror—a death she'd have the benefit of but not the blame.

And in his chair, Randal's face went white beneath his freckles and his whole frame began to rock while, with every lunge and quaver, the nonmaterial bonds around his chest grew tighter and the snakes (stupid snakes who never understood anything) began querulously to complain that it was Randal's bet and wonder what was wrong as cards fell from his twitching fingers.

Strat was out of Ischade's, where he shouldn't be but mostly was at night, just taking off his clothes when the damned door to her front room opened with a wind behind it that nearly doused the fire in her hearth.

Accursed Haught, her trainee, stood there, arch mischief glowing in his eyes. Strat hitched up his linen loinguard and said, "Won't you ever learn to knock?" feeling a bit abashed among Ischade's silks and scarlet throw pillows and trinkets of gem and noble metal—the woman loved bright colors, but never wore them out of doors.

Woman? Had he thought that, said it to himself? She wasn't exactly that, and he'd better remember it. Haught, once slavebait, looked at Strat and through him as if he didn't exist as he entered and the door closed behind him of its own accord.

"Best remember that you're mortal, Nisi boy. And that respect is due your betters, be you slave or free," Strat warned, looking at his feet where, somewhere in a confusion of cushions, his service dagger lay buried. Best to teach this familiar some manners before he'd have to do worse.

But behind him he heard a stirring and a soft step as sinuous as any cat's. "Haught, greet Straton civilly," came her voice from behind him and then her hand was on his spine, pouring patience into him where patience had no right to be.

"Damned kid comes and goes like he owns the—"

Haught was abreast of him, then, speaking to the necromant beyond. "You'd want this warning, if you weren't so busy. Want to be ready. Trouble's on the way."

Then something unspeakable happened: Ischade, hushing the Nisi exlave, came round Strat and did something to the other man, something that included not quite touching him but circling him, something Strat didn't like because it was intimate and didn't trust because he could tell that information was being exchanged in a way he didn't understand.

Abruptly, the creature called Haught turned in a

flare of cloak and arrogance and the door opened wide, then shut again behind him, leaving candles flickering huge shadows upon the wall and a chill in the air Strat was expecting Ischade to dispell with a caress.

But she didn't. She said, "Ace, come here. Before the fire. Sit with me."

He did that and she cuddled by his knee in that way she had, so much a woman then that Strat could barely refrain from pulling her onto his lap. She looked up from under the darkness that veiled her and her eyes clamped on his: "What I am, you know. What I do, you understand better than many. What life Janni has with me, his soul has chosen. Someone is going to come here, and if you don't tell him all of that, the result will not sit well with you. Do you understand?"

"Ischade? Someone? A threat to you? I'll protect you, you know—"

"Hush. Don't promise what you'll not deliver. This one is a friend of yours, a brother. Keep him from my doorway or, despite what I'd like to promise you, he'll become a memory. One that will hang between us in the air forever." She reached up toward his face.

He jerked his head back; she lay her head upon his knee. He couldn't tell if she was crying, but he felt as if he would, so sad was she and so helpless did the big Stepson feel.

An hour later, outside her door, stationed like a sentry, he began to wonder if her creature hadn't lied. Then his big bay, tied at her low gate, let out a challenge and some horse answered from the dark.

Sword drawn, he sidled down to calm the beast, wondering what in hell he was supposed to do about something she hadn't explained, when a darkness separated from the midnight chill and a tiny coal, red-hot, seemed to bobble toward him in midair.

Closer it came, until the soft radiance of Ischade's hedges caught its edges and he made out a mounted man smoking something—pulcis, by the smell of it, laced with krrf and rolled in broadleaf.

"Hold and state your business, stranger," Strat called out.

"Strat?" said a soft voice full of distaste and some measure of disbelief. "Ace, if it's really you, tell me something a man would have had to fight on Wizard-wall to know."

"Ha! Bashir can't hold his liquor, is what—not even laced with blood and water," Strat responded, then added, "Stealth? Niko, is that you?"

The little coal of red grew brighter as the smoker inhaled and in its flare Strat could see the face of Nikodemos—bearded, but with scars showing like white tracks among the hair, just where those scars should be.

A surge of joy went through the Stepsons' leader: "Is Crit with you? The Riddler—is Tempus come back?" Then he sobered: Niko was the problem Ischade'd sent him out here to deal with. Now her distress, and her cautions, made good sense.

"No, I'm alone," came Niko's voice soft as a winter gust as sounds and the movement of the smoke's coal let Straton know the Sacred Bander was dismounting.

They had a bond that should have been deeper than Straton's with Ischade—that *had* to be. Straton considered alternatives as Niko tied his Aškelonian to the fence on the other side of Ischade's gate from where Strat's bay was tethered, and vaulted over the hedge, then grinned: "Not good form to enter a witch's home through a portal she's chosen. How'd you find out about this? No matter—I'm glad to have your help, Ace. Janni's going to be, too."

So that was it—Janni. All Straton's mixed feelings about Ischade's minions roiled around in him and kept him speechless until he realized that Niko was reaching over the fence to get a bow and bladder of naptha and rags from his horse's saddle.

"Niko, man, this isn't the time or the place for the talk we've got to have"

Stealth turned and as Strat bore down upon him, the Bandaran fighter said, "Strat, I've got to do this. It's my fault, in a way. I've got to free him."

"No, you don't. From what? For whom? He's fighting a war he still has a stake in—fighting it his way. I've fought beside him. Stealth, things are different here from the way they were upcountry. You can't make any headway without magic on your—"

"Side?" Niko supplied the missing word, his face glowing red from the coal of the smoke between his lips. Then he dropped the smoke and ground it under his heel. "Got a girlfriend, do you, Straton? Crit would beat your ass. Diddling around with magic. Now either help me, as your oath demands, or step aside. Go your way. I owe you too much to make an issue of what's right and wrong between us." Niko's hand went to his belt and Straton stiffened: Niko was an expert with throwing stars and poisoned metal blossom and every kind of edged weapon Strat knew enough to name. The two were thought to be, by Banders, of nearly equal prowess, though Strat's was fading as he aged, Niko's coming on.

"Whatever I'm doing, Stealth, is worse than what you've done? Don't I remember some fight up at the Festival, one in which you protected the Nisibisi witch from a priestess of Enlil?"

That stopped Niko's hand, about to lever a bolt to ready in his crossbow. "That's not fair, Ace."

'We're not talking fair—we're talking women. Or

womanish avatars, or whatever they are. You leave this one alone—she's on our side; she's fought with us, for us . . . saved Sync from Roxane, for one thing." Suspicion leaped into Straton's mind, suspicion enough to chase the memory of Janni's tortured shade. "Roxane didn't put you up to this, did she? *Did* she, Stealth?"

Niko, a flint in one hand, naptha bladder in the other, paused with the bladder poised above the rags on his arrow's tip. "What difference does that make? What's going on here, anyway? Randal's disappeared and no one's looking for him? You're sleeping with a necromant and no one gives a damn?"

"You stay around, and you'll find out. But I can guarantee you're not going to like it. I don't. Crit wouldn't. Tempus would bust all our butts. But he's not here, is he? It's you and me. And I'm bound to protect this . . . lady, here."

"More bound to her than to me? Sacred—"

Niko stopped and stared, his mouth half open, at something behind Strat, so that the big fighter turned to see what Niko saw.

On Ischade's doorstep, beside the necromant swathed in her black and hooded robe, was Janni—or what remained of Janni. The ex-Stepson, ex-living thing was red and yellow and showing bone; things glittered on him like fireworks or luminescent grubs. He had holes for eyes and too-long hair and the smell of newly-turned earth preceded him down the steps.

Despite himself, Strat looked over his shoulder at Niko, who slumped against the waist-high fence, his eyes slitted as if against some blinding light, his crossbow pointing at the ground.

Strat heard Ischade murmur, "Go then. Go to your partner, Janni. Stay awhile. Have your reunion."

Then, louder, "Strat! Come in. Let them be alone. Let them solve it—I was wrong; it's between these two, not us."

And then, as Niko threw the bow up to his shoulder and took fluid, sudden aim at Ischade—before Straton could put himself between her and Niko's arrow or even thought to move—Ischade was beside him, facing Niko with a look on her face Strat had never seen before: deep pain, compassion, even acknowledgement of a kindred soul.

"So you're the one. The special one. Nikodemos, over whom even the god Enlil and the entelechy of dreams contend." She nodded as if in her drawing room, sipping tea at some civil table. "I see why. Nikodemos, don't choose your enemies too quickly. The witch who sent you here has Randal—is that not a greater wrong, a deeper evil, than giving the opportunity for vengeance to a soul such as Janni, who craves it?"

Ischade waited, but Niko didn't answer. His gaze was fixed on the thing that shambled toward him, arms outstretched, to embrace its erstwhile partner.

Strat, were he the one faced with love from such a zombie, would have run screaming, or shot the bow, or lopped the head off the undead who sought to hold him.

But Niko took a deep breath that Strat could hear, so shuddering was it, dropped the bow, and held his own arms out, saying: "Janni. How is it with you? Is she right?"

And Strat had to turn away; he couldn't watch Niko, full of life, embrace that thing who'd once ridden at his side.

And when he did, Ischade was waiting there to take Strat's hand and cool his brow and usher him inside.

But no matter the depth of her eyes or the quality

of her ministrations, this time Straton knew he had no chance of forgetting what he saw when a Sacred Band pair was reunited, the living and the dead.

Niko was drinking off his chill in the Alekeep, which opened with the rising sun, when he realized that somebody was drawing his picture.

A little fellow with a pot belly and black circles under his eyes, who was sitting in the beamed common hall's far corner, was looking at him too often, then looking down at a board he held on his lap.

Just the day barman was present, so Niko didn't try to ignore a problem in the making. He'd had too rough a night, at any rate, to have patience with anyone—let alone a limner who didn't ask permission.

But when he was halfway to the other man, his intention clear enough, the day barman reached out a hand to stay him: "I'd not, were I you, sir. That's Lalo the Limner, who drew the Black Unicorn that came alive in the Maze and killed so many. Just let the scribbler be."

"As far as I know, I'm alive already, man," Niko said. "And I don't like having my picture scrawled on anything—walls, doors, hearts. Maybe I'll turn the tables and draw my sign on that fat, soft belly . . ."

By then, the little, rat-faced limner was scrabbling up, running for the door, his sketching board under his arm. Niko didn't chase him.

He went back to his table and sat there, digging in the wood with the point of his blade the way Janni used to do, thinking of the meeting he'd had and wanted to forget with a dead thing happy to fight beyond mortal battles at the bidding of the necromant, wondering if he should—or could—find a way to put Janni's soul to rest despite its assurances that it willed to be the way it was. Did it know? Was it really

Janni? Did the oath they'd sworn still obtain when one respondent wasn't a man any longer?

Niko didn't know. He couldn't decide. He tried not to drink too much, but drink dulled the picture in his mind's eye, and at nightfall he was still sitting there, trying unsuccessfully to get thoroughly drunk, when the priest known as Torchholder happened to come in with others of his perfumed breed, all with their curl-toed winter shoes and their gaudy jewelry.

Torchholder knew him, but Niko didn't have the sense to leave before the High Priest of Vashanka recognized the fighter who'd been with Tempus at the Mageguild's Fete two winters past.

So when the priest sat down opposite him, Niko raised his head from the palm on which he'd been propping it and stared owlishly at the priest. "Yeah? Can I help you, citizen?"

"Perhaps, fighter, I can help you."

"Not if you can't lay the undead, not a chance of it."

"Pardon?" Torchholder was watching the half-drunk Sacred Bander closely, looking for some sign. "We can do whatever the god demands, and we know you are pious and well disposed to—"

"Enlil," Niko interrupted firmly. "Gotta have a god, around here, so I'm making it plain: mine's Enlil, when I need one. Which is as infrequently as possible." Stealth's hand went to his belt and Torchholder froze in place.

But Niko only patted his weaponsbelt and brought the hand back to the table, where he propped his chin on it. "Weapons'll do me, mosttimes. Other times . . ." The Sacred Bander leaned forward. "You any good at fighting witches? I've got a friend I'd like to get out of one's clutches . . ."

Torchholder made a warding sign with practiced

fluency before his face. "We'd like to show you something, Nikodemos called—"

"Ssh!" Niko said with exaggerated care, and looked around, right and left, before leaning forward to whisper. "Don't call me that. Not here. Not ever. I'm just visiting. I can't stay. Too much magic. Hurts, you know. Dead partners that aren't dead. Ex-partners that aren't ex. . . . Very confusing—"

"We know, we know," soothed the priest with wicked eyes. "We're here to help you sort it out. Come with us and—"

"Who's we?" Niko wanted to know, but two of Molin's cohort already had him by the armpits. They lifted the only mildly protesting fighter up and eased him out the door to where a carriage with ivory screens was waiting and, after some little difficulty, convinced him to allow them to boost him inside and close the door as he staggered to a padded bench within.

Before him, on the other side of the carriage, were two children, one on either side of a harried looking woman who might once have been beautiful and whom Niko, who liked women, vaguely recalled: a temple dancer. The two children were hardly more than babes, but one of them, the fair-haired, sat right up and clapped his little hands.

And the sound of those hands clapping rang in Niko's ears like the thunder of the god Vashanka, like the Storm God's own lightning that seemed to issue from the childish mouth as the boy began to giggle in joy.

Niko sat back, slouched against the opposite corner of the wagon, and said, "What the . . . ?"

And though the child was now just a child again, another, deeper voice, rang in the Stepson's head, saying, *Look on Me, favorite of the Riddler, and take word back to your leader that I am come again. And that I would take advantage of all you have to give before the little world that is thine suffers unto perishing.* The boy from whose mouth the words could not have issued was saying, "Sowdier? Hewo? Make fwiends? Fwiends? Take big ride? Water place? Soon? Me want go soon!"

Niko, stone sober, sat up, looked at the woman sharply and then nodded politely, as he hadn't before. "You're that one's mother? *That* temple dancer— Selyaha, the First Consort who bore Vashanka's child." It wasn't really a question; the woman didn't bother to answer.

Niko leaned forward, toward the two children, the darker of whom had his thumb in his mouth and regarded Niko with round black eyes. The fair child smiled beautifully. "Soon?" the boy said, though it was too young a child to be discussing anything as sensitive as Niko knew it was.

He said, "Soon, if you're worthy, boy. Pure in heart. Honorable. Loving of life—*all* life. It won't be easy. I'll have to get permission. And you've got to control—what's inside you. Or they won't have you in Bandara, no matter how they care for me."

"Good," said the fair child, or maybe just "Goo;" Niko wasn't sure.

These were toddlers, the both. Too young and, if Niko's *maat* was right and a god had chosen one as His respository, too dangerous. Niko said to the woman, "Tell the priests I'll do what I can. But he must be taught restraint. No child can control his temper at that age. Both of them, then, must be prepared."

And he pushed on the wagon's door, which opened and let the sobered fighter out into the blessedly cold and normal Sanctuary night.

Normal, except for the presence of Molin Torchholder and the little scribbler, whom the priest held by the collar. "Nikodemos, look at this," said the priest without preamble as if Niko were now his ally—which, so far as Stealth was concerned, he indubitably was not.

Still, the picture that the scribbler, who was protesting that he had a right to do as he willed, had scribbled was odd: it was of Niko, but with Tempus looking over his shoulder and both of them seemed to be enfolded in the wings of a dark angel who looked altogether too much like Roxane.

"Leave the picture, artist, and go your way." It was Niko's order, but Torchholder let go of the bandy-legged limner, who hurried off without asking when or if he'd get his artwork back.

"That's my problem . . . that picture. Forget you've seen it. Yours, if you want what the god wants, is to get those children schooled where they can be disciplined—by Bandaran adepts."

"What makes you assume I want any such—"

"Torchholder, don't you know what you've got there? More trouble than Sanctuary can handle. Infants—one infant, anyhow—with a god in him. With the power of a god. A Storm God. Can you reason out the rest?"

Torchholder muttered something about things having gone too far.

Niko retorted, "They're not going any further unless and until my partner Randal—who's being held by Roxane, I hear tell—is returned to me unharmed. Then I'll ride up and ask Tempus what he wants to do—if anything—about the matter of the godchild you so cavalierly visited upon a town that had troubles enough without one."

The architect-priest winced and his face screwed

up as if he'd tasted something sour. "We can't help you with the witch, fighter—not unless you want simple manpower."

"Good enough. As long as it's priest-power." And Niko began giving orders that Torchholder had no alternative but to obey.

On the dawn of the shortest day of the year, Niko had still not come back to Roxane.

It was time to make an end to Randal, whom she despised enough—almost—to make the slight dealt her by the mortal whom she'd consented to love less stinging.

Almost, but not quite. If witches could cry, Roxane would have shed tears of humiliation and of unrequited love. But a witch shouldn't be crying over mortals, and Roxane was reconstituted from the weakness that had beset her during the Wizard Wars. If Niko wouldn't come to her, she'd make him notorious in hell for all the lonely souls his faithless, feckless self-interest had seen there.

She was just getting the snakes to put aside the card game and fetch the mage when hoofbeats sounded upon her cart-track drive.

Wroth and no longer hopeful, she snatched aside the curtain. The day was bright and clear as winter days can be, with a sky of powder blue and horsetail clouds. And there, amazingly, was Niko, on a big sable horse of the sort that only Aškelon bred in Meridian, his panoply a gleam as it came within orb of all her magic.

So she had to shut down the wards and go outside to greet him, leaving Randal half unbound with only the snakes to guard him.

Still, it was sweeter than she'd thought it could be, when anger had consumed her—ecstasy just to see him.

He'd shaved. His boyish face was smiling. He rode up to her and slipped off his horse, cavalry style, and slapped its rump. "Go home, horse, to your stable," he told it, then told her, "I won't need him here, I'm sure."

Here. Then he was staying. He understood. But he'd not done anything she'd asked.

So she said, "And Janni? What of the soul of your poor partner? How can you leave him with Ischade—that whore of darkness? How can you—"

"How can you torture Randal?" Niko said levelly, taking a step closer to Roxane, hands empty and outstretched. "It makes it so hard for me to do this. Can't you—for my sake, won't you let him go? Unharmed. Unensorceled. Free of even the taint of hostile magic."

As he spoke, he pulled her against him gently until she pushed back, fearful of the burns his armor could inflict. "If you'll get rid of that—gear," she bargained, trying to keep her hackles from rising. He should know better than to come to her armored with protections forged by the entelechy of dream. Stupid boy. He was beautiful but dumb, pure, but too innocent to be as canny as his smile portended.

She waved a hand behind her. "Done." And as she spoke, a howl of rage and triumph issued from inside and something, with a crash, came bursting out the window.

Niko gazed after Randal as the mage ran, full-tilt, into the bushes. He nodded. "Now it's just the two of us, is that it?"

"Well . . ." she temporized, "there are my snakes, of course." She was primping up her beauty in a way he couldn't see, letting her young and girlish simulacrum come forward, easing the evil and the danger in her face and form. By all she revered, did she love this boy with his hazel eyes so clear and his

quiet soul. By all she held sacred, the feel of his hand
on her back as he ushered her into her own house in
gentlemanly fashion was unlike the touch of any
man or mage she'd ever known.

She wanted only to keep him. She sent away the
snakes, having to discorporate one who objected that
she would then be defenseless, open to attack by
man or god.

"Take that silly armor off, beloved, and we'll have
a bath together," she murmured, preparing to spell
water, hot and steaming, in her gold-footed tub.

And when she turned again, he'd done that and
stood before her, hands out to strip her clothes away,
and his body announced its intention to make her
welcome.

Welcome her he did, in hot water and hot passion,
until, amid the moment of her joy and just before
she was about to begin a rune to claim his soul
forever, a commotion began outside the door.

First it was lightning that rocked her to her foundations, then thunder, then the sound of many running feet and chanting priests as all Vashanka's
priesthood came tramping up her cart-track, battle-
streamers on their standards and horns to blow the
eardrums out of evil to their lips.

He was as nonplussed as she. He held her in his
arms and pressed her close, telling her "Don't worry,
I'll take care of them. You stay here, and call back all
your minions—not that I don't think I can protect
you, but just in case."

She watched him dress hurriedly, strapping on his
armor over wet skin, and run outside, his weapons at
hand and ready.

No mortal had ever come to her defense before.
So when, snakes by her side and undeads rising, she
saw them wrestle him to the ground, disarm him,
put him in a cage (no doubt the cage they'd meant

for her) and drive away with him, she wept for Niko, who loved her but had been taken from her by the hated priesthood.

And she planned revenge—not only upon the priesthood, but upon Ischade, the trickster necromant, and Randal, who should never have been allowed to get away, and on all of Sanctuary—all but Niko, who was innocent of all and who, if only he could have stayed a little longer, would have proclaimed in his own words his love for her and thus become hers forevermore.

As for the rest—now there *would* be hell to pay.

DREAM LORD

"When I count to three and snap my fingers," Aškelon's voice came to Niko from afar, "you will awake, refreshed and unharmed, remembering everything that you saw and heard."

Snap.

Niko's eyes came open of their own accord. Over Aškelon's head he could see the gray telltales of dawn on the distant horizon, as if someone had veiled the sea for marriage.

He took shuddering breaths and waited for the strange sensations of the trance to subside. His body still felt like a shell, a suit he'd donned that was stiff and unfamiliar. His breath was entering his lungs and exiting his nose in a different way than it normally did when he was awake; his belly and his chest rose and fell in harmony with that deeper breathing. His eyes could no longer see any more than what was directly to the front and sides of his head.

While he'd been in the altered state that Aškelon had brought him to, he'd been able to see three-hundred and sixty degrees around his person. He'd seen himself, uncharitably at times. He'd seen the witch, Roxane, who'd come to a foul pass subsequently—a fate Tempus had helped design.

Where Roxane was now, Niko couldn't say. She'd been trapped thereafter. Trapped and exorcised and . . . driven out of body, if not mind, by the combined efforts of god-sworn soldiers, magicians, vampires and even Jihan the Froth Daughter. So Roxane was no threat; she should trouble him no longer. But the part of him that once loved the witch, despite all she'd done, still loved her.

Was it Roxane's freedom that Aškelon had shown him? Was there some flicker of salvation held out to that sold soul, simply because Niko had loved her? Was love freedom, then, as well as entrapment? Was there hope for all men if there was hope for such as she?

Niko looked at Aškelon and the dream lord was smiling pensively, watching him fondly as a mother a sleeping child.

In the trance he'd seen all his Sacred Band brothers and realized he missed them. And seen too that none of them were any freer than he.

He said, "If freedom is unattainable in life, then what is life's meaning? What's the point? The purpose?"

"The meaning of life, Nikodemos, is to live life with meaning. The purpose of life is merely to live it, perhaps to give it."

And for those of us that *take* it?" Niko was a fighter, had always been, would always be.

"Death is a doorway, Niko, that leads to an adventure greater than any you have ever known. Like the gateway in your rest-place, it is on the path of every man. When you come to death, you will understand it. Not before. When you give death, you give of your own life—every time. Yet there is no world large enough on which all men could live forever."

"Not even Meridian?"

"Ah, Meridian . . . there is a place great enough to hold the dreams of every man who ever lived. And dreams are what make us different from the beasts of the field. Dreams, Nikodemos, are worth living for."

"And dying for?"

"Sometimes," said the dream lord, and seemed to flicker, as if his substance was not quite as wholly present as it had been just moments before.

Niko ignored this trick of the predawn light. The light had been like that in the place that Aškelon had taken him, so like his rest-place, from which he'd dared to remember Strat's plight, the witch's worst, the storm children and Janni's terrifying accommodation with his fate.

"Sometimes, you say? When?" Niko pressed, wanting Aškelon to absolve him, on the post, for all the deaths on his account and all the suffering he'd been party to inflicting. He'd never wanted that before. But he'd never been so deep inside himself, where life as an abstract force was precious and holy, where all things had a harmony and all men a place. And because he needed some proof from Aškelon, before he got in any deeper with the dream lord, that the entelechy of the seventh sphere was a representative of good, not evil.

Not evil . . . not like the witch.

But when he looked up, Aškelon was positively ephemeral, translucent, fading away.

Niko said sharply, "Don't do this to me. Not again. Don't disappear. Not now. Not if you want me—"

"I want you. You must want yourself," came the gusty voice out of Aškelon's near-departed throat. Like the wind, those words buffeted Niko as he watched Aškelon fading.

The dream lord had come in the flesh, walked up

the cliff, been here and touched him. Now he was dissolving like a ghost or a figment.

Niko reached out to grab the translucent wrist of the dream lord, and his fingers closed on thin air. "Wait!" Niko demanded. "Don't leave me now! How will I find you again?"

"In your dreams," Aškelon said, now just a face hovering over the seaward side of the cliff. "Whenever you need me."

Niko had thought Aškelon was going to ask him to ride away in the dolphin-prowed barque. He shouted, "But I don't understand why you're doing this, after all you taught me! Please—"

"Tempus," was the single word formed by the disembodied lips of Aškelon, before the dream lord faded entirely away.

TEMPUS

The dawn light was still tricky, diffused with mist, its reds and golds full of the shimmer of the sea when the cloud descended out of the west.

It was a long cloud, a pink-tinged cloud as tall as a temple and it floated down Ennina's peak until it covered everything but Niko and the cabin at his back.

The young Bandaran fighter didn't move to run as the cloud slithered along the ground toward him, then stopped. He merely watched as the cloud rolled in upon itself and the sun came up somewhere behind it, giving a bloody tinge to the roiling mass hovering between the Sacred Bander and the sea.

Such clouds came from the gods, not from magic. Such clouds came from the west or east, never the north or south. Such a cloud had brought Abarsis to Sanctuary and the will of Enlil into play among younger, more savage gods.

This cloud was no exception. It rolled itself into a fleecy funnel and at the end of that funnel could be seen another land, terrain much different from Ennina's gentle overlook of the placid sea.

There were spires within the cloud and domes and ragged hills. There was a horseman in the cloud, on a horse of misty color with a dappled crest and nightblack mane. There was a second horse behind the first, and perhaps another on a tether, but it was the rider of the first steed who seemed to force the very cloud to shrink away.

Out from the cloud came the gray horse, picking his way with lowered head and distended nostrils over unfamiliar ground. Its rider's head nearly brushed the arch of cloud above and that head wore a helmet crowned with boar's teeth. His shoulders were as broad as the horse's chest and strewn across them was a leopard-skin mantle, moth-eaten from ancient times.

Behind, as the first horse's hindquarters gained solid ground, a second steed trumpeted a greeting. This horse was sable, and behind it was another like it.

Nikodemos rose to his feet when the horse-call sounded, and waved a greeting as if nothing unusual were happening.

But it was. The rider waved back, turned in his saddle to make sure all three horses were on solid footing, and spoke a gruff word softly. Upon its utterance, the cloud began to whirl in upon itself. The rider took another loop on the horses' tether just before the cloud became a whirlwind and consumed itself, spinning out of existence with an ear-aching "pop."

"Life to you, Tempus," called Niko from the shelter of his cabin's porch.

The rider dismounted then, holding the gray Trôs horse by the bridle and letting it nuzzle his palm. "And to you, Stepson. And everlasting glory." The old formula came hard to Tempus's lips, as if it had become some travesty of meaning—still, the words must be spoken.

Tempus held out his hand to Niko and the youngster came forward to grasp it. The sable stallion shouldered its way forward to greet its master, and soon there was a confusion of man greeting man and horse greeting man that hid the emotion all were feeling.

Finally, with the sable's head pressed against his chest and his glistening eyes on the far horizon, Niko asked, "What brings you here, commander—by cloud and on the heels of Aškelon?"

"So, he's been here," Tempus said, not answering Niko's question, watching the youth closely. "To politic for your allegiance, no doubt."

"To . . . teach, he said," Niko replied and met Tempus's gaze. "I didn't run. Or fight it. I wasn't ready. I have to learn how—" Niko's eyes burned with intensity. "I haven't betrayed anything."

Yet, Tempus thought but didn't say. "Nor will you. The god of the armies thinks it's time you returned to active duty. You saw the cloud. You see me. Are you ready to mount your horse and go back to the World?"

Tempus had brought boys to Ennina in the past. This time he'd come to collect a man. The Storm God wanted to give Nikodemos a choice, that was certain. Arriving on the heels of Aškelon made this plain. Gods didn't believe in coincidence; they created it.

The sable horse nuzzled Niko, its beloved master, and whickered softly. He rubbed the spot under its jowls and it stretched its head, eyes half closed in pleasure. "To take the mission we discussed before I brought the children here? I'm as ready as I'm going to be."

"Ready enough," said Tempus, deciding not to force a discussion of Aškelon and his teachings. When Niko was finished becoming whatever Niko would become, there would be time for such talk. Tempus had all the time in the world, and more. "Shall we get Jihan, then, and depart?"

"Jihan? She's on the main island," Niko said, startled. "With the children, still. And there's no way out of here by horse—"

Tempus bared his teeth. "The gods want you, Nikodemos, as much as any specter from the land of dreams does. We'll wait for Jihan a few minutes longer—she saw the cloud; she knows its meaning. You should, too. We promised the emperor we'd sortie into unknown realms. It suits me—the unknown has a benefit over the well-known: it's not familiar enough to be disappointing."

"Disappointing," Niko repeated, his eyes focused inward. "Sometimes I'm sure that's what I am to you. And sometimes—" Niko held up his hand to forestall anything Tempus might say. "—sometimes I am that, I know. So that unshared knowledge doesn't become betrayal, I must tell you what Aškelon said . . ."

"Go on."

"He said your sister's left him; served her year; dissolved their marriage. She's abroad in the realm. Some realm."

"The realm? Is that what he said? Exactly?"

"I . . . I don't remember, exactly, what he said. But abroad."

"There are many realms, Niko, accessible from Aškelon's domain. Where she is, she is. She's not our problem until she wants to be. And as for betrayal, don't be so hard on yourself." Tempus knew Niko like the son he'd never wanted; even now the younger man was worrying over what it would mean to have spent time under Ash's tutelage.

"I—he showed me things about myself. About the witch. And you. And the adepts did, also. I'm not the same as I was before."

"None of us are ever what we were before, Stealth." Using Niko's war-name brought emphasis to a lesson Tempus had to teach. "And as for betrayal—there must be love, and understanding, to betray. Most men haven't the wit or the honor for betrayal: not to know it when they see it; not the stomach to apprehend it as they do it. Most men, blind and dumb in their self-centeredness, don't betray; they merely disappoint.

Niko looked at him out of that shapely skull with eyes as wide as any Tempus had ever seen, and as tortured. "I know what I'm doing. I'm choosing—or choosing not to choose. My heart is still with you, commander."

"A good place for a right-side partner's heart to be, Stepson," said Tempus gruffly as the third horse on the tether nickered and all three mounts danced about.

And then, before Niko could respond by more than the slow, spreading smile that threatened to engulf his face, Jihan's beautiful, bronze head and then her shapely form can into sight as she climbed into view.

"Well," said the Froth Daughter, hands on her hips, "it's about time, lover." She glared at Tempus in mock impatience. "You've got your partner, I see, and his horse and mine. What's holding us up then? I've had my fill of babies and monks and twaddle. Let's get out into the World and see what wrongs we can find to right." She grinned. "Or vice versa."

"Right away, Jihan," said Tempus, with a man-to-man wink at Niko, who'd shed the last vestige of his boyhood on Ennina and was about to realize it.

As they mounted up and in the west a cloud began to boil, a cloud big enough for three horses with riders, Tempus watched it, ignoring his rightside partner Nikodemos and Jihan with equal fervor.

He'd send the adepts a gift or two—they'd done him a good turn, teaching both his companions that life was never simple, happiness never where you thought you'd left it, and right and wrong no more fixed than the clouds in the sky.

Niko had survived the dream lord and Jihan had outgrown her obsession with babies. The Bandarans had turned a sensitive boy into a man and a spoilt brat into a woman. Well, into the simulacrum of a woman. It was reason enough to send a herd of cows, or even a pair of breeding Trôs horses, to the Bandaran adepts.

As the cloud lowered to whisk them away, Tempus had just a moment to wonder if, having reclaimed these two whom he loved above all others, it was a sign that he'd freed himself of his curse.

But then he realized that it didn't matter, that if it was true today it might be untrue tomorrow, and spurred his doubtful Trôs horse into the maelstrom.

Its front feet clopped one last time on Ennina's rocky ground, then were silent, muffled by the cloud. Its back feet did the same, and he couldn't hear its hooves any more. Before him was unknown miasma, from behind wafted the sound of Niko's sable, following the Trôs into the funnel.

And then Tempus couldn't hear the sable's hooves beat either, or Jihan's mount, behind his.

He twisted in his saddle, for a moment fearing some trick of the gods. But both Niko and Jihan were still there, riding serenely behind him as the cloud swallowed up the last wisps of Ennina and there was nothing left to differentiate what lay behind them from what lay before.

Here is an excerpt from Vernor Vinge's new novel, Marooned in Realtime, *coming in June 1987 from Baen Books:*

The town nestled in the foothills of the Indonesian Alps, high enough so that equatorial heat and humidity was moderated to an almost uniform pleasantness. Here the Korolevs and their friends had finally assembled the rescued from all the ages. At the moment the population was less than two hundred, every living human being. They needed more; Yelén Korolev knew where to get one hundred more. She was determined to rescue them.

Steven Fraley, President of the Republic of New Mexico, was determined that those hundred remain unrescued. He was still arguing the case when Wil Brierson arrived. ". . . and you don't appreciate the history of our era, madam. The Peacers came near to exterminating the human race. Sure, saving this group will get you a few more warm bodies, but you risk the survival of our whole colony, of the entire human race, in doing so."

Yelén Korolev looked calm, but Wil knew her well enough to recognize the signs of an impending explosion: there were rosy patches on her cheeks, yet her features were otherwise even paler than usual. She ran a hand through her blond hair. "Mr. Fraley, I really do know the history of your era. Remember that almost all of us—no matter what our present age and experience— have our childhoods within a couple hundred years of one another. The Peace Authority"—her lips twitched in a quick smile at the name—"may have started the general war of 1997. They may even be responsible for the terrible plagues of the early twenty-first century. But as governments go, they were relatively benign. This group in Kampuchea"—she waved toward the north— "went into stasis in 2048, when the Peacers were over-thrown. That was before decent health care was available. It's entirely possible that none of the original criminals are present."

Fraley opened and closed his mouth, but no words

came. Finally: "Haven't you heard of their 'Renaissance' scheme? In '48 they were ready to kill by the millions again. Those guys under Kampuchea probably got more hell-bombs than a dog has fleas. That base was their secret ace in the hole. If they hadn't screwed up their stasis, they'd've come out in 2100 and blown us away. And you probably wouldn't even have been born—"

Yelén cut into the torrent. "Hell-bombs? Popguns. Even you know that. Mr. Fraley, getting another hundred people into our colony will make our settlement just big enough to survive. Marta and I haven't spent our lives setting this up just to see it die like the undermanned attempts of the past. The only reason we postponed the founding of Korolev till megayear fifty was so we could rescue those Peacers when their bobble bursts."

She turned to her partner. "Is everybody accounted for?"

Marta Korolev had sat through the argument in silence, her dark features relaxed, her eyes closed. Her headband put her in communication with the estate's autonomous devices. No doubt she had managed a half dozen fliers during the last half hour, scouring the countryside for any truant colonists the Korolev satellites had spotted. Now she opened her eyes. "Everybody's accounted for and safe. In fact"—she caught sight of Wil standing at the back of the amphitheater and grinned—"almost everyone is here on the castle grounds. I think we can provide you people with quite a show this afternoon." She either hadn't followed or—more likely—had chosen to ignore the dispute between Yelén and Fraley.

"Okay, let's get started." A rustle of anticipation passed through the audience. Many were from the twenty-first century, like Wil. But they'd seen enough of the advanced travelers to know that such a statement was more than enough signal for spectacular events to happen.

From his place at the top of the amphitheater, Wil

had a good view to the north. The forests of the higher elevations fell away to a gray-green blur that was the equatorial jungle. Beyond that, haze obscured even the existence of the Inland Sea. Even on the rare, clear day when the sea mists lifted, the Kampuchean Alps were hidden beyond the horizon. Nevertheless, the rescue should be visible; he was a bit surprised that the bluish white of the northern horizon was undisturbed.

"Things will get more exciting, I promise." Yelén's voice brought his eyes back to the stage. Two large displays floated behind her.

"As Mr. Fraley says, the Peacer bobble was supposed to be a secret. It was originally underground. It is much further underground now—somebody blundered. What was to be a fifty-year jump became something . . . longer. As near as we can figure, their bobble should burst sometime in the next few thousand years; they've been in stasis fifty million years. During that time, continents drifted and new rifts formed. Parts of Kampuchea slid deep beneath new mountains." The display behind her lit with a multicolored transect of the Kampuchean Alps. The surface crust appeared as blue, shading into yellow and orange at the greater depths. Right at the margin of orange and magma red was a tiny black disk—the Peacer bobble, afloat against the ceiling of hell.

Inside the bobble, time was stopped. Those within were as they'd been at that instant of a near-forgotten war when the losers decided to escape to the future. No force could affect a bobble's contents; no force could affect its duration—not the heart of a star, not the heart of a lover.

But when the bobble burst, when the stasis ended . . . The Peacers were about forty kilometers down. There would be a moment of noise and heat and pain as the magma swallowed them. One hundred men and women would die, and a certain endangered species would move one more step toward final extinction.

The Korolevs proposed to raise the bobble to the

surface, where it would be safe for the few remaining millennia of its duration. Yelén waved at the display. "This was taken just before we started the operation. Here's the ongoing view."

The picture flickered. The red magma boundary had risen thousands of meters above the bobble. Pinheads of white light flashed in the orange and yellow that represented the solid crust. In the place of each of those lights, red blossomed and spread, almost—Wil winced at the thought—like blood from a stab wound. "Each of those sparkles is a hundred-megaton bomb. In the last few seconds, we've released more energy than all mankind's wars put together."

The red spread as the wounds coalesced into a vast hemorrhage in the bosom of Kampuchea. The magma was still twenty kilometers below ground level. The bombs were timed so there was a constant sparkling just above the highest level of red, bringing the melt closer and closer to the surface. At the bottom of the display, the Peacer bobble floated, serene and untouched. On this scale, its motion towards the surface was imperceptible.

Wil pulled his attention from the display and looked beyond the amphitheater. There was no change: the northern horizon was still haze and pale blue. The rescue site was fifteen hundred kilometers away, but even so, he'd expected something spectacular.

The elapsed-time clock on the display showed almost four minutes. The Korolev pattern of bomb bursts was still thousands of meters short of the surface.

President Fraley rose from his seat. "Madame Korolev, please. There is still time to stop this. I know you've rescued all types, cranks, joyriders, criminals, victims. But these are *monsters*." For once, Wil thought he heard sincerity—perhaps even fear—in the New Mexican's voice. *And he might be right*. If the rumors were true, if the Peacers had created the plagues of the early twenty-first century, then they were responsible for the deaths of billions. If they had succeeded with their Renaissance Project, they would have killed most of the survivors.

Yelén Korolev glanced down at Fraley but didn't reply. The New Mexican stiffened, then waved abruptly to his people. One hundred men and women—most in NM fatigues—came quickly to their feet. It was a dramatic gesture, if nothing else: the amphitheater would be almost empty with them gone.

"Mr. President, I suggest you and the others sit back down." It was Marta Korolev. Her tone was as pleasant as ever, but the insult in the words brought a flush to Steve Fraley's face. He gestured angrily and turned to the stone steps that led from the theater.

The ground shock arrived an instant later.

320 pp. • 65647-3 • $3.50

To order any Baen Book by mail, send the cover price plus 75 cents for first-class postage and handling to: Baen Books, Dept. B, 260 Fifth Avenue, New York, N.Y. 10001.